Far from Home

Sheila Newberry was born in Suffolk and spent a lot of time there both before and during the war. She wrote her first 'book' before she was ten – all sixty pages of it – in purple ink. Her family was certainly her inspiration and she was published for most of her adult life. She spent forty years living in Kent on a smallholding with her husband John, and had nine children, twenty-two grandchildren and six great-grandchildren. Sheila retired back to Suffolk where she lived until her death in January 2020.

Also by Sheila Newberry

Sheila
NEWBERRY

Far from
Home

ZAFFRE

First published in Great Britain in 2005 by Robert Hale Ltd as
The Little Train Home
This edition published in the UK in 2022 by
ZAFFRE
An imprint of Bonnier Books UK
4th Floor, Victoria House, Bloomsbury Square, London, England, WC1B 4DA
Owned by Bonnier Books
Sveavägen 56, Stockholm, Sweden

A CIP catalogue record for this book is
available from the British Library.

ISBN: 978–1–83877–689–3

Also available as an ebook and in audio

1 3 5 7 9 10 8 6 4 2

Typeset by IDSUK (Data Connection) Ltd
Printed and bound in Great Britain by Clays Ltd, Elcograf S.p.A.

Zaffre is an imprint of Bonnier Books UK
www.bonnierbooks.co.uk

To Joyce and John Moir,
our friends forever

PROLOGUE

November, 1923

Foghorns resounded mournfully in the dark, deep waters beyond the port of Ipswich. The wooden Thames barges had discharged their cargoes earlier to the tall dockside mills. Grain harvested on the great prairies of North America was still brought under sail on the last stage of the journey from London.

A sulphurous odour overlaid the familiar ambience of brewers' malt and yeast, which pervaded the area. Local folk avowed this was healthy, even as they coughed.

The swirling fog occluded the view from the attic window through which Elin peered. The barges were safely in dock, she thought, but only recently she'd seen them outlined against a spectacular evening sky. Before they were lowered, the sails of the Cranfield mill barges, decorated with a full moon, were entrancing.

Heavy footsteps now echoed along the cobbled path, which led to the row of substantial red-brick villas set well above a poorer area. Then Elin heard cursing as Buttle fumbled with the door lock. She pulled the curtains and turned towards the bed.

'Shush!' She cautioned the two dark-eyed, small boys, smoothing their covers. Their stepfather mustn't suspect that they were fully dressed, apart from their boots.

She snatched up her pinafore to conceal her good frock and then went resolutely downstairs to meet her employer, who was hanging his coat and hat on the hallstand.

'Your supper's in the warming oven, Mr Buttle,' she said politely.

'*She* ain't deigned to come back then,' he stated, looking at his gold fob watch.

Elin shook her head. She couldn't lie or say she was sorry. She'd quaked in bed last night when Buttle and his young wife, Erminia, had quarrelled bitterly in the sitting room below. When screaming began, then thumping, she'd crept into the boys' room.

After Buttle stormed out of the front door, Erminia, sobbing, ran upstairs to her bedroom. Elin told the little boys to stay put, then she went to see if she could help. Erminia was throwing clothes into a suitcase. By the gas-light, Elin had been shocked to see her bruised face, the swollen bleeding lips.

'Erminia! You must call the bobby!' Elin had exclaimed.

'No! I've had enough trouble. I'm getting out while I can. You should, too.'

'Where are you going?'

'Best not to say. I'm sorry to involve you, Elin, because things have been a bit better here for me since you came to help me with the boys, but—'

'He's a violent man, Erminia, especially when he's been drinking. What can I do?'

'I . . . can you bring the children to me tomorrow night? Meet me at the dock gates.'

'What time?' Elin heard herself say calmly.

'About nine. After Buttle's had his supper and gone out to drink with his cronies. You must carry on as normally as possible, Elin, so he doesn't suspect anything.'

Now, Buttle muttered: 'Foreign bitch. She should be grateful, me taking her on with kids in tow when her first husband drowned at sea. She married me for my money, Elinor Odell, but I wasn't good enough, being a bookie. Then she cuckolded me.' He grabbed at Elin's arm, twisted it painfully behind her back. 'She tell you who *he* is?'

'No . . .' Elin managed. It was true. She took a deep breath. 'Let me go, please.'

To her surprise, he released her.

'Where are the kids?'

'They're in bed. They're upset about their mother leaving, of course.'

'You're fond of 'em, ain't you?' His tone had changed, was almost wheedling.

'Yes, Mr Buttle.' She thought fearfully, *he's much stronger than me.*

'Then you'll stay on and do the necessary, eh?'

Elin didn't like the way he leered at her. She nodded again mutely.

'*She* yelled when I yanked out some of her black mane. Coarse stuff, not like yours.' Elin flinched as he touched her strawberry-blonde hair, recently cut to a short, wavy bob. He continued, 'I'll make it worth your while, Elin. Meantime, I'll keep the kids here for a bit. Make her sweat. You understand?'

'I ... think so, Mr Buttle.' She was relieved when he moved away.

'Good. I'll eat now, then have a bath before I go out. I'll see *you* when I get back.'

He'd locked the doors, back and front, she discovered to her dismay when it was time to make their escape. There was no bathroom in the house, so the copper in the scullery provided hot water for his tub. Then she saw that he'd left the scullery window ajar to release the steam. Elin kicked the pile of clothes and damp towels out of the way. It relieved her feelings. She opened the window as wide as she could, almost choking as she breathed in the acrid air. She pushed her basket case and the boys' bundles out of the window on to the adjacent flat roof of the coal shed. The plaintive mewing of a cat made her jump.

'Here, Bruno, you first; up on the sill, dangle your legs outside and slide down, it's not far. Then wait for me. Now you, Bertie.' She must try to make a game of it.

'Side gate's locked,' Bruno told her when she joined them.

'We'll have to climb over the top then, won't we. I'll go first this time, and catch you in turn, eh? Bruno, you'll have to give Bertie a leg-up, then manage by yourself, there's a good boy. I'll have to throw the baggage over the gate and hope for the best.'

She was handicapped by her skirts, she thought. The boys, she hoped, would be inconspicuous in dark over-coats. She had covered her bright hair with a scarf.

Twenty minutes later they stood, luggage at their feet, by the big gates. At this hour the docks were seemingly deserted, but there were men still aboard the boats, or patrolling with swinging lanterns. It was a raw night. Elin hugged the shivering boys close to her on either side, praying that Erminia would come.

Three figures approached, gradually becoming visible. Two men and Erminia.

The boys ran into her outstretched arms. 'Mamma!'

'Shush!' Erminia whispered, as Elin had the night before. She turned to Elin. 'Thank you – I knew I could trust you! Did you have any trouble in getting away?'

'A little,' Elin admitted. She had caught and torn her sleeve on a nail in the gate.

'These are my brothers,' Erminia said. 'Alex, Mario – this is my brave young friend, Elin. Will you come to Mario's house with us?'

'There are three more children with my wife there,' the older man said. 'But we can make room, I promise you.' He smiled reassuringly at Elin.

She had decided earlier where she would head for.

'Thank you for your kind offer, but I can go to my sister and brother-in-law, at the other end of town.'

'You mustn't walk that far alone in the dark. Alex will see you safely there, eh?'

'Of course.' Alex, dark and good-looking like his sister, took Elin's arm.

'I … I'm not sure,' she faltered, remembering her grandmother's strictures.

'Oh, you can trust my little brother! He is studying law,' Erminia assured her.

'One day perhaps.' Alex smiled. 'I am a clerk in a solicitors' office.'

'We'll see you again soon. Say goodbye to Elin, boys,' Erminia told them.

Another half-hour or so passed as Elin and Alex took shortcuts down mean streets of terraced cottages where the front doors opened directly on to the narrow pavement. The two did not converse much, concentrating on their direction. Light and noise spilled from the corner pubs; a jangle of piano music from one. Two men were wrestling in the doorway of another. They were now walking along a road with flaring gas-lamps. They were on the last lap, when they turned off into an unlit crescent.

Suddenly feeling very weary, Elin climbed the steps to the end house.

Then Jenny was hugging her and calling to Alex at the gate: 'Come inside, do!'

Jenny's husband Ted was sitting at the table that dominated their small living room. He was halfway through a steaming plateful of tripe and onions. He was employed at one of the flourmills; he brought in a decent wage, with working overtime. Jenny didn't have to go out cleaning like many of the women round here.

Jenny was twenty-two, six years older than Elin; their mother, Delia, had died when her sister was born. Their grandma had looked after the family, and Jenny had helped out with the baby. There was a close bond between them. That was why Elin had jumped at the chance of living nearer Jenny, Ted and little Billie, when she'd left her home in Langford, a village near Southwold, last September for her first job as a mother's help.

Ted nodded to the visitors. Wisely, he didn't ask questions, but continued eating.

Jenny busied herself pouring out two more cups of stewed tea. She brought them over to the iron-framed rexine-covered settee, where Elin and Alex sat.

'Drink up! Anything to eat? No? Ted's having a late supper. Billie was tucked up before he got in from work. Now, take your time, then you can tell me why you've come here, Elin, when you should be in bed yourself.'

The fire was made up; Elin was relaxing at last in the warm room.

'Mr Buttle attacked his wife. She managed to escape to her family last night. Alex is Erminia's brother. He kindly walked me here.'

'Your sister is full of spirit,' Alex put in. 'She brought the children to the docks to be reunited with Erminia this evening. She took a big risk, because Buttle is a nasty piece of work. You can be proud of her, Mrs Drake.'

'Jenny, please! Oh, I am. It's a shame it had to end like this, but you can stay with us, Elin, eh, Ted?' Ted nodded again, swigged his tea. 'You must take your time looking for a new post, Elin – make sure it's right for you this time.'

'I ought to go. Thank you for the tea.' Alex said.

They stood for a moment on the doorstep. Alex didn't say that they would meet again. He just smiled and said softly, 'Goodbye and good luck always, Elin.'

On impulse she whispered, 'I won't forget you,' adding, 'or Erminia and the boys.'

'Your eyes are very blue,' he said unexpectedly. He looked serious now.

Then he was gone.

'Shut the door,' said Jenny, 'you're letting the cold in!' Then, noting her sister's bemused expression, she added, 'You'll meet him again, I'm sure of it. I saw the way he looked at you, Elin.'

PART ONE

ONE

Belle, Elin's grandma, was busy in the pantry with last-minute baking when Elin arrived home on Christmas Eve, but the front door was, as always, unlocked. The double-fronted, pink house in Suffolk, in the centre of the village opposite the church, had red pantiles that sheltered the bedrooms in the eaves.

To one side of the house was a long workshop with an iron roof. Inside was a run of benches and gleaming tools. Partitioned off was the paint shop, where two old men of indeterminate age refurbished the traps and carts brought in for repair. Behind that was a yard where tree trunks, ramrod-straight, were stacked until sawn to size over a pit for new wheels. The forge where the wheel rims were fitted belonged to an independent blacksmith. Elin's dad had inherited the house and living from his father, but now, like the Ipswich bargees, he clung on to the old skills, while business declined for R. ODELL & SON; WHEELWRIGHTS. He had no son to follow on.

Elin trod quietly along the hall, where she glimpsed in passing the glowing logs in the sitting room fireplace. *A real welcome home*, she thought, *after the chilly evening walk along the lanes from the station*. However, as usual, she'd enjoyed the last part of the journey from Halesworth along the narrow-gauge line of the Southwold Railway where the little train leisurely traversed the heath. Snow was definitely in the air.

'*Surprise!*' she sang out, as her little, plump grandma whirled round from the table, rubbing the flour from her hands, intent on untying her apron, to receive visitors.

'Oh, it's *you*,' she said, but the smile on her face betrayed her pleasure. 'Expected you home before this, Elin.' She permitted her granddaughter to kiss her cheek.

'Sorry, Grandma, I got caught up with all the excitement in Ipswich. Billie wanted me to stay with them, but I said you and Dad would expect me here.'

'Billie, what a name for a little girl,' her grandma said, turning back to the dough.

'I know, Grandma, you hoped she'd be named Belle, after you! Can I help?'

'Take your coat and hat off first. I made your bed up; I reckoned you'd come. How long will you stay?' Belle cut pastry rounds for mince pies.

'Until the New Year, if you'll have me. Then I really must look for another job. I can't expect you to keep me now I'm grown up.'

'What are you hiding under that cap, I wonder?'

'Had my hair lopped, Grandma. I guessed you wouldn't approve.'

'Got to go with the times,' Belle said unexpectedly. 'Seen your dad?'

'Not yet. Heard him sawing away in the log shed. Didn't want to startle him.'

'Doesn't matter about *me*, eh? Hungry, Elin? There's sausage rolls cooling.'

Elin sat down opposite her grandma. They drank from bluebird-patterned cups, the remaining two from Belle's wedding-gift tea service. The pastry was flaky and pale gold, plump with coarse-cut sausage meat, savoury with sage. Elin looked around the pantry-cum-kitchen, with the cream-painted dresser, scored table, cool marble slab for pastry, the bread oven in the wall, and the Belfast sink by the window. The weekly baking took place here; daily cooking on the range in the living room. The nearby bakery provided the wherewithal to roast larger joints, like the Christmas goose, already delivered there, to cook slowly overnight.

'I missed you, Grandma, I missed your cooking,' Elin said, clearing her throat.

'You haven't changed that much then, that's good. I missed you, too.'

'Here you are then!' Elin's dad exclaimed when he came in. His head and shoulders were powdered with snow, already melting in the warm room. 'Just in time, eh?' His eyes, as blue as her own, twinkled at her as he bent to kiss her.

'Still got your fierce moustache,' she said ruefully, trying not to wince.

'But you've lost your curls. At least you haven't painted your pretty face.' He turned to Belle. 'I spread rock salt on the path and the step, in case the snow lies. Well, Elin, you can pull my boots off, eh, and tell me what's going on in the town!'

Richard had a special cup with a rim to accommodate his moustache. He was a big man, with a ready smile. He took great gulps of the scalding tea

'I'm real pleased to see you,' he observed, as she wrestled with his hefty footwear. 'Home for good, are you? Plenty for you to do here, helping your grandma, you know.'

'The Buttles' wasn't the place for me, though I enjoyed looking after those little boys, but I mean to find a better job, with nice people, Dad.'

'Why not train to be a nurse, like your mother was before I married her?'

'Or a teacher?' Belle put in. 'You're bright enough for that.'

'I can be a bit of both, with the right family. I've had a taste of independence, I don't want to give up because of a bad start.' She smiled at them. 'Don't worry, I'll be back to see you as often as I can. This is my home, after all.'

Later, after supper, they moved to the sitting room, to comfortable chairs with feather-filled, brown-velvet cushions, drawn close to the leaping flames of the fire. Elin, like the others, slipped off her shoes and stretched out her stockinged feet. All the familiar ornaments were on the mantelshelf over the ruby-red tiles, she thought sleepily: the miniature Southwold lighthouse, the plaster black-and-white spaniels, one with a chipped ear, the ormolu clock protected by its transparent dome, and the model covered wagon with working wheels, made by her father when he was his own father's apprentice. Tucked in a corner of the gilt-framed mirror was a picture of ducks on a rush-fringed stretch of water, painted on card, entitled: *School Pond*. The youthful artist had been her late mother. That small watercolour had fostered her own interest in wild fowl on the local marshes. She knew little of her mother's life before she had come here, before she married her dad. There had never been mention of any relatives on the other side. Richard Odell's life history was, of course, here, like his mother's. No mysteries there.

'I ordered this magazine for you from the newsagent's in town,' Belle said, reaching behind her cushion. 'Mrs Sides said the advertisers are all bona fide.'

The expression was typical of one who, unusually for her generation and modest upbringing as a girl among four brothers, had received a sound education. She'd determined that her granddaughters would emulate her.

'*The Lady*, I've heard of it,' Elin said, turning the pages. She thought privately that the articles were suited to the mature reader. No romance! Here were the *Situations Vacant*. She read them carefully. She was on the second page before she exclaimed: 'Listen! How about this?'

FAMILY TIES TO SOUTHWOLD.
APPLICANTS FROM THIS PART OF SUFFOLK
PREFERRED FOR THE POST OF NURSE/
COMPANION/GOVERNESS TO BOYS, AGED FOUR
AND THREE YEARS, AND A BABY GIRL,
TWO MONTHS OLD.
MOTHER, A JOURNALIST, WORKS PART-TIME
FROM MIDDLESEX HOME. FATHER WORKS
IN LONDON.
SUCCESSFUL APPLICANT TO LIVE AS ONE OF
THE FAMILY.
OTHER HELP EMPLOYED.
HOLIDAYS SPENT AT FAMILY HOME IN
SOUTHWOLD.
INTERVIEWS TO BE HELD THERE FROM FIRST
WEEK OF JANUARY, 1924.
APPLY: BOX NUMBER . . .

'Sounds all right,' Belle observed. 'What with living as one of the family. There'll be no post until after Boxing Day, remember.'

'The letter will have to go via the magazine,' Elin said. 'I hope I'll be in time.'

'What about references?' her dad reminded her gently. 'You're unlikely to get one from that rogue Buttle. Unless his wife writes one for you. Got her address?'

'No, I'm afraid I haven't. But I'll explain, and I have my letters from the school and the parson. Let's forget it for the moment! Anyone joining us for dinner tomorrow?'

'Aunt Ida, as usual.' This was Belle's widowed sister-in-law who lived close by in the cottage where Grandma was born, to where she had returned for a while after her son married. 'And we've invited Mrs Goldsmith and her son – you haven't met them yet – they moved into Church Cottage in October. She's a widow, her husband was an army chaplain. He was killed in the war,' Richard said, a trifle too casually.

Elin shot a glance at her grandmother, but could read nothing from her expression.

'They won't be over until after the morning service, about midday,' Belle said. 'That will give us time to pre-pare the vegetables and lay the table. Ida will come earlier to help. Are you accompanying me to the midnight mass tonight, Elin?'

'I hope to, if I can keep awake.' Elin yawned. She thought, *I shall miss Jenny's little Billie diving to the bottom of her cot to retrieve her bulging stocking. It's not so long*

*since I did the same, but those days are past now I'm sixteen
and a working girl.*

*

Frances Goldsmith was tall and imposing with hennaed
hair plaited round her head. Her pendant earrings swung
and sparkled as she greeted Elin coolly, as if meeting
Richard Odell's daughter was of little importance. Her
son, after stamping his feet on the doormat, turned to
murmur 'hello'. He shook hands with them in turn.

'Come in by the fire.' Belle ushered them into the sitting
room. Elin's dad had banked it up well when he went to
bed, and stirred the glowing embers first thing. She added:
'Elin will entertain you. Dinner is almost ready, but you
must drink a toast to Christmas. Richard will pour whatever you fancy, then he'll fetch the goose.'

Elin stood by the array of polished glasses on the table.
Mrs Goldsmith and her son both requested sherry; her
father had cider; Elin her usual ginger beer. Dad downed
his quickly, then departed with a glass apiece for Belle
and Ida.

'You weren't at church this morning,' Mrs Goldsmith
stated.

Elin flushed. 'We went to the midnight service,' she said
defensively, relieved that Mrs Goldsmith hadn't been there
to observe her falling asleep during the sermon.

'And I attended neither,' Luke, the son, put in, grinning at Elin.

'You were too long at the Plough last evening,' his mother said disapprovingly.

Luke shrugged his shoulders. He was sallow-skinned, with floppy brown hair; a couple of years older than Elin.

'Say it, Ma – I am missing a father's guidance, eh? That's hardly my fault.'

Mrs Goldsmith ignored this.

'I was a staff nurse at the hospital where Delia, your late mother, trained,' she told Elin. 'We were friends at that time. It's quite a coincidence she lived here, too.'

Elin was intrigued, but something warned her to be cautious, not to ask questions.

'Oh,' she replied. Then: 'Dad's calling us – dinner is obviously about to be served!'

'I look forward to it, as you had a part in preparing it,' Luke said gallantly.

'I'm only responsible for the vegetables, I must admit. But I did pick the sprouts and shake the snow off them first thing! Follow me!'

There was homemade redcurrant jelly and plenty of fresh mustard on the side of each plate, salt from a tiny spoon, slices of white meat, curls of pink ham, roast potatoes and parsnips, sprouts, bread sauce and plenty of gravy, all piping hot. Mrs Goldsmith dabbed her mouth with her white linen napkin, taking her time over the meal. At last, the dinner plates were cleared and the Christmas pudding was doused with brandy and flamed impressively, before being served with thick yellow custard and cream.

Elin and Aunt Ida stacked the plates. Mrs Goldsmith sat with a pained expression on her face. Elin suspected that her boned corset was constricting her full stomach.

'We'll wash up and make the tea,' Belle told their guests. 'Why don't you retire to the sitting room with Richard and take your ease?'

'I feel like a walk rather than a nap,' Luke said quickly. 'How about you, Elin?'

'Yes, you go, too. We can manage, can't we, Ida?' Belle decided for Elin.

'Don't venture too far,' her dad advised. 'Snow's holding off, but it's very cold.'

Elin donned her red woollen cap, which matched the Christmas jumper knitted by her grandma. She hoped Luke wouldn't notice the puckered darn on the sleeve of her coat, a reminder of her recent escape from the Buttle house.

'Glad I brought my college scarf, as Ma insisted,' Luke said.

'You're at college then?' Elin asked as they trudged along the deserted street.

'I was.' He didn't enlarge on that. 'Shall we go down to the river?'

'We shouldn't walk in the water meadow, it's very boggy at this time of year.'

They leaned on the rough brick wall of the hump-backed bridge. There was the glint of ice on the water in the weak winter sunlight, but the outlook was bleak.

'Look, a paddle of ducks,' Elin observed, for something to say. 'Widgeon, I think, by the short necks and legs. They don't upend; they graze a lot on the grass. I always love to see them, pointing like arrows, rising straight up from the water. '

'I haven't heard that before; a *paddle* of ducks – it's a good description.'

'D'you like it here?' Elin asked him.

'I do, now I've met you,' Luke said frankly. 'Not many other young people around.'

'Some didn't come back from the war. Those my age mostly go elsewhere to find work, unless they come from a farming family. I'll be off again shortly, I hope.'

'Perhaps it's just as well . . .'

'Oh, what do you mean?'

'My mother intends to hook your father,' he said frankly. 'She's had enough of moving about, pretending my father left us well provided for when he didn't. We're only here for six months, due to the kindness of the parson who knew him. If Ma succeeds, both of us would be well advised to leave, go our own way.'

'I think you're mistaken. Dad's not interested in marrying again. He's over fifty.'

'And you assume that's too old? Love doesn't come into it, where Ma is concerned. Your grandmother won't be around forever, and you'll get married—'

'How do you know that?' she demanded. 'Look, I don't think we should be discussing this, but if Mrs Goldsmith believes Dad is a good catch, well, she's mistaken. Business is not nearly as good as it was. The motorcar is seeing to that.'

'We'd better go back. I can see you're riled. I apologise, Elin.'

'I should think so,' she said huffily, stalking ahead of him.

After the Goldsmiths departed late that evening, and while her father was escorting Aunt Ida home, Elin helped her grandma with the final washing-up in the pantry.

'What do you think of Frances Goldsmith, Elin?' Belle asked.

'I'm not quite sure,' Elin answered warily. She could guess what was meant.

'Nor am I,' Belle said, rinsing the glasses. 'But I reckon *she*'s made up her mind ...' She paused, looking at Elin thoughtfully. 'Watch out for that young man, he's rather wayward, I hear. His college decided not to have him back next term.'

'Don't worry, Grandma; I won't give him another thought if I get that job!'

'Get that letter written then, tomorrow – we'll be on our own, I hope. The Goldsmiths are spending the day with

24

the parson and his wife.' Belle suddenly looked sad. 'We're coming to the end of an era, Elin. You won't be living here any more, just visiting from time to time, and I'll end up back with Ida, I suppose.'

'Oh, Grandma! After you worked so hard bringing up Jenny and me, and looking after Dad. Mrs Goldsmith said she and my mother worked together as nurses, by the way.'

'Your mother never mentioned the name Frances,' Belle said drily.

'I'd like to find out more about her – but not from Mrs Goldsmith!'

'Some things are best left alone,' Belle said, but she didn't enlarge on that.

TWO

1924

There were no cows on the common in January. That vast three-cornered area between the marshes was almost deserted. There were no holidaymakers larking about and picnicking under the trees or strolling across to the harbour, no white-clad cricketers at the crease, no tennis balls lobbed by young ladies gleefully throwing restraint to the winds in their new short skirts. Even winter football practice was restricted as local players had to earn a living, at sea, or with the Sole Bay brewery. The heady aroma wafted through the streets as in Ipswich, but here folk also enjoyed salty breezes. The brewery drays with the plodding great horses were a sight to see.

Elin's father drove her in the pony and trap to her appointment in one of the big houses looking out over the common. Parked in the driveway was a gleaming green motorcar. Elin had been feeling nervous during the short journey, silently rehearsing what to say, but now she was reassured by the sight of a small blonde boy wobbling on the lower strut of the front gate, waving them to stop.

'She's here!' he called over his shoulder, jumping down and opening the gate.

'Hello,' he greeted Elin, 'I'm Charlie, and you're going to look after me.'

'Oh, I do hope so,' Elin replied, taking to him immediately.

Mrs Lambert, baby in arms, younger son clinging to her skirts, came out to greet Elin.

'We'll see you later then,' she said cheerfully to Richard. 'Do come in,' she added to Elin, with an encouraging smile. 'Please excuse the havoc caused by the boys. Miss Odell, may I introduce my husband; he'll take the boys for a walk so that we two can talk in peace.'

Marian Lambert was slender and elegant in a calf-length navy skirt with a loose cream wool overshirt, belted Cossack style. Her husband towered over her. He had cropped hair and was clean-shaven, like most men of his age since the war.

'I have faith in my wife's judgement at all times,' he told Elin. 'She is in control of all matters domestic. Charlie, Jack, get your coats on and we'll stroll down to the pier.'

They heard the front door close. 'Please sit down, Miss Odell,' said Mrs Lambert. 'Would you like to hold Peggy while I disappear for a few minutes into the kitchen to make us a pot of tea? Then we can get to know one another, eh?'

This is a little test, Elin realised, as she took the baby. She gently adjusted the shawl to look down into Peggy's wide-open blue eyes. Instinctively, she cupped and supported the baby's head with her left hand.

'Hello, Peggy,' she said softly.

Later, after Peggy was settled in her hooded Moses basket on wheels in the cosy nook by the fire, Mrs Lambert poured tea and offered shortbread biscuits to Elin.

'I was impressed with the information given in your letter. You are very young to take on shared responsibility of three children, for we would naturally be working together, but you were frank about why you left your previous employment. You dealt courageously with a difficult situation, which shows maturity beyond your years.'

'I was entrusted to look after those little boys to the best of my ability. I couldn't let them down, I had to take them to their mother,' Elin said firmly.

'I must say I was particularly struck by the way you described your escape: "*I gathered the children under my wing, then we scaled the locked back gate . . .*" I was relieved to learn that the only casualty was your coat!'

'That was soon mended,' Elin told her, blushing at the extravagant quote.

'You like sewing? That's good. Needle and thread are much plied in our house.'

'My grandma taught us how to darn our father's socks when my sister, Jenny, and I were quite small. It came in very useful when I was seven, and a friend dared me to slide down a big heap of builders' sand on the grass verge on our way home after Sunday school,' Elin confided. Later, she would wonder what on earth had made her relate this tale to a prospective employer.

'I'm intrigued; tell me more!'

'Well, I was wearing new lace-trimmed drawers, and not only were they gingery from the sand, but I'd ripped them. Later, I rubbed the marks with Pears soap, but first I crept upstairs to my room, pulled the curtains and got out my little sewing box . . .'

'Why did you close the curtains, I wonder?' Marian mused.

'Grandma didn't let us sew or knit on the Sabbath! I thought God wouldn't see me then, but I had to take the drawers off before I mended them, because the tear was at the back and anyway, you mustn't sew things when you're wearing them.'

'Another of your grandma's strictures, I imagine? I hope you will teach my children to be resourceful, too, as well as responsible, Elinor – if I may call you that?'

'My family call me Elin,' she said, in a rush. Did this mean she had the job?

'You talk of your grandma, Elin; I gather she brought you up?'

'My mother, who was a nurse before she married, died when I was born.'

'That's sad, I'm sorry. But your grandmother obviously did very well with you. Shall I tell you my own background? My parents were medical missionaries in Africa. As small children my brother and I were sent back home to boarding school. We spent all our school holidays here in Southwold with our great-aunt in this house. When she passed away it was left to my brother, Mark, and me.

'I was eighteen in 1914. My parents had by then returned to this area. My father found retirement irksome. His services were called on during the war, and he has continued to minister to the sick, locally. My brother joined him recently.

'I didn't get to the Front, but as a Red Cross nurse I cared for the wounded in one of the big houses near here, which was taken over as a convalescent home. That's where I met my husband. He says he determined to recover quickly, so he could ask me to marry him, before any of the other patients had the same idea. We married in 1917.'

'I thought you were a journalist,' Elin put in.

'I gave up nursing when the war ended, but I missed it. Mr Lambert is an accountant for a large publishing concern. I've always enjoyed writing, so he suggested me for a weekly column in one of their magazines for young mothers. Shush – a touch of nepotism, I'm afraid! I'm Sister Serena, that being the name of my predecessor. I hide behind her elderly, wise image, still at the top of the page. I write on a different health topic each week and deal with readers' queries. I also answer personally a selection of the unpublished letters. This all takes me three mornings a week, hence my need for a children's nurse whom I can trust completely. I feel we could work together very well if you are willing to be guided by me. Well, Elin, may I welcome you as one of the family?'

'Oh, yes please!' Elin made up her mind instantly, like Marian Lambert.

'Now let's discuss the essentials, eh; wages, hours and duties. My husband has to return home by train tomorrow as he doesn't drive. We'll join him next weekend. Is that convenient for you?'

'Of course, I shall look forward to it!'

'If possible, I'd like you here with me for a day or two first, to get used to the children, because it will be necessary for you to travel by train with Charlie and the baby to Liverpool Street station, where you'll be met by my cousin Miss Clements. She has kindly offered to provide lunch to fortify you for the rest of the journey.

'I'll drive straight home in the car with our luggage and Jack, who prefers to leave the small talk to his brother so isn't so distracting! However, you'll find Charlie more of a help than a hindrance, I'm sure. He knows all the ropes.'

Mrs Lambert has a lovely smile, Elin thought, *it lights up her face so you don't notice her rather prominent nose, only her bright eyes, and tawny hair . . .*

'I can come the day after tomorrow, Wednesday, if you'd like me to?' Elin offered.

Then Charlie and Jack rushed in, clutching treasures in gloved hands, which they held out to Elin.

'Let me take off your coats,' their father said. 'They're all damp from the spray. The waves were pounding the pier so we walked along the top of the beach.'

'These are for you, Miss Odell – so you'll like us and stay, not go off like our last nurse who said we were ... what was it, Mummy?' Charlie asked.

'Precocious,' Marian said ruefully, adding apologetically, 'I'm afraid I omitted to tell you that, Elin.'

'Well, *I* was called that in my day,' Elin told them, unaware that her new employers were amused at that from one not so old herself. 'So I'll soon have the measure of you two. Thank you for the shells, boys, they're very pretty.'

'Like *you*,' Charlie said.

*

'It all seems to have happened so quickly,' Belle sighed, pressing the pleats in Elin's best skirt with a damp cloth and much hissing from the flat iron. 'Off to Southwold tomorrow. They're expecting a lot of you to make that long train journey to London.'

'Oh, Grandma, it's only a hundred miles! About four times the journey to Ipswich.'

'But you've still got to go on to where the Lamberts live.'

'Mrs Lambert's cousin, Miss Clements, is meeting us at Liverpool Street. We'll go by taxi across London to her flat for lunch before we catch the next train.' It was time to change the subject. 'Mrs Lambert's brother is taking the boys out tomorrow afternoon while we wheel Peggy along to the shops to choose my uniform. Mrs Lambert says it must be smart and to my liking, as well as practical!'

'She sounds a generous lady. Some employers expect you to provide your own.'

'Hello?' A loud, carrying call from the hall. 'Anyone at home?'

'Oh, dear, it's Mrs Goldsmith! Wonder what she wants?' Belle whispered.

'I'll see, shall I?' Elin offered. She closed the pantry door behind her.

'I didn't expect to see you,' Frances said ungraciously. 'I thought you had started your new job. I only wish Luke could be as lucky.'

'I wouldn't have been accepted for the situation if I was unsuitable,' Elin flashed back. 'I certainly appreciate my good fortune. Can I help you, Mrs Goldsmith?'

'I wish to talk to your father, but he is not in the workshop.'

'Probably at the forge. Did you try there?'

'A great carthorse standing in the doorway . . .' Mrs Goldsmith blew her nose. 'All that *heat* – and I'm not an animal lover. Aren't you going to ask us in to wait?'

Elin became aware that Luke, looking fed up, was lurking behind his mother.

'Of course. Come in the sitting room, I'll just tell Grandma, then I'll fetch Dad.'

Luke hung back. 'I'll go with you, Elin.'

'Don't say anything out of turn to Richard, then,' his mother said sharply.

'I was glad to hear your good news,' Luke said, as they walked down the street. 'I envy you. It looks as if *I'll* be stuck here for some time yet.'

'I'm looking forward to all the challenges – beginning with the journey to London, with young Charlie and the baby! But this place will always be home to me, Luke. I don't see it as you do. Mrs Lambert feels the same – she likes to say hello every time she visits here, to old Southwold Jack! *That* Jack – I don't think *her* Jack was named after him – is a wooden automaton who strikes St. Edmund's clock bell and looks as if he's imbibed too much Adnam's ale. He's over five hundred years old; survived the Reformation . . .'

'Give me a chance to say I've made his acquaintance, too!' Luke reproved mildly.

The huge horse was backing out from the forge when they arrived, and there was Elin's dad, wheel at the ready, chatting to the blacksmith.

'Dad, Mrs Goldsmith is waiting at home to see you.'

'I'm busy just now, I'm afraid, Elin.'

'We'll make a start, get the bellows working,' the burly blacksmith suggested. 'Leave the wheel with me and the boy, come back in half an hour, eh?'

Richard had some news for Belle and Elin at supper that evening.

'I expect you're wondering what Frances had to say. Well, she asked me if there was any chance I could take her lad on as my apprentice.'

There was silence for a moment, then Belle observed:

'Can't see him suiting you, Richard. What does Luke think about it?'

'Give him his due, he's willing to give it a try. That decided me. He starts next week. I warned Frances the pay is next to nothing, but I'd do my best with him.'

'He could be trouble,' Belle warned.

'I like him,' Elin put in unexpectedly in Luke's defence, surprising herself.

'One thing could lead to another,' her grandma stated, looking at Richard. Then she turned to Elin. 'Just as well *you* won't be around, Elin, my dear . . .'

The neat string-tied parcels were piling up on the counter of Denny's in the market place. This high-class outfitters was rightly dubbed the Harrods of Southwold.

Two winter-weight dresses, one saxe-blue, the other grey, with detachable white collars and cuffs, proved a perfect fit for Elin. For walking out to shops or the park, there was a splendid dark-blue cape with military style brass buttons.

'We must find a neat little hat to match,' Marian told Elin, smiling to see her face flushed with excitement. 'And warm stockings and stout shoes – we're in a rural part near the Thames; it's muddy down our lane when it rains.'

'It's not like a uniform at all!' Elin said ingenuously.

'Good. I'm so glad you approve. Well, we must make tracks home because Mark and the boys are looking forward to crumpets and chocolate cake for tea!'

Elin hadn't met Marian's brother earlier because she'd been upstairs changing Peggy ready for the outing. This was a last-minute affair after the baby had taken her bottle, because she'd regurgitated a little milk over her pram suit. 'You live and learn,' as Elin said ruefully to her replete charge.

Marian had mentioned, prior to his arrival, that Mark was a year and a half her senior and that they'd been inseparable as children.

'Perhaps you should know that my brother's wife has suffered from a recurrent mental illness since they married early in the war,' she'd added. 'She decided to leave him several years ago. At the moment, Ann is in a nursing home. Mark visits her there regularly. It's all very sad.'

Mark's motorcar drew up outside the house as they opened the front door.

Elin gently removed the baby's bonnet and adjusted the shawl. The useful travelling- cot-cum-perambulator was wheeled into the alcove. Peggy was asleep. Elin turned, almost colliding with Mark, who was eager to say hello to his niece.

'Peggy's the first girl in our family since my sister was born,' he observed. 'I sent the boys to wash their hands before tea. We've been messing about down by the ferry at Walberswick, but we didn't see any crabs. Marian says I'm to toast the crumpets.'

'Oh, that's *my* job, the hand washing,' Elin said, 'but thank you. I'll fetch the crumpets for you. Here's the toasting fork.'

It seemed like a feast, crumpets oozing butter, soft chocolate cake with fudge topping, freshly made by Eastaugh's specialist bakery in the high street.

'The boys will need a bath; all sticky fingers and chocolate-smeared faces!' Marian said. 'Would you like to tackle the two of them together, Elin, please?'

The bath was roomy and there was plenty of hot water from the newly installed gas geyser. Elin, protected by a rubber apron, soaped and sponged the energetic children, splashing and having fun. There was a tap on the door.

'May I come in?' Mark called. 'Marian dispatched me with the warm towels, she's giving the baby her bottle.'

Elin was flustered. 'Oh, that's—'

'*Your* job, I suppose!'

He has a nice smile, like his sister, thought Elin.

Charlie and Jack, in their pyjamas and dressing gowns, went downstairs to say goodnight to their mother. Mark stayed for a moment as Elin rinsed and wiped the bathtub.

'I'll be off shortly, Elin; glad to have met you.'

Elin went into her room to collect herself; to hang up the new dresses. *He's very good-looking*, she thought. *I feel – oh like I did when I said goodbye to Erminia's brother after he'd escorted me to Jenny's. Two attractive men: one I'm unlikely to see again, and the other, well, he's a married man . . .*

THREE

Elin was to see Mark again much sooner than she'd expected. On Friday evening she was assisting Marian with the packing-up when the telephone rang in the hall.

'That was Mark,' Marian said when she returned. 'He's offered to drive you and the children to catch the mainline train. My father will take the morning surgery. Mark will be here after breakfast at half past eight, so it won't mean such an early start for you.'

He's thoughtful, like his sister, Elin thought.

'That's a relief,' she said aloud.

Mark arrived promptly, when Elin was packing a shoulder bag with necessities for the baby and a few things to keep Charlie amused on the journey.

There was a pleasant surprise for Elin as they sat in the waiting room at Ipswich station with ten minutes to spare before the London train steamed in. Elin cuddled tiny Peggy in her blanket cocoon. No pram – that was packed in Marian's motor. It was a cold and blustery morning, but they were keeping warm by a good fire when the door opened wide, caught by the wind.

'Jenny! I didn't expect to see *you*!' Elin exclaimed.

'I took a chance. I hurried over and bought a platform ticket.' Jenny smiled. 'I left Billie with Ted, she's cutting a tooth and is rather grizzly; I daren't tell her I was off to see her favourite auntie.'

'Well, give her a big hug from me when you get back, won't you.'

'Of course I will! So this is baby Peggy, Elin, and you are Charlie, eh?'

'And you must be Elin's sister. You look so alike,' Mark put in, amused.

'Oh, Jenny – this is Mrs Lambert's brother, Dr Clements. He drove us here.'

'How d'you do,' Jenny said demurely. Her slight nod signalled approval to Elin.

When they heard the train approaching, Charlie nudged Elin.

'Remember, Elin, to ask the guard to warm up Peggy's bottle in water from the boiler. Then Mummy says you won't have another peep out of her.' He took his duties seriously.

'Good idea,' Mark offered, 'but leave that to me. I'll see you safely aboard first.'

When Elin and her charges were settled in their reserved seats, they waved at Mark and Jenny.

'Have a good journey!' Jenny was holding on to her hat in the wind.

'I'll give your sister a lift home. Good luck!' Mark called.

Elin's big adventure had begun.

Miss Celia Clements was a few years older than her cousin Marian. Charlie spotted her on the platform, porter in attendance, when they arrived at their destination.

'That's Aunt Celia, she's my godmother, for my sins, Daddy says, and her fox fur smells doggy, but she sprays scent behind her ears. She's bossy, but I like her.'

'Train's on time,' Celia observed, pulling her glove back over her gold wristwatch. 'Has young Charlie been well behaved, Miss Odell? To the taxi please, porter. Charlie, hold my hand, your governess has enough to do with the baby.'

'I'd never even been in a motorcar before this week!' Elin confided in the cab. They drove along in fits and starts through the heavy London traffic, to the accompaniment of blaring horns and shouts from an eclectic range of vehicles, many still horse-drawn. 'Doesn't all this noise give you a headache?' she asked frankly.

'Oh, you hardly notice it after a while,' Celia replied. 'I've lived and worked here since the war. The bright lights and the nightlife compensate for the frustration of mark-ing time as a woman in a man's world in a big corporation. Cousin Mark sometimes visits me. You'll see him often at the Lamberts. The boys adore him. It's such a shame he hasn't children of his own. We both seize any chance to spoil Marian's family.' She tapped on the glass screen to alert the driver: 'As you'll see, I live in a sober apartment, over an insurance company, no less.'

The lofty ceilings and the sash windows in Celia's flat were tempered by fresh white paintwork, contemporary wallpaper and furniture in golden oak and bamboo. The interior wasn't sober at all. There were so many fascinating objets d'art that Charlie was in his element, picking them up and asking Celia about her latest acquisitions.

'Don't tell him not to touch,' she said, noting Elin's apprehension that something might be dropped and broken. 'He's learning to appreciate style, if not cost.'

Tiny triangular-cut sandwiches were soon unwrapped from greaseproof paper and arranged on two large dishes on the oval table.

'I ordered the food first thing from Fortnum and Mason. More palatable than my cooking, I have to admit. I usually eat out. I hope you like smoked salmon, Miss Odell? The egg-and-cress sandwiches I know are Charlie's favourite. I am very partial to the chocolate éclairs, myself. Milk for Charlie and coffee for us – eat up, before Peggy stirs and demands her bottle.' Peggy lay on the sofa, bolstered with cushions.

Elin was feeling really hungry, for it had been hours since breakfast. The sandwiches constituted a light lunch, even the éclairs were insubstantial; puffs of choux pastry filled with cream and topped with dark chocolate. Still, there were two each, and the coffee was steaming and sweet. Celia had mastered that. Elin was getting a taste for it.

Celia replenished the small cups.

'Charlie, in the big chair with you – let your lunch settle, eh? The comic papers are for you to look at.'

'I can *read* – well, nearly,' Charlie reminded her, but he settled down obediently.

Celia fitted a cigarette in a long holder, drew deeply as she lit it.

'Marian disapproves of smoking, but I took it up after my fiancé was killed in Mesopotamia. Still, I count myself more fortunate than Mark. His future is uncertain. He visits his wife most Saturday afternoons, or I expect he'd have driven you all the way.'

Peggy was murmuring that it was time for another feed before they went on their way.

Marian arrived on the platform with a coach-built perambulator as the train departed, while Elin cautioned Charlie to stand well back!

'I wrapped a hot-water bottle in flannel to warm the blankets – here, let me take Peggy. You did well, Elin, quite a baptism of fire bringing the children home! Now to stretch your legs; it's a fair walk from the station, but one Charlie always enjoys.'

'Where's Jack?' Charlie was disappointed not to see his brother.

'He stayed at home with Daddy. Mrs Bunting's busy getting high tea.'

Something substantial, Elin hoped, as her stomach grumbled impolitely.

The firm pram mattress was in three sections. Under the middle was a well where the travel bags fitted snugly. Peggy was soon tucked in, then shielded by the mackintosh cover and hood.

'Put your handbag in the basket,' Marian advised Elin. 'Would you like to push?'

'Only three miles to go!' Charlie volunteered, with a grin. His mother shook her head at him.

'Not even a mile, Charlie! I felt like stretching my legs, too, after all that driving. Four and a half hours, with just a short break.'

'Glad I decided to wear my walking shoes, then,' Elin said. She was already aware that Marian firmly believed in fresh air and plenty of exercise for her family.

They took the footpath by the river; past the ferry and a couple of unoccupied houseboats moored at a distance from the lock gates. Across the Thames there was a long ribbon of neat timber-built bungalows with gardens sloping down to the waterside.

'No smoke from the chimneys,' Marian observed. 'The bungalows are deserted in winter. In the summer, children in the gardens wave at us as we pass by—'

'And we wave back,' Charlie finished.

There were glimpses of a distant church spire as the track widened into a lush green sward, marked by the muddy pram wheels. There was the smell of damp vegetation, darkening skies overhead, then welcome lights as at last they turned into a lane with a development of modern detached red-brick houses with garages within secluded grounds. Homeleigh was at the end, before the road veered right.

'Green Lane: convenient for the local shops in Overbridge village,' Marian pointed out. 'Our nearest town is Staines.'

*

The house was not quite as Elin had expected. The compact kitchen housed a New World gas cooker, a clothes copper with wringer attached, a tall larder cupboard and an icebox. Instead of a table there was a tiled counter with two stools set underneath. No comfortable clutter as in her grandma's pantry; here, crockery and pans were stowed away in wall cupboards. Hot water was provided by a gas heater over the sink.

The swing door connected with the breakfast room, a misnomer, for all family meals were taken here. This was a comfortable room, with latticed windows overlooking the back garden, an oval table in the centre; the baby's crib and high chair; a toy cupboard with an invitingly open door and cretonne-covered easy chairs in the alcoves either side of the brass guard which shielded the fire. The far wall was dominated by a rosewood piano with frayed pink silk behind fretwork panels and candleholders.

'Not one of my accomplishments,' Marian remarked cheerfully, noting Elin's interested glance. 'But I'm pleased you play. My parents presented us with the piano when Charlie was two and told us to make sure *he* learned! So, I hope you won't mind teaching him his scales when – and if – you have time?'

'Oh, I'll find time, and so will he!' Elin assured her.

'Now, just a quick look round the rest of the house so you can get your bearings, and then we'll have our fish pie in here. Mrs Bunting'll keep an eye on the baby.'

The separate dining room where the adults had their evening meal was also used as a study by Marian during her writing mornings, and by her husband, when he brought work home.

The formal sitting room was where the adults retired to after dinner. Elin felt much more at ease in the cosy breakfast room, with all the children's toys.

There were four bedrooms. Peggy's cot was in her parents' room, off this was a dressing room, which had been adapted for Charlie's use. Elin was to share her room with Jack, who sometimes woke in the night. Elin's bed had a soft down quilt.

'I hope you don't mind, Elin? You can screen off his bed to give yourself some privacy, or when you want to read at nights,' Marian said. 'I believe children sleep more soundly when they aren't isolated. In a few months Peggy should be ready to move into the dressing room, then Charlie and Jack can share the room next door to you.' She indicated the closed door, then the last bedroom along the corridor beyond the bathroom. 'Spare room, for visitors – usually Mark or Celia!'

'It's a very nice house, and I do like my room,' Elin said happily.

It was past ten that night when she shaded her bedside lamp with a scarf and, sitting on the edge of the bed in her nightgown and dressing gown, wrote to her grandma as she'd promised, to let her know that she had arrived safely, that all was well, and ending with 'all my love to you and Dad'. Then she pencilled a shorter note to her sister: 'I do think that Dr Clements is nice, don't you?'

She'd post the letters in the morning; now she slid under the covers, said her prayers and switched off the light, hoping that Jack was as tired as she was and would sleep through the night.

FOUR

Elin soon settled into the Homeleigh routine. She really did feel like one of the family. It was Mrs Bunting, the housekeeper, who kept the household wheels smoothly oiled. She and her niece Clover Butt, known as Clo, the maid, not much older than Elin, arrived at seven each morning, except on Monday, the big wash day, when they came an hour earlier. Then the copper bubbled and the kitchen windows steamed up. They were cheerful workers. Clo came and went during the day, while her aunt carried on alone.

'Clo has responsibilities at home,' Marian observed to Elin, when she was unexpectedly missing one lunchtime. 'We'll serve ourselves, thank you, Mrs Bunting.'

When Elin went downstairs to breakfast, little boys in tow all washed and dressed, she'd hear the bathroom door close. Mr Lambert was preparing for his day in the City, while Marian bathed the baby in the basin in their room, warmed by a gas fire.

After settling the boys at the table, Elin went into the kitchen. She fitted the previous day's well-rinsed bottles in the holder in the sterilising pan and set it to boil. She appreciated how easy it was here, to light the burner with a single match. After breakfast she'd mix the formula milk, fill the bottles and later store them in the icebox. She considered privately that it was a pity that Marian, who was such a good mother, had decided not to nurse her baby herself. Billie, at almost two, still received that comfort from Jenny when she was fractious or overtired.

Homeleigh, she thought, was bright and cheerful even at this time of year due to the electric lights. They had gaslighting at home now, but oil lamps and candles stood at the ready, for gas mantles burned out at inconvenient times.

Elin had always enjoyed a cooked breakfast at home, even during wartime rationing, which had ended only three years ago. They kept their own hens. Fish, tiny local fried sprats, were often on the menu. Here, the meal began with half a cupped grapefruit, adorned with a diced glacé cherry, not Grandma's thick porridge. Scrambled eggs were kept warm in a covered dish; toast taken from a china rack, then spread with a pat of butter. Marian poured the tea; the boys drank juice from oranges squeezed by Clo. It was a leisurely meal and Elin couldn't help thinking: *I won't have to do the washing-up!* She'd even move to an easy chair to give the baby her bottle.

Mr Lambert made his excuses after his second cup of tea, then rolled the newspaper he had been reading. He didn't communicate much during breakfast. He kissed his sons, who still would be toying with their crusts, on their foreheads, then ruffled Peggy's downy hair, as Elin massaged the baby's back to relieve any wind.

'Be good for Elin, eh?' Elin quickly suppressed the odd feeling that he might pat her on the head, too.

'You're in charge, Elin.' Marian smiled. 'When I drive my husband to the station.'

Elin did the baby's washing by hand, except for the napkins, which were soaked in a bucket in the bathroom before boiling. She enjoyed swishing the small garments in gentle soap flakes and patting the woollens into shape before they were laid out to dry flat in a folded towel. At home, Preservene household soap was used not only for washing clothes, but for most domestic cleaning. Shredded, Belle swore by it for hair-washing, but copious rinsing with rain water from the butt outside was necessary. They'd had mains water for a few years now, but Belle believed soft water was best.

Then it was time for Elin and the boys to go along Green Lane to the shops in Overbridge with Mrs Bunting's daily list. There was always something needed though the tradesmen called weekly. Marian went into the study to work.

When they returned, it was lessons in the breakfast room for Charlie and Jack. Their fingers pointed at the words in the Early Primer; there was copying and colouring in and the rivalry of reciting of numbers. At 10.30 they had a break; Clo brought milk and biscuits. Elin relaxed, with

Peggy in her arms, and they watched the boys set up their clockwork train track and let off steam themselves.

Marian joined them for lunch, nursery food like shepherd's pie or macaroni cheese followed by spotted dick and custard, or wobbly pink blancmange. In the kitchen, Mrs Bunting and Clo perched on their stools and ate their share at the counter. After the meal, Peggy and Jack were taken upstairs to have their rest. If she'd had a disturbed night with the baby, or a headache from concentrating on her writing, Marian, too, slipped off her dress and shoes and cat-napped on her bed for an hour or so.

From 1.30 until 2 p.m., Elin and Charlie practised at the piano. He was keen to learn, but fortunately, Elin thought, his feet dangled well above the 'loud' pedal. Even so, she noticed that Mrs Bunting firmly closed the kitchen door during these sessions.

Then it was time for the afternoon walk along the riverbank – unless it was raining or foggy – with a bag of stale bread for the ducks, except on Thursdays and Saturdays, when Elin had her afternoons and evenings off, and every other Sunday. The other staff departed after tea. Dinner was cooked by Marian, while Elin bathed and undressed the children so they'd be ready for bed when their father arrived home. Often she would be so absorbed in reading the boys a stirring story that she would literally jump when Mr Lambert's deep voice enquired: 'Am I allowed to listen in?'

Elin rather felt she was intruding when she joined her employers for dinner.

'Soup, Elin?' Marian asked, dipping a ladle in a round pot.

It wasn't soup as Elin knew it at home, made with stock and thick with chunks of vegetables, this was simply prepared from Marmite and hot water.

'If it was good enough for the troops and kept them going despite all that mud in the trenches, well, it's good enough for us,' Marian observed. Belle would have called it wishy-washy!

To follow, there was good plain cooking, nothing too heavy on the stomach at night, Marian decreed, so it was lamb chops, boiled potatoes and greens, or braised beef without the dumplings. Elin learned to eat her fill of sandwiches and homemade scones and rock cakes – chocolate fudge cakes were obviously holiday treats – at teatime, so she was not too hungry three hours later. There might be an apple tart provided by Mrs Bunting as a change from the usual stewed fruit, served with custard left over from lunch, and to round off the meal, always cheese and biscuits, with coffee.

Elin scraped and stacked the plates in the kitchen for the morning helpers to deal with. Then, she left the Lamberts in the drawing room and went yawning off to bed as Mr Lambert lit a cigar and poured port for himself and sherry for his wife.

Another long, full day, she thought. *I hope young Jack sleeps through, but I'm so happy to be treated like one of the family . . .*

It was one of those dismal, dark winter afternoons where the pavements were puddled from sudden fierce showers of icy rain and folk did not linger outside the bright shop windows in Ipswich. Not only were they cold, their pockets and purses were empty.

Jenny, in new but cheap shoes, which she now discovered let in water, was glad that young Billie was protected by the pushchair hood, though it was difficult to steer with one hand while she struggled to hold on to her brolly with the other. At least she'd achieved her object at the butcher's: a late Saturday afternoon bargain for Sunday dinner. Ted had gone off earlier to see his parents at the other end of town. They'd had a few words about that because he'd said the weather was too nasty to take Billie with him. He didn't realise that Jenny would have been glad of the break. *Elin is off duty this afternoon*, she thought. Still, she felt remorse now for flaring up as she had; Ted's father had chronic chest trouble, so common in these parts. His little mother looked older than her years from caring for him. Ted liked to slip a couple of coins in her apron pocket. She knew the drill: no fags for his dad, but a bottle of stout to build her up.

'Want to get out,' Billie protested, fiddling with the restraining straps.

'No!' Jenny said firmly. Billie was being a trial today, no mistake.

The next moment, the child had freed herself from her harness and jumped clear on to the pavement. The pushchair tipped up and Jenny tripped and fell, gashing her knee on the spinning back wheel.

'*Billie – stand still!*' she yelled frantically.

She was assisted to her feet.

'Don't worry,' the man in the belted raincoat, collar up round his face, said reassuringly. His voice was vaguely familiar. 'Look, a kind lady has hold of your little girl. Thank you,' he added, as Billie was returned to her mother.

The pushchair was righted, the newspaper parcel of meat and the brolly retrieved.

'I have the car parked round the corner; you've had a shock and I'm afraid your leg is bleeding profusely. I'll take you home and then bandage you up, Mrs Drake—'

'Dr Clements!' she realised. 'Oh, thank you!'

He lifted Billie up. 'Hold on tight, I need a hand free for the pushchair.'

'Oh, no, I can manage that—' Jenny insisted.

'You can hang on to the handle, too, it'll help you along.'

Jenny sat in the passenger seat of the car with Billie. She felt awkward, and concerned about what the neighbours might think, seeing her arrive home in style.

'My husband is out but he will be back shortly,' she managed when they drew up outside her little house. 'I'm not sure I ought to—'

'I think in the circumstances he will agree that you are right to invite me in!'

Billie was entertained by the sight of her mother having her leg bathed and iodine applied. Mark first unfastened and peeled off the torn, soaked stocking adhering to the wound. Even so, despite his professional attitude, Jenny was affected by involuntary trembling. Ted would have been too embarrassed to perform such an intimate task.

'There, you'll do,' he said, straightening up. 'Now, swing your feet up on the sofa, and if Billie will show me what's what in the kitchen, I'll make the tea.'

He stayed to drink a cup himself, and they made polite conversation.

'How is your sister?' he asked.

'Oh Elin is very well – I miss her, of course, and so does Billie.'

'There are just the two of you?'

'Our mother died in childbirth.'

'It must have helped Elin, having a caring older sister,' he observed.

'There's six years between us. When I left home for my first job at sixteen, Elin was only ten, so she became like an only child. She's certainly Grandma's favourite.' *That sounds childish*, she thought.

'You are very alike, so I can't imagine why that should be.' He was openly staring at her mass of fair hair, with damp, curling tendrils escaping the prim knot.

'Not in some ways . . .' She didn't enlighten him further.

Billie clunked him on the arm with a wooden toy to get his attention.

'Ouch!' He winced. 'She's a determined girl like her mother and aunt, Jenny!'

He called me by my first name, she thought, blushing. And like her sister, she added silently: *I mustn't forget he's a married man . . . and I'm well and truly wed, too . . .*

Ted was rattling the letterbox. She lowered her feet to the ground, hobbled to the door. The knee was stiff now under bandages made from torn strips of sheet.

Mark followed her to the door.

'Perhaps you'd like to come with me to my sister's sometime to see Elin?' he said quietly in her ear, as she turned the knob.

'Oh ..' she said, then: 'Ted, you remember Dr Clements – he gave me a lift home from the station the day I saw Elin off on the train. I took a tumble when Billie and I were out this afternoon and he saved my bacon – well, the belly of pork, anyway!'

Ted was unsmiling, ungracious. Mark made his excuses and went on his way.

'I told you not to go out,' Ted told Jenny heavily.

'You're not my keeper,' she flashed back.

'I'm your husband, don't you forget that.'

This was unlike Ted, laying down the law. She realised he was jealous. She must let the remark go.

'I expect you want your supper?' she asked, limping to the stove.

His arms went unexpectedly around her from behind, hugging her tight.

'I'm really sorry, love.' She instantly recalled the first time he'd said those words. It was soon after they met. Jenny was in her first job as a mother's help in Ipswich. Ted's mother worked for her employers, and through her she met Ted. They were a pair of innocents, and soon after she discovered she was pregnant with Billie.

She turned and kissed him. 'I know you are. Let's have an early night . . .'

'We haven't had many of those since Billie was born,' he said meaningfully.

Grandma was disappointed that we had to get married in a hurry, she thought, *me with my wedding posy hiding my bump, and Elin, as my bridesmaid, stealing all the lime-light. I hope Elin won't make the same mistake.*

*

'You should go out on your afternoon off, Elin,' Marian worried, after Saturday lunch. 'Otherwise the boys will take advantage of you being around to amuse them.'

'I don't mind, really,' Elin assured her.

'Look, let me treat you and Clo to the pictures; nice to have company, and you like her, don't you? I'm sure Clo's mother will keep an eye on things at home.'

'I would like to see Charlie Chaplin in *The Kid* – I know it's not his latest picture, but my sister saw it in Ipswich and said it was lovely, even though it was sad.'

'I'd agree with that. Celia and I went to see the film in London. We're always a few years behind in our little cinema! It's not a patch on the Palace in Southwold!'

'I hope your mother won't mind you going out,' Elin said to Clo as they hurried off to the afternoon performance.

'Oh, she won't, but *he* might,' Clo answered. She looked shyly at Elin. 'I reckon you've not been told, then? I've got a little lad, see, and me mum's a bit rough and ready with him, like she was with me and my brothers and sisters – I'm the youngest. I can see you're thinking I'm just a girl myself, like you, but little BP surprised everyone, including me, when he came along eighteen months ago. Mrs Lambert was good to me, giving me a job when I got the sack from the other one. She gave me her baby clothes, 'cause then Peggy wasn't even thought of, and her boys' outgrown clothes and that.'

'BP. What does that stand for?' Elin wondered.

'Well, I named him Robert Baden Powell, Butt being so short 'cause I figured he'd have a lot to live up to then, and a good name helps you get on in life, don't it.'

'I prefer Butt to *Buttle*! My last employer was a nasty piece of work,' Elin said quickly to cover her surprise at these revelations, as they arrived at the cinema.

As they settled into their seats in the second-to-front row, Elin thought: *I suppose all that happened to Jenny, too. At the time I was too naive to realise why she had a baby so soon after she and Ted were married. Probably little BP's father scarpered, and Clo is better off without him. I'm content with my lot as it is.*

The film was the heart-wrenching tale of a kid abandoned by his mother, then adopted by the Little Tramp. Both girls dabbed their eyes throughout the film.

*

The little package addressed to Mrs Jenny Drake came in the second post three days later. Jenny was relieved it hadn't come earlier before Ted left for work. She opened it wondering what it contained. A pair of sheer silk stockings! No note, but she guessed who had sent them. She couldn't wear them of course, else she would arouse Ted's suspicions – the stockings they replaced were cheap rayon.

FIVE

Elin wrote to tell Grandma about going to the cinema, and the film:

I suppose it's really only pictures shown in a hut, nothing grand, but when the lights go down, you get transported – if that's the right expression? Anyway, Mrs Lambert said we should make it a regular outing as we enjoyed it so much. She says I need to have fun with a friend my own age, as otherwise I might start mumbling two-times-two in my sleep! This is the job I dreamed of when I was at the Buttles'. Here I really am treated like one of the family . . .

She omitted to tell Belle about Clo's baby. She'd worry, Elin thought, that her beloved granddaughter might be led astray, yet she knew her grandmother to be a compassionate woman who quietly provided practical help to village girls in that situation. Belle's steel knitting needles were clicking most evenings as she turned the heels of tiny white socks or fashioned the crown of a lacy patterned bonnet.

Clo's friendship was expressed by the occasional whole cherry on Elin's breakfast grapefruit. In return, Elin requested and was given a useful remnant of bottle-green corduroy from the sewing pieces. Marian provided a pattern and in her spare time Elin made warm dunga-rees for young BP.

'Use the machine,' Marian advised. 'You do enough darning by hand.'

Elin soon learned to treadle, and when the Singer whirred along neat hems, she thought happily: *maybe I'll make a party dress next, for Billie, not me!*

'Oo-er...' was all Clo could manage, when Elin gave her the gift for BP. They were in the kitchen, where Clo was washing up, and Elin was warming Peggy's bottle.

Mrs Bunting nodded her approval.

'Fit the little tyke a treat, they will, Elin,' she said gruffly.

Clo smiled ruefully. 'He is that; got to learn his man-ners, like Charlie and Jack.'

Early on Saturday morning Elin was woken by an urgent tapping on her door. She stumbled out of bed and padded barefooted to see why she was being summoned. Marian stood there, torch in hand, whispering to Elin to follow her to her bedroom.

By the light of a bedside lamp, she saw Mr Lambert, in navy-blue silk pyjamas, sitting up in the double bed. His expression was impassive.

Elin averted her gaze quickly, wishing she had paused to put on her dressing gown, as she tiptoed round the bed to the baby's cot.

'Peggy's very restless, won't take her bottle. I believe she's caught Charlie's cold, he *would* kiss her goodnight. She's running a temperature. I'll undress her and hold her while you sponge her down with lukewarm water.'

The baby's skin was burning hot, her limbs trembling. They worked in silence, damping down the fever. Several times Elin changed the water in the basin, then continued the soothing, cooling trickling of water. Eventually, Marian gently dried the baby with the towel she was lying on.

'She'll do,' she whispered wearily. 'I'll pop her into a clean gown while you change the sheets on her bed; we'll cover her lightly, but leave her quilt rolled back for now. Thank you, Elin, I couldn't have managed without you . . .'

The connecting door opened and Charlie stood there, rumple-haired and sleepy.

'Is it morning?' he asked, then gave an explosive sneeze.

'I'll see to him.' His father spoke at last, reaching for his dressing gown. As he made to pass Elin, smoothing the clean linen, she felt a slight pressure on her back. The warmth of his hand seeped through her nightdress to her skin. It was disturbing.

'You must get back to your bed, Elin,' Marian said. 'When Charlie's settled, I'll ask my husband to make tea. Would you like a cup?'

'No, thank you,' Elin said hastily. She didn't want Mr Lambert coming into her room after what had just occurred, even though Jack was asleep in his corner.

'Try and get back to sleep then; Mark is coming tomorrow – oh, today! He seems in need of a sympathetic ear . . . He can look the baby over for me, that's a comfort.'

I'm not sure I want to see him either, Elin thought. *Maybe I'll go to Clo's to spend my afternoon off, I know she wants me to meet young BP.*

'Come back to bed, Marian,' Mr Lambert repeated mildly.

Marian pretended to sip her tea, sitting on a chair by the cot.

'Turn the light out if it's bothering you,' she said at last. 'I've got my torch in my pocket.' Did he realise she had seen him touch Elin? she wondered. Was it her own fault? Peggy's birth had been traumatic, a breech presentation; Marian had needed stitches for a bad tear. Was she expecting too much of him to be patient? She must be watchful, for Elin's sake, and his. They couldn't afford to lose Elin.

All the advice I give to others, she thought, *including my brother, rejected by his wife; but I can't talk this over with anyone, not even with the love of my life.*

*

'You go off directly after lunch,' Mrs Bunting suggested. 'I'll see to the clearing-up.'

Elin tactfully put on what she now thought of as her Buttle coat, not the smart cape. Clo changed from her black dress and white apron into her own shabby clothes.

'Don't worry about Peggy,' Marian reassured her, as Elin peeped into the Moses basket. 'She's snuffly, but not feverish now, thank goodness. Enjoy your time off.'

Clo and her aunt lived in the older, less salubrious part of the village, which had been considerably extended by speculative building since the advent of the railway. They went up an alley that was in stark contrast to the well-kept, affluent main street. Clo pointed out her aunt's neat mid-terrace brick house but they had to walk on up a steep slope to a straggle of ancient cottages, which looked forgotten and forlorn.

The front door swung open on creaking hinges. Waiting politely in the dark narrow hallway while Clo told her mother they had a visitor, Elin's nostrils were assailed by a pungent odour – a combination of various unpleasant things including ammonia from unwashed nappies. She was really glad now she wasn't wearing her new clothes.

'Ma says to come in,' Clo said, removing her threadbare jacket, then the warm scarf that her employer had given her for Christmas. 'Take off your coat.' She tossed the garments on to a chair on top of a pile of indeterminate clothes.

Clo's mother was a thin woman in her fifties with a wan, lined face. She rose from one of the two sagging armchairs in the living room, said a husky hello to Elin, coughed as she wiped cups with a rag, then poured stewed, bitter tea from a pot.

'Ignore the hounds,' Clo said. 'They only bite each other.'

Two aged black mongrels eyed each other balefully from their respective corners on either side of the stove. Both emitted a low, continuous growling.

'Every night, just at the time my old man use ter come home from the pub, them animals get up and have a fight. Make more noise than *he* did, in his cups. When one makes the other yelp, they change corners and shut up. Devils, they are,' Ma said.

'living room, I reckon,' said Clo with feeling. 'Fang and Grump, I call 'em. Have a chair,' she offered Elin, pulling one out from the table. She rubbed the seat with her sleeve. 'Bit hard, I'm afraid, but BP's taken over the other armchair.'

As Elin's eyes adjusted to the gloom, for the oil lamp was not yet lit, she saw Clo's little boy in his new dungarees, sprawled asleep, as if he had fallen in action. She hoped she'd concealed her surprise at his glossy black curls and apricot skin, reminiscent of the dark good looks of her film hero, Charlie Chaplin, but Clo picked up on it.

'He's beautiful, ain't he? His father was a waiter at the hotel where I worked after I left school. I was learning to be a chambermaid, but got sacked when the manager found out. The waiter'd already gone back to Greece, not knowing the trouble he'd put me in. That's why Ma and me give my boy a name to live up to, Elin,' she said proudly. 'He's real forward for his age.'

'Too clever by half,' Ma remarked fondly.

'Elin's a natural with children,' Clo informed her mother. 'I reckon you'll want a big family of your own one day, eh, when you meet the right feller?'

Elin went very pink. She thought, but couldn't say, in view of Clo's circumstances: *I'm not seventeen until March, plenty of time for that.*

She said instead: 'The young Lamberts – well, I'm content to look after them for as long as they need me.'

BP's eyes seemed to snap open. They were large, almost black; his expression was instantly animated, mischievous. He slid down from the chair and pointed at Elin.

'Who's that?' he demanded.

'This is my friend, Elin, from where I work, the one what made you them trousers.'

He shot across the room and leapt on to Elin's lap, gave her a smacking kiss.

'Tell me a story,' he demanded, and of course, she obliged. He was indeed a beautiful, affectionate child, a credit to his young mother, even though there was a spreading damp patch on the seat of the new dungarees, as Elin soon ruefully realised.

'It'll be dark going down the lane,' Clo said anxiously, when it was time for Elin to leave. 'You ought ter brought a torch. Want me to come with you?'

'Of course not, you've got BP to feed and put to bed. I'm not nervous.' Elin wasn't too sure that was true. 'I enjoyed myself, thank you. I'll see you on Monday.'

It was later than she'd realised, getting on for eight o'clock by the time she left the lights of Overbridge and its dwellings behind and turned into the long, winding tree-lined lane that led towards the new houses. There was no footpath and as she brushed against the hedgerows water from the recent rain dripped down her neck, causing her to shiver. Then she spotted a beam of light ahead, heard footsteps approaching.

'Hello, who's that?' she called out, her voice wavering.

'Mark Clements. I arrived after you'd gone out. Marian asked me to look out for you. Sorry if I frightened you.'

'You didn't,' she said unconvincingly, as he tucked her arm in his.

They walked a way in silence, then she said: 'Is Peggy all right?'

'A trifle grumpy. I'm to tell you Marian intends to get off to bed early, herself.'

'Oh, good, she was up most of the night . . .'

'So were you, I hear. Maybe Marian was tired of listening to all my troubles.' He paused, then, 'You may know something of those. I came to tell Marian my wife is improving following her recent shock treatment.'

'But that's good news, isn't it?'

'It is, indeed. However, she has decided that she won't be returning to me; she feels our marriage was a mistake, she wants to end it,' he stated flatly.

Elin wasn't sure how to respond to this. After all, she didn't know him that well.

'Oh, I might as well tell you the rest of it – Marian thinks I am being too impetuous. Our father wants to semi-retire and is offering me the practice. I'm tired of our nice middle-class patients, I feel I shall be free now to do something worthwhile with my life. I went to see a friend recently in Ipswich, whom I met during my medical studies – by the way, by chance I bumped into your sister and niece that day, did she tell you?'

'No,' Elin said, wondering why Jenny hadn't mentioned it in her last letter.

'My friend has a surgery in a deprived area, he needs a partner, why not me?'

'Won't your parents be upset?'

'I left home when I joined the Army, then I married Ann. I only went back on a temporary basis. I suppose I really knew early on that Ann and I were not compatible, but if we'd had a child, we would have made the best of it. Marian, who seems to have the perfect marriage, was shocked when I said I'm glad it's over. What do *you* think, Elin Odell?' he challenged her, taking her by surprise.

'Most people would say I'm too young and inexperienced to have any opinion.' She was really embarrassed now by his frankness.

'Oh, I think you were born wise!' They had almost reached the corner, could see the lights of Homeleigh. He stopped, turned, his breath warm on her face. 'If you were a few years older,' he whispered.

'But I'm not. Grandma says we all have to make mistakes before we settle down.'

'Your grandma is right. I apologise, I didn't mean—'

'You asked for my advice. Well, I think you're doing the right thing,' Elin said.

He drew her close, planted a chaste kiss on her cheek.

'I *do* like you, Elin Odell!'

If you were a few years older . . . well, one day she would be, Elin thought.

Mr Lambert opened the front door as they crunched along the gravel drive.

'Oh, good, Mark, you've found her. Elin, help yourself to supper if you're hungry.'

'Thank you, I'm starving,' Elin said gratefully. She'd missed both tea and dinner; nothing had been forthcoming at Clo's house. She didn't blame them for that as her visit had been a last-minute affair.

'I'm afraid my wife has succumbed to this wretched cold in the head,' Mr Lambert added. 'You're on duty this Sunday aren't you? If she isn't any better in the morning, I shall insist she spends a day in bed. Well, goodnight, Elin.'

'Goodnight, Mr Lambert. Dr Clements, thank you for walking me home.'

As she left them, Elin heard her employer say: 'I'd like a chat with you Mark, *now*, please. I understand you are going off tomorrow morning. We'll go in the study. You upset Marian earlier, you know . . .'

*

A lady from the Welfare called on Jenny. She pronounced Billie to be well nourished and progressing satisfactorily. However, she'd really come to remind her mother that it was time for Billie to be vaccinated against smallpox.

'I thought that there wasn't a real need nowadays,' Jenny said tentatively.

'This disease is not eradicated yet. Parents must still be vigilant.'

'I suppose I don't, well, want her to have a great weal on her arm like this.'

Jenny rolled her sleeve up, showed the offending mark on her own upper arm.

'The modern procedure is much improved. A tiny silvery scar, that's all.'

'But suppose she takes it badly?'

'I'll be honest. She may well be out of sorts for a few days. Only a small number of children have a severe reaction. Billie is a strong, healthy child; don't worry!'

That afternoon they went down town to the surgery. *Like taking a lamb to slaughter*, Jenny thought fearfully. Grandma's Bible sayings were never forgotten, likewise her remedies for minor ills. They only visited the doctor when they really had to.

'Doctor Wade is out on a call,' the motherly receptionist told Jenny. 'The new doctor is extremely busy. Please take a seat, I'm afraid you are in for a lengthy wait.'

Billie was very fidgety indeed after two hours had passed, even tiring of watching the dispenser/receptionist selecting the medicines from the cabinet behind her counter.

'Strawberry or lemon?' she asked, when children's cough linctus was required. Jenny recalled that the taste was the same, despite the colouring, as the corks were pushed with a squeak into the neck of each bottle. Jenny and Billie were the last to be seen.

'You!' she exclaimed in astonishment when she saw Mark at the doctor's desk.

'I saw your name on the panel list,' he said, 'but thought it best not to call on you.'

'After the way my husband reacted?' Like Elin, Jenny believed in being frank.

He nodded. 'Didn't Elin tell you I was moving here? I saw her recently.'

'No, she didn't.' But then, Jenny thought, *I didn't tell her I saw him, either* . . .

He busied himself with preparations for the vaccination.

'You're not too worried about this, are you?'

'My mother was a nurse. She believed in vaccinations – she had me done, as a child,' Jenny said. *He looks weary*, she thought, *it must have seemed an endless day.*

'Hold her close and reassure her. I'll be as gentle as I can . . . there, that's done.'

Billie let out an outraged yell. Then she plucked urgently at her mother's blouse, for Jenny's coat was undone. Embarrassed, Jenny looked at Mark.

'Go ahead,' he said. 'I'll just let my receptionist know that she can leave, and I'll lock up now surgery is over. I live here; Dr Wade moved when he married recently.'

Jenny nursed her daughter for a few minutes until she calmed down. She wasn't quite buttoned up when Mark returned. He busied himself tactfully at his desk.

'Now, as a friend, not a patient, would you like to come upstairs for a cup of tea?'

'What made you decide to come here?' she asked when he set the kettle to boil, and they sat on an ancient examination couch, which Jenny guessed doubled as his bed. He obviously hadn't acquired any furniture of his own as yet. It was a spartan flat.

'Well, the new government, under Ramsay MacDonald, talks about providing more, cheaper housing for the masses, but they don't seem to have considered the plain fact that the slum areas need clearing first . . . There is still a great need for dedicated doctors for poorer folk.'

'You aren't thinking of me and my little family in that sense, surely? Ted has a job, we have a nice place.' *Not as comfortable as my dad's house though, and money's always tight*, she thought.

'Don't sound so fierce! Medical care is costly; there are too many unemployed. It seems the situation will get worse. More strikes are inevitable, according to the *Daily Herald*, the favoured paper in our waiting room. Moscow and Stalin are much in the news, but as doctors we are more concerned with our patients than politics.'

'Ted's a Liberal if anything, not a Socialist! You know, I didn't mean – oh, I'm *sure* you're doing the right thing, working here.'

'There's another reason. My wife wants to dissolve our marriage. So I've decided to devote myself to a worthwhile cause.'

Jenny gulped the hot tea.

'I must go. Ted will be home shortly.' Then she added, before she had time to think about it: 'Elin's very young still, even though she is so capable . . .'

Would he read between the lines? She rose, picked up the sleepy child.

'I am aware of that. My sister knows how fortunate she is to have her. Don't worry, I'm too busy to visit Marian often. Shall I carry Billie downstairs for you?'

She nodded, and held her breath as he took the child from her arms. His face was very close to her own for a brief moment. *He hasn't shaved today*, she thought; *he's pale under the stubble. He's been rejected by his wife, it will take time for him to heal.* Clattering behind him down the uncarpeted steps, she still felt hot and bothered.

'Send a note for Dr Wade to call if there is any problem,' Mark told her.

SIX

Sometimes Elin felt guilty, observing how hard Clo worked in the house, even dealing with Elin's laundry along with the family's. Although Marian was always considerate to the daily helpers, Elin knew herself to be in a more privileged position. She and Marian worked in harmony; she appreciated being asked for her opinion when there was a minor problem with the children. Elin was left in charge when Marian travelled to London for the day, once a fortnight, to see her editor. Mrs Bunting cheerfully accepted this situation and on these occasions they all sat down to a relaxed lunch together.

This was the case the day before the family were to depart for Southwold for the Easter break. It was still only March, with blustery weather, but Elin was happy because she would be with her own family for a few days. In all, they'd be away for two weeks.

'Clo and me'll do the spring-cleaning while the house is empty next week, till the master gets back,' Mrs Bunting said, adding more water to the teapot.

'You deserve a rest, too,' Elin exclaimed, concerned.

'Well, we won't have to cook apart from his dinner and I can see to that, so it'll be a nice change, dearie. Clo can spend more time with BP. You all packed up?'

'Just about. Life's easier now Peggy's sitting up and only needs one bottle during the journey. Miss Clements is joining me and the children on the train from London. She's staying with us in Southwold for a few days. My dad's collecting me Thursday evening. Mr Lambert should be there by then, he's coming straight from the office.'

'And Mr Mark? We miss seeing him nowadays.'

'I think he's spending Easter with the family. But I won't be there, of course.'

'Mmm . . .' Mrs Bunting squeezed the last cup of tea out of the pot. 'He's got an eye for you, like *someone else* I could mention . . .' She glanced at Charlie, to see if he was listening in, but he was whispering and nudging his brother.

'Please can we get down from the table?' Jack asked after his prompting. The children usually had to sit there until the grown-ups were finished.

''Course you can,' Mrs Bunting told him. 'Looking forward to all them chocolate eggs, are you, boys?'

'Yes! Even Peggy can have a little one this year, Mummy thinks,' Charlie said.

Elin glimpsed the wistful look on Clo's face as she collected the plates. She had a surprise package for Clo to take home; she knew BP would love his milk-chocolate egg wrapped in gold foil. She'd bought one for Billie, too, of course. This morning she'd helped the boys make their parents a special card, and to paint faces on hard-boiled eggs for tea. They'd receive plenty of chocolate eggs next Sunday.

Charlie would be off to school in September; Jack was bound to miss his brother. When the time was right, Elin intended to ask Marian if BP might keep him company during the mornings. He was a bright little boy and it was never too early to start lessons.

Richard and Mark arrived at the house in Southwold within minutes of each other. Charlie was watching out as usual. Elin was all ready to leave, her case in the hall. Celia went out to greet them, while Elin gave the boys a hug and Peggy a kiss.

'We'll miss you,' Marian said, 'but enjoy your holiday, won't you?' She tucked an envelope in Elin's pocket. 'A little something for your birthday on Saturday, Elin dear. May it be a happy one! We'll celebrate with a chocolate cake when you return!'

Elin encountered Mark in the hall. He smiled.

'You look well!'

'And you look thin!' she said impulsively, as he shook her hand.

'Like me, he doesn't eat properly, living on his own,' Celia said from behind him.

'That'll be remedied while you're here,' Marian assured them.

Elin's dad wasn't thin, he was as big and bulky as ever, and pleased to see her. He helped her up into the trap, and tucked a blanket over her knees. Then she waved to the family watching from the doorway.

The pony clopped along and Elin snuggled up to Richard.

'Missed you, Dad!'

'Missed you, too.' He cleared his throat. 'Got something to tell you. I should have written, but it all seemed to happen at once . . . I asked Grandma to leave it to me. Frances – Mrs Goldsmith – and I are getting married on Easter Monday. She and young Luke moved in with us a week ago. I thought it would be nice to tie the knot while you are home. Jenny and Billie are arriving on Saturday – they'll be with us for two days, but going home after the ceremony. Your grandma's already moved back with your aunt, despite me asking her to stay.' He flicked the reins; the pony turned into the village street. 'Say something, Elin, please. I know it must be a shock – a surprise—'

'Not a shock,' she said in a matter-of-fact way, realising she should have heeded Luke's warning at Christmas. 'Now Jenny and I are grown up, you've a right to think of yourself, Dad, to be happy . . .' *I really have 'left home' now*, she thought. *Dad hasn't mentioned my birthday on Saturday, either, but at least Jenny and Billie will be here.*

'You don't mind, then?' He sounded relieved.

She shook her head, hoping that would reassure him. Then: 'Does Jenny know?'

'Yes, although it doesn't concern her as much.'

Why not? Elin wondered. *Because she's married herself?*

They were entering the yard where the pony was stabled. Richard lifted her down and hugged her for a brief moment.

'Be nice to Frances, Elin, won't you?'

The back door opened and Frances stood there wearing Grandma's apron and drying her hands on a cloth. The look she gave Elin was triumphant, but Richard was unharnessing the pony and didn't see.

'Supper is served,' Frances said mockingly.

It was short commons: tinned ham from the grocer, and lumpy mashed potato.

When she visited her grandma at Aunt Ida's on Good Friday, Elin shed the tears she'd been holding back.

'Oh, Grandma, why don't you come home?' she pleaded.

'It wouldn't be the same, dearie. Aunt Ida and I get on well. I look after the house, while she tackles the garden. She's out there now picking you a birthday posy. '

'Frances can't even cook! She's taken my room till after Monday, and Jenny and Billie'll be in your room for two nights – but there'll soon be two empty bedrooms—'

'And where have they put *you*?' Belle enquired sharply.

'Oh, I'm in one of the rooms under the eaves; Luke has the other one.'

'Not very suitable, the two of you up there. I don't trust that boy.'

'Dad seems pleased with the effort he's made at work. Wouldn't *anyone* rebel a bit with a mother like that?' Elin asked.

Belle sighed. 'Perhaps. Look, Elin, I'll make an effort, just as I did when your dad married your mother. Ida and I'll be round for your birthday tea tomorrow. Jenny'll be with you by then, and young Wilhelmina, eh? She'll lighten things up.'

'No one calls her that! Ted wanted a boy and he'd fixed on the name William—'

'So, Billie it had to be, I know. But she's named for the Dutch Queen, no less.'

'My mother – she wasn't difficult like Frances, was she? You liked *her*?'

'Yes, of course I did. But I suppose I didn't really know her long enough to think of her as a daughter . . . we didn't share many confidences.'

Her dad had remembered her birthday after all. He presented her with a lacquered trinket box with her initial in gold. There was an ornate card with embossed purple pansies and a fringed bookmark signed *With Love from Dad and Frances*. There was quite a post, too, with cards from the Lambert children and their parents; one from their cousin, Celia; a glossy card with playful white kittens on the front from Jenny and family; beribboned cards from her grandma and Aunt Ida. There was also an unexpected postcard from Mrs Bunting, Clo and BP. 'With love to our friend', the message said.

Later she'd show her dad, when he was on his own, the golden guinea in the little suede bag, given to her by Marian with the note: 'For a rainy day!'

At breakfast time, Luke, who had been absent most of the day before, came down yawning in his dressing gown, hair uncombed, and handed her a small parcel. Elin felt his mother's disapproving gaze on her as she unwrapped it. A little box contained a paste brooch in the shape of a flying duck with a glittering simulated ruby eye.

'It's very nice,' Elin faltered. 'Thank you, Luke.' She opened the lacquered box and placed the brooch inside. 'There, my first trinket!' How could she say she didn't like that baleful red eye? There was something she hadn't noticed before at the bottom of the box; she left it where it was, aware that Frances was still watching. It was the picture on card that her mother had painted of 'School Pond'.

'Just a family party when your sister arrives,' Richard said. 'I hope that's all right?'

Before Elin could answer, Frances spoke.

'We'll have the big celebration on Monday, of course,' she said. 'The wedding reception is being held at the Red Lion Hotel.'

Luke murmured wickedly in Elin's ear: 'May the wine run like water, then!'

'Eat up, everyone,' Richard said. 'There's still a lot to do. It was a bit of luck seeing Mrs Lambert's brother when I fetched you, Elin. He said he'd be glad to collect Jenny and Billie from the train at Southwold and drive them here.'

Jenny looked young and pretty, with newly washed hair, too slippery to put up, hanging down her back and tied with a red ribbon which matched the glossy red cherries decorating her straw boater. She held firmly on to Billie's tugging hand as they watched the train depart.

'Grandad will be here in a moment,' she said.

'Hello again.' Mark smiled. 'I offered to meet you, I hope you don't mind?'

The sun was shining, there was more than a hint of spring in the air, and Jenny said primly that she didn't mind at all.

'It's very kind of you.'

He didn't drive them straight home, but along the sea road, so that Billie could see the waves rushing and receding on the beach and a couple of distant boats on the dark-green water. Billie, of course, wanted to stop and go paddling, but Jenny reminded her that she was wearing her best clothes; that it was breezy down there, this afternoon.

'Dad will wonder where we are,' she said. *And Ted would be furious*, she thought, *if he knew I was sitting beside another man in a motorcar. Especially if he knew how fluttery inside I felt when Mark looked at me like that, earlier on.*

'I know what you're thinking,' he said softly. 'Because I feel the same.'

Elin enjoyed her birthday evening with the family. It was good to see her grandma in her old armchair, with Billie on her knee, reciting one of the poems she remembered from her own childhood. Even Frances seemed to mellow a little, but she withdrew from the company around nine o'clock, saying that she needed her beauty sleep.

'*I'm* not going to bed, yet,' Billie insisted, and for once she got her way.

Luke disappeared after his mother went upstairs, and Richard sighed when he heard the front door close.

'He won't be back till devil's dancing hours,' he said.

By ten o'clock the party was breaking up. Belle and Ida went back to the cottage, Jenny carried her little girl off, Richard made the fire up and Elin collected up her gifts to take up to her new bedroom.

'Goodnight, Dad, and thank you for a lovely birthday.' She gave him a hug.

Unexpectedly he responded.

'I wish your mother could have been here . . .'

'So do I. Thank you for her picture. See you in the morning!'

She had been sleeping for two or more hours, when she suddenly awoke and became aware that there was someone in her room. She felt for the torch under her pillow, turned it on, and directed the beam to the end of the bed. Luke was clinging to the rail, swaying and grinning foolishly.

'Go away, you're drunk,' she hissed. She threw the bedclothes back, scrambled out of bed. He lurched towards her.

'Let me stay, I'm lonely . . .'

'If you touch me, I'll – I'll hit you with this!' Elin brandished the heavy torch.

'I'm tired, I won't do anything – promise—'

'You certainly won't!'

His response was unexpected. He caught hold of her arms, tried to propel her backwards to the bed. As they struggled, she was aware of his beery breath, but also his superior strength. She'd dropped the torch – it was out of reach. In her panic she cried out and he clapped a hand over her mouth. Somehow she wriggled free; she brought her fist up and struck him on the jaw. He gasped, then fell on the floor.

She fled from the room, closing the door behind her; she crept down the attic stairs to the mid-landing room where Jenny and Billie were. *Thank goodness that my dad's and Frances's rooms are down the next flight*, she thought. *I hope they are sound asleep.*

She tapped tentatively on the door, then opened it. Jenny was shushing Elin as she bent over Billie's truckle bed. The night-light flickered in the draught.

'What's wrong, Elin?' she asked, alarmed.

'Can I get in bed with you, Jenny?' Elin was visibly shaking.

'Something happened? D'you want me to wake Dad?'

'No, please don't! I'll tell you in a minute . . .'

Her sister held her close, stroked her hair soothingly while the whispering went on.

'He was too drunk then, to do anything much; it sounds as if you were a match for him. I don't suppose he'll recall any of it in the morning, eh, Elin?'

'I knocked him out,' Elin said ruefully, then she couldn't help joining in Jenny's giggles. 'He was still breathing!'

''Course he was. It serves him right!' Jenny gasped. 'I expect he just passed out. They were wide awake now, wanting to talk.

'You haven't heard then, why he left college in disgrace?' Jenny asked.

'No. Have you?'

'Grandma told me. She warned me to be wary of him, too. He got the principal's daughter in the family way. It was all hushed up, but he had to go, of course.'

'Oh, why are men like that? Why do they drink too much?'

'Not all men, Elin. Not our dad; not my Ted. You'll find a good 'un, Elin.'

Elin couldn't say: *Like Mark, but that can't be, of course . . .* or Jenny might want to know more.

'I hope so,' she said instead. 'Perhaps you know something else I don't, Jenny.' She told her sister what Belle had said about not knowing her mother well.

'They should have told you,' Jenny said, after a lengthy pause. 'She's not my real grandma; Dad's . . . well . . . not my real dad. But I know I love them and they love me as if they were. I believe my father was a doctor at the hospital where Mother was training to be a nurse and that they couldn't marry because he already had a wife. She had to foster me out, and eventually moved away to Suffolk. Dad met her in the outpatients department when he had an ingrowing toenail removed – how unromantic, eh? I was nearly three years old before we were reunited, when she married him. That's why there's a gap between me and you. Our mother was only married to Dad for three more years; I hardly knew her either. But I'm so glad I've got *you* as my sister, and you . . ?'

Elin was finding all this difficult to take in, but she instinctively responded:

'So am I, Jenny. We must stick together, now Dad's marrying Frances.'

SEVEN

'So here you are!' Richard exclaimed. 'I took up your tea, Elin, and found you'd gone! Looked in Luke's room, but he was sound asleep, still in his clothes. He must've had a rough night. Anyway, it's nice to see my three girls together. I'll put the tray on the side.'

It was a tight squeeze, in the single bed, with Billie larking about between her mother and aunt, but there were plenty of pillows to prop them up.

'Girls!' Jenny said ruefully. 'It's nice of you to include me in that!'

When Richard went downstairs to riddle the stove, Elin had a sudden thought.

'Jenny, do you think Frances knows what you told me last night – about our mother?'

'I imagine she'll find out eventually if she doesn't already know. She's the sort to hold it against *me*, don't you agree? Anyway, I don't think either of us will be encouraged to think of this as our home, after tomorrow.'

'Did you tell Ted when you got married?'

'Yes, of course – husband and wife shouldn't have secrets from each other. I needed my birth certificate before we married, so Dad and Grandma had to tell me the truth. I only have a few vague memories of when I was very young.'

'Why didn't Ted come with you for Easter – for the wedding?' Elin asked.

'He had to work on Saturday morning, then his parents expected him as usual.'

They walked down to the bridge during the morning to show Billie the ducks.

'Billie won't need any dinner after eating all that chocolate egg,' Elin remarked. 'Just as well, as Frances is cooking the goose—'

'Oh, I didn't know we were having goose,' Jenny said.

'We're not! Roast beef. Can she ruin that?'

'I reckon she could . . . did you actually mean, she's *cooked* her goose, I wonder?'

The wedding was at eleven on Monday in the church. It was the second of three that day, so the bell-ringers were kept busy. Elin and Jenny left Billie with Belle and Ida early on, then joined the flower-arrangers. Inside the church, the shafts of sunlight streaming through the stained-glass windows set the dust motes dancing, and haloed the yellow daffodils on the sills, still sparkling with dew. Their scent mingled with furniture polish.

They helped tie white ribbons to the wrought-iron posts supporting the lamps at the ends of the pews. They left as the bells signalled the advent of the first wedding but lingered outside to watch the arrival of the young bride, face hidden by her lacy veil. She wore a low-waisted dress with white stockings and shoes. They stood back from other onlookers, conscious of their pinafores, with dusters tucked in pockets.

Later, heads turned in church, as Frances came up the aisle to join Richard, unfamiliar in his dark suit and wing collar, with his best man, Cobb the blacksmith, beside him. Frances wore a costume in fine ivory shantung with the skirt just skimming her ankles, and a matching hat decorated with creamy silk roses. Luke, who had been acting as usher, his mother being given away by her brother, slid quietly into the front pew beside Elin. He gave her a little nudge, smiled at her.

She thought, with relief, oh good, he doesn't remember Saturday night . . .

It was a short ceremony, being a second wedding for both bride and groom. No homilies from the parson about marriage being for the procreation of children, or advice on give and take. They were all conscious that the next service was scheduled for noon, and that guests were already gathering outside the church.

Jenny was intent on trying to restrain her daughter from escaping into the aisle and following her grandfather when he escorted his new wife to the altar. She was already thinking ahead to when Mark would arrive to drive them back home after the reception.

'I have our return tickets for the train,' she'd exclaimed, when he offered the lift to Ipswich, before leaving them last Saturday afternoon.

'But that would mean leaving the party early, eh, and someone taking you to the station? Your father can suggest a time, I'm sure.'

She worried what Ted would say. Was she foolish to agree to seeing Mark again?

The reception was held in the dining hall of the super-ior Red Lion in the village. This one-time coaching inn had prospered since the motorcar had given the middle classes easier access to the coast. Frances had arranged it all, and it was obvious to his daughters, from their dad's anxious expression, that he was no doubt wonder-ing how on earth he would pay for the feast. None of his friends were present, apart from Cobb. Frances had invited those she considered of standing in the village, like the vicar, the doctor, the retired colonel and his wife who'd recently moved into the Grange, and the vacuous Honourable Hubert, shabby relict of the one-time lord of the manor, and his snobbish wife. They all used the cor-rect knives and forks, of course, except for Hubert who dripped soup from his spoon down his starched white dicky front. But at least he didn't throw bread rolls, like bored young Billie, at those sitting aloof across the table.

'That lot's only here for the meal,' Jenny murmured to Elin. 'And the dyspepsia.'

'I wish I was going back to the Lamberts tonight . . .'

'What, you'd leave me on my own with the honeymoon couple, Elin?' Luke teased her. He was seated on Elin's other side. He'd already imbibed three glasses of wine, and the toasting and the champagne was still to come.

'What honeymoon?' Elin retorted, unaware how prophetic these words were.

As the wedding party emerged from the hotel, Elin spotted Mark's car in the forecourt.

'There he is, Jenny!'

'Will you take my bag over to the motor, then, Elin, while I say goodbye?'

'Did all go off well?' Mark asked Elin, getting out to greet her.

She glanced over her shoulder to see if anyone was in earshot.

'It was quite a day,' she said with feeling.

'The family send their love, look forward to seeing you tomorrow.'

'And I can't wait to see them! Oh, here's Jenny . . .'

Richard and Belle were there, too, to give Jenny and Billie a last hug.

As the motor drove off, and they waved, Luke lurched into Elin, then clutched her arm.

'Sorry . . . can you walk me home? Mother isn't speaking to me, apparently . . .'

'I'm not surprised,' Elin said, as she guided him along the street to the house.

Once inside, she gave him a little push as they arrived at the foot of the stairs.

'Go to bed. No going out again to the Plough. I'm going to stay with Grandma overnight.' *I don't think she'll mind,* she thought. *I'll just wait to tell Dad. Frances won't want me around this evening.*

'I'm taking you back to . . . Southwold . . . tomorrow,' Luke mumbled.

'I know you are. I'll be back here by mid-morning.'

Mark drove through the gloaming, until they reached the outskirts of Ipswich, where the dazzle of lights began.

'Nearly there,' he said. 'Billie asleep? Haven't had a peep out of either of you for most of the way.'

'I was thinking, you know, about Dad; hoping he'll be happy . . .'

'But you don't think that's likely, do you?' he asked frankly.

'No, I'm afraid I don't. It's the end of our family, as we've known it.'

'You've got your own family now though, haven't you. A husband and a child . . .'

'Of course I have!' *Is it enough?* she asked herself. *It seemed so, until I met you.*

He stopped the car outside her house. It was dark now, but the house was unlit.

His hand brushed inadvertently against her thigh.

'Forgive me,' he apologised.

'Real silk,' she whispered. 'The stockings you sent me, Mark. I've still got a scar on my knee, as a reminder of that day . . . I must go.'

'Have your key ready. Your husband appears to be out.'

'Still at his mother's,' she said, but suddenly anxious. This was unlike Ted.

'I'll see you safely inside then,' Mark insisted.

The gaslight flared, and he stood beside her, sleepy Billie in his arms, as she read the scribbled note on the table. There were some silver coins beside the message:

Sad news. Dad passed away last night. Staying with Ma until arrangements made. Best not to bring Billie there yet. Will be in touch about funeral. Love Ted.

Jenny's legs seemed to buckle. She sat down abruptly on the settee.

'Ted's dad has died. He won't be home tonight,' she stated. 'You'd better go.'

'Of course. Will you be all right?'

She nodded. 'I must put Billie to bed. Goodnight, and thank you for the lift.'

He stopped at the door.

'When will I see you again?' he said urgently.

'I don't know,' she said flatly. 'Goodnight,' she repeated.

He put out a hand, gently touched her quivering mouth.

'You know where I am,' he said, as he opened the door, 'if you need me.'

'Goodnight, Richard,' Frances said firmly, opening the door to Elin's old bedroom.

'But, I thought . . .' Then a feeling of sheer relief washed over him. The whole day had been a charade. She'd got what she wanted; a home, husband and security, hadn't she? It might be a loveless marriage, but he'd look after her as best he could.

'Goodnight, Frances.' Not even a perfunctory kiss. He trod heavily upstairs.

Of course, he thought, as sleep eluded him that night, folk might say that Delia, his first wife, had married him for precisely the same reasons. But Delia had been a generous, strong-minded, loving young woman, like her daughters now. She'd stirred the hidden passion within a shy bachelor and he was grateful for the precious time they'd had together, before it was tragically curtailed.

*

It was breezy in the trap. Elin held on to her hat. The pony knew that inexperienced hands were flicking the reins, and she slowed down to amble along the lanes.

'Luke, you look awful this morning,' she remarked candidly.

'Come out with it then: tell me to give up the demon drink!'

'Well . . .'

'I've got to get my courage up to tell your dad I'm leaving, too, Elin.'

'He'll be disappointed, because you're doing well at work, but—'

'But I'm being realistic, aren't I? Mother's about to wash her hands of me.'

'Did she love your father?'

'Perhaps she did, early on. But after I was born, they didn't share a bedroom.'

'That's not a real marriage,' Elin put in impulsively.

'It wouldn't do for me. I'm of a passionate disposition.' He glanced at her slyly.

'I know all about that. Aren't you ashamed of yourself?'

He ignored that. 'Gee up!' he urged the pony. 'No point in hanging about.'

There was Charlie, waiting by the gate.

'She's here!' the cry went up.

Marian came out with Peggy in her arms, and Celia with Jack. Luke, assisting Elin to alight from the trap, said in a low voice that he wouldn't come in, that he was going home to pack, then to break the news that he was leaving.

'So it's goodbye,' he said, and before Elin could open the gate, he pulled her close and kissed her full on the lips. Then he stepped up into the trap and drove off.

Scarlet-faced and confused, she turned to Marian crying: 'Oh, it's good to be back!'

Late that evening she and Marian met unexpectedly in the kitchen.

'Did that young man make a nuisance of himself over the weekend?' asked Marian.

'Well . . . he tried, but . . . I wouldn't allow it.'

'I'm glad,' Marian said. She gave Elin's arm an affectionate squeeze. 'We don't want to lose you, Elin, not for a long time yet, because you really are an important member of our family. Although I realise that a pretty, talented girl like you will have plenty of offers.'

'There are offers, and *offers*,' Elin said ruefully.

Then the tears began and Marian was hugging her.

'Take your time – you can confide in me,' she was saying. 'Everyone else has gone to bed. My husband and Celia need to be up early tomorrow to travel back to London. Fortunately, they've arranged for a taxi to Ipswich. I only popped in here for a glass of water, and whom do I find tidying up? You.'

'Now Dad's married again, and Grandma's moved out, well, I don't feel as if I have a family and a home to return to. Frances has even taken over my bedroom. Not only that – I suppose it's only just sinking in – there's something I didn't know about my mother, but Dad still hasn't said anything about that. Jenny had to tell me, and you see, it really affects her much more than me . . . '

Marian waited patiently for the rest of the story to spill out.

EIGHT

Ted was naturally very cut up about losing his father. As the only surviving son, he told Jenny, it was his duty to insist that his mother came to live with them. He was shocked when his wife displayed a certain resistance to this plan. Jenny was forced to explain herself to him, aware that she would hurt him.

'I know how close you are to your ma, Ted, particularly now, but . . . well, you must realise that she's never really accepted me. She didn't want you to leave home, to marry me, oh, don't deny it, it's true. That's really why I encouraged you to visit them by yourself, and later with Billie; I was always the odd one out.'

'How can you say that?' he demanded. 'Look, it's my house, and if she wants to join us, that will be the end of it.'

'All right,' she said miserably. But it wasn't all right, and she feared that things would never be the same again. They were growing apart, *and it's my fault*, she thought.

It was an uneasy alliance. Mrs Drake took over the cooking, and the spoiling of Billie. She sat up with the young couple at nights. The only private moments they had were in bed, and then Jenny had to remind Ted that the walls were only lath and plaster, and that his mother, despite other frailties of age, retained sharp hearing.

'You ought to be thinking of adding to your family,' Mrs Drake reproved Jenny one day. 'Billie could do with a brother or sister. Too fond of getting her own way, that one.'

And whose fault is that? Jenny wanted to say.

One Saturday afternoon in late April she'd had enough. She left Ted and his mother to deal with the latest tantrum, and said firmly that she was going out.

It was a warm day, but she didn't wait to change out of her faded blue cotton housedress. She hoped Mrs Drake wouldn't notice her lack of stockings. She did plonk her hat on her untidy, loose hair. Being fair-skinned, she had to guard against the sun.

'Where're you going?' Ted called after her, belatedly anxious.

'Don't know. But . . . I'll bring back some fish and chips later, eh?' She had her basket on her arm. 'After Billie's gone to bed,' she added meaningfully.

She didn't intend to go downtown, but she did. She climbed the side steps to the flat above the doctors' surgery, now silent and closed for the weekend after the busy morning.

Jenny knocked twice before the door opened, glad that the street below was deserted. Then Mark stood there, and it was obvious that she had woken him from a nap, because his hair was as rumpled as her own, and he was in his shirt-sleeves and braces.

'I thought it must be an emergency,' he said.

'It is, oh it is! Can I come in?'

Before she knew it, she was weeping against his shoulder, and he was leading her gently to the couch, and saying something about making tea. He sat her down and took off her hat, tossed it on the cluttered table.

'Slip off your shoes, put your feet up,' he suggested. 'Then you can tell me all about it . . .'

It spilled out: the tension with her mother-in-law, Billie's paddies.

'She sounds like a typical two-and-a-half-year-old,' Mark observed. 'Marian's boys went through a stage like that. But children have to know who's in charge. You *are* a good mother, Jenny, you must believe that. Here, drink your tea and you'll feel better.'

'I'm all hot and sweaty,' she said, just as she had to Grandma, as a child.

He put the cup down and stroked her hair back from her damp forehead, then let his hands slip to her shoulders, drawing her to him. She closed her eyes, anticipating what would happen next. Knowing she wouldn't resist. His lips caressed her neck, her face, lingered on her mouth.

'Jenny, you're so sweet,' he whispered huskily. He straightened up. 'It would be all too easy to give in to the heat of the moment, wouldn't it? But could either of us live with the guilt? My marriage is over, but it still exists on paper. Your husband is as devoted to your daughter as you are; he wouldn't allow you to take her from him, to come to me. You're still fond of him, aren't you? Go home, and forget what so nearly happened.'

*

Jenny walked along in a daze. The smell of deep-fat frying and the queue outside the local chip shop suddenly brought her to her senses. She waited her turn, then hurried home with her newspaper parcel in her basket.

The door opened as she stepped up to it. Ted stood there, his shirt sleeves rolled up, looking dishevelled.

'Where's your hat?' he demanded.

She thought quickly.

'I took it off,' she mumbled. 'I must have left it on the park bench . . .'

'So that's where you've been!' He grabbed her arm and hauled her inside the house. Mrs Drake was nowhere to be seen, but there was an outraged yell from upstairs.

'Ignore it. Billie's in her cot. She can stay there until she calms down. I thought you'd left me . . . oh, Jenny!' he said, his face reddening as he struggled with emotion.

She put the basket on the hallstand, wrapped her arms around him, embraced him fiercely, aware of the pounding of his heart.

'Don't you know me better than that?'

They went through into the living room. The table was laid for supper. The vinegar and sauce bottles were placed prominently.

'Oh, you expected the fish and chips to walk here by themselves?' Jenny teased, through tears of relief.

'Look, Jenny, I'm sorry for how things have been lately. I've moved Ma's bed and things downstairs into the front room – after all, we don't use it much. We'll rearrange things to make her really comfortable, tomorrow. Ma can be private when she wants, in her own room, and we—'

'I know what you mean,' Jenny said quietly.

'Before I call Ma and fetch Billie down to eat her chips – well, is everything all right now?' he asked anxiously.

Go home, Mark said, forget what so nearly happened . . .

'As all right as it ever will be,' Jenny assured him.

Mark didn't notice the straw boater with its jaunty bunch of cherries for some time. He picked it up, picturing it perched on a tangle of curly hair, framing a glowing face. He guessed she wouldn't return to claim it, and how could he take it to her house? Sighing, he hung the hat on one of the coat-hooks on the back of his door. He didn't need that to remind him of the softness of her skin, the pulsing of her throat, the urgency of her response before he'd come to his senses.

*

In September, Elin, Jack and Peggy waved to Charlie as he climbed into Marian's motor, looking serious and unfamiliar in his new green blazer and cap. This was to be his first day at prep school, a few miles' drive away in town.

'I'm so glad we decided not to send him to boarding school. I can still remember that feeling in the pit of my stomach on the first day of each term, knowing I wouldn't be going home that night,' Marian confided to Elin. 'Charlie won't have to go through that.'

'Here comes BP, right on cue,' Elin observed, opening the front gate to admit Clo and her little son. Clo had hurried home for him, while Marian drove her husband to the station.

'Into the playpen, Peggy; you boys can enjoy the toys while you get acquainted,' Elin said. 'I must tackle the washing before Peggy has her sleep, and you two, lesson time.'

She also wanted a few minutes to herself to read the letter from Jenny that had arrived earlier. She hadn't seen her sister since the wedding at Easter. Jenny was expecting her second child around the new year. Jenny wrote:

Actually, it has been a help having Mrs Drake here. I feel so tired most of the time. I am much bigger than I was when carrying Billie. Ted keeps saying I should see the doctor, but, after all, it should be easier the second time around.

Anyway, when it happens, I would like you to be with me. Grandma has not been too well, as you know, so I can't ask her. I think she has sort of given up since Frances took over at Dad's place, don't you?

I have been tactful (I hope!) and suggested to Mrs Drake that she will have enough to do with Billie and Ted and the house. We have booked the midwife. She thinks the baby might be early – around Christmas.

Will you ask Mrs Lambert if she could spare you then, please?

It was good that Jenny considered she was mature enough now to be with her during labour, Elin thought. She was sure Marian would agree, because she would be entitled to time off then. And much as she loved her dad and her grandma, she didn't want to spend Christmas with Frances. Maybe they would have Luke home then, but she doubted that. Grandma wrote that they'd seen or heard nothing of him since the wedding.

Another thought struck her: should the doctor be needed, she could send for Mark. He'd been too busy to visit the family in Southwold during the summer. She longed to see him again. Marian had mentioned that his divorce proceedings had begun.

Time to wash out Peggy's rompers – everyday wear now that the little girl was crawling – and Elin mused, as she hung them out to dry in the garden, that a session on the piano would be good this morning. Charlie's progress in that respect had been slow, but now he would have music lessons at school; however, she had hopes for Jack and young BP.

On Marian's return, before she retreated to her study to work, Elin made her report.

'The boys pounded the piano enthusiastically!'

She couldn't say: 'BP's a natural. He can already play a couple of chords, even with pudgy baby hands, and when I amused them with a rendition of "Three Blind Mice", he demanded to be shown how to play that, too.' Or that she was really missing Charlie. They had bonded right from the start. She was not as close to Jack, perhaps because he clung more to Marian, and Peggy was still a baby. Being one of the family was not always easy.

Celia was joining the Lamberts for Christmas. The day before Christmas Eve, she accompanied Elin, Charlie and Peggy from London to Ipswich. She encouraged Elin to use her first name, saying: 'We're friends after all, aren't we? "Miss Clements" sounds middle-aged, all stiff and starchy!' Elin enjoyed her pithy comments about the other travellers' peculiarities and Charlie joined in the muffled mirth.

It's strange, Elin mused, *although I think of Mrs Lambert as Marian, I wouldn't dream of calling her so. And as for Mr Lambert, well Marian refers to him as that, too.*

Mark was there to meet the train, to ferry Celia and the children to Southwold, where Marian and Charlie were already ensconced.

After settling the family in his motor, he escorted Elin to a waiting taxi.

'Oh, I could have walked to Jenny's,' she exclaimed. 'It's not far.'

'Certainly not, it's already getting dark. Marian said to look after you.'

'Have you seen Jenny at the surgery?' Elin asked anxiously.

He shook his head. 'I heard she was pregnant, of course, through Dr Wade. Most mothers prefer to have the midwife in attendance. Why, are you worried about her?'

'I don't have reason to be; I suppose it's just a feeling I have . . .'

'Ah, female intuition – not to be disregarded, by the way. Send for Dr Wade if you consider it's necessary. I shall be back on call overnight and tomorrow, but hope to be with my parents on Christmas morning,' he added.

He opened the taxi door. 'In you go . . . Elin, happy Christmas – take care of Jenny . . .'

'I will,' she assured him. He walked back to the car, with a final wave.

'Any minute now,' Jenny said optimistically. 'I'd like to get it over before Christmas Day, so I can enjoy my dinner . . . I expect that's what Stanley Baldwin said when they called

the general election last month and he became prime minister again. Our new baby will be a little Conservative, eh?'
But Elin didn't even smile at her joke.

She looks very pale, Elin thought, *and her ankles are
swollen. Could it be tonight?*

'We're going to have a baby, Auntie Elin,' Billie told her.
'Daddy says we can wet it's head with Tizer. It's a new drink
with lots and lots of bubbles. They tickle your nose.'

'I know. My boys are mad about it, too. We have it with
our Sunday roast.'

'I'm giving the baby my old toys; I'll get some more for
Christmas, Mummy says.'

'Aren't you lucky,' Elin said, hugging her niece. Marian
had advised her to make sure Billie had extra cuddles right
now; a good excuse to do so, she thought, happily.

'Supper. Ted's favourite – hotpot,' Mrs Drake announced.
It sounded like a challenge.

'Scrag-end of mutton,' Jenny murmured in Elin's ear.
'She's teaching me thrift.'

'I scraped the carrots,' Billie said, 'I sit up at the table
now, the baby's going to have my high chair and sleep in
my cot: I've got a new bed beside yours, Elin.'

'Oh, how grown-up you are these days!' Elin exclaimed.
She turned to her sister. 'Mrs Lambert said to ask you if
you'd like Peggy's Moses basket on wheels? Peggy's outgrown it. She brought it with her, anyway, and we just
have to let her know.'

Before Ted could say that he 'preferred to provide for his own family, thank you', Jenny clapped her hand to her mouth and said faintly that she felt sick.

The WC was outside in the yard. Elin pushed back her chair.

'I'll take her,' she offered, thankful to leave her own half-eaten meal, for it was swimming in grease.

'How d'you feel now?' she asked her sister, when the nausea had passed. They were shivering in that sentry-box-like edifice tacked on to the coal shed, with the overpowering odour of carbolic and the wind whistling through cracks in the walls.

'It's started, Elin – backache. I didn't want to cause any fuss until Billie is in bed.'

Ted was hammering on the door. 'Are you all right, Jenny?'

Jenny was consumed by waves of pain. Elin answered for her.

'No, she isn't. We must get her upstairs. Your mother can distract Billie while you run for the midwife.'

Ted pushed open the door. Then: 'My God! The floor's awash.' He grabbed hold of his wife as she sagged into his arms. 'I've got you, Jenny, love, lean on me . . .'

'My waters have broken – oh . . . oh . . . it's all happening too fast,' Jenny managed.

Mrs Drake rose to the occasion.

'Billie can sleep in my room tonight,' she offered. 'Then she won't hear what's going on, up top. I've a new book to read to her.'

The midwife arrived, plump and cheerful.

'Let me see what's what, eh? Your sister can spread this bundle of newspapers on the mattress, and, Father, get the kettle on!'

The pains continued unabated, but the midwife worried that little progress was being made. The first stage of labour was going on too long and her patient was becoming increasingly distressed. She didn't tell her that the baby's heartbeat was erratic.

She turned to Elin, rubbing her sister's back as the spasms struck.

'Send Mr Drake for the doctor – and tell him to hurry,' she advised, in a whisper.

Ted was sitting by the stove, his head in his hands, while the array of pots and kettles steamed and spat boiling water on the hotplate.

'Ted – go for Dr Wade . . .' Elin gasped.

He looked up. She saw that his eyes were puffy and red-rimmed.

'What's wrong?'

'I don't know . . . oh, please go! Get on your bike and ride like the blazes!'

There was a light on upstairs at the doctor's house. His wife pushed up the window sash and called down to the frantic man banging on the front door.

'Doctor's already out at a confinement – go round to the surgery, Dr Clements lives in the flat above – tell him, I sent you – good luck!'

'Jenny!' the doctor exclaimed, when he should have said, 'Mrs Drake'. 'I'll come, of course. I told Elin I would, when I saw her earlier at the station.'

Ted thought, in his anguish, *it's my fault Jenny's in this state. She didn't want another baby yet, but I insisted. How could I be so selfish? Her own mother died in childbirth.*

Ted pedalled furiously, the tail light of the doctor's car was no longer visible, but he tried to keep up. He'd recognised the doctor as the one who'd bandaged his wife's leg that day. He'd resented that act of kindness, because he was jealously aware that other men found her attractive. She'd only married him because of Billie . . .

Jenny heard her name repeated in a deep, masculine voice, but she couldn't manage to reply. The nurse wiped the sweat from her face, shifted her up on her pillows.

'There, there, my dear – Doctor's here. He'll get that baby born.'

She struggled as a cloth soaked in ether was held over her nose. Then mercifully she slipped into unconsciousness.

Elin retreated to a corner of the room as, in silence, the doctor and midwife worked to deliver Jenny's baby. Forceps glinted silver under the ceiling light; the baby was eased slowly into the world. Jenny seemed to be abandoned, as all attention now centred on the baby, not yet breathing, held up by the heels to be slapped into life with a feeble cry.

Unwashed, the baby was wrapped in sheeting, its eyes and nostrils cleared with cotton wool by the midwife, then handed to Elin to hold.

Mark was now urgently attending to Jenny. The bed was rattling. She was in shock, shaking uncontrollably. He called to the midwife.

'She's haemorrhaging – pass me my bag! Is there a telephone nearby?'

'My house, over the road . . . lights are on, so my husband's back from the pub. I'll get Mr Drake to run over there and tell him to ring the hospital, shall I?'

'Yes, and bring back all the towels from the linen cupboard, we must try to stem this.'

Jenny was coming to, threshing about and murmuring incoherently. Mark spoke to her, clearly and calmly.

'Your baby is safe in Elin's arms, Jenny. But you need to go to hospital because you have lost a lot of blood and you need special care.'

'What . . . is it . . .' she asked.

'You have a new daughter, Jenny.'

'Ted . . . will be so . . .' Her voice trailed off.

He was there, standing in the doorway, afraid of what he might see.

'Here he is,' Mark said gently, stepping aside. 'Tell him the good news yourself.'

Ted travelled in the ambulance across town with Jenny and a doctor from the hospital, while Mark followed in his car with Elin in the back seat, still holding the baby.

'I don't know how Billie slept through it all,' Elin said after a while.

'Jenny's mother-in-law was a real gem,' Mark answered. 'She made sure of that.' He paused, then: 'You got more than you bargained for tonight, eh, Elin?'

'I was only concerned for Jenny, I didn't have time to feel frightened, Mark.' She shifted the baby in her arms. 'She's very tiny – will she be all right?'

'They'll examine her thoroughly at the hospital, but Jenny will be their first concern.'

'Will you wait there with us?'

'I'm afraid I have to get back in case I'm needed elsewhere. Jenny will be staying put for a few days, I imagine. When you know she is safe and comfortable, you should go home – the hospital will arrange a lift for you. Billie will need you tomorrow.'

When they arrived at the maternity ward, Jenny was already being wheeled away to an examination room. Ted walked alongside the trolley. A nurse took the baby from Elin, and another nurse wrote down the details at a desk.

Elin went with Mark to his car.

'Thank you for saving Jenny's life, and the baby's.'

He gave her an unexpected hug.

'You're a special girl, Elin. It seems we have a lot in common, despite me being older, if not wiser. We are both on the fringe of family life, caring for other people's children. I imagine it will stay like that, for me, if not for you.'

NINE

In the New Year, when Elin was due to return to work, Belle came to take her place. Jenny and the baby were still in hospital. Ted met Belle at the station and wheeled her suitcase home on his bike. She used a stick now, which was something new.

'How are things, boy?' Belle asked. All young men were 'boys' in Suffolk, and Ted, in his middle thirties, was not yet considered 'a good old boy', like his father-in-law.

He hesitated, then: 'Ma and Elin have been a great support. I hope it won't be too much for you, helping us out – that's why we didn't ask you earlier . . .'

She ignored that. 'And young Billie? How has she taken all this?'

'She misses Jenny, of course she does, but Elin has taken her to the hospital twice.'

Belle paused to catch her breath.

'Legs don't go as well as they did . . . do you know yet when Jenny and the baby will be coming home?'

'Jenny will be back shortly, we hope. But . . . well, I have to tell you . . . the baby's not doing as well as she should. She'll have to stay in hospital for a bit, for some tests.'

'Doesn't the little soul have a name yet? Any idea what's wrong?'

'She's what they call a blue baby. We can't make up our minds what to call her.'

'She ought to be baptised, my dear, just in case . . .'

'I know that, but Jenny doesn't.'

'She'll have to be told sooner than later. What's your mother's name?'

'Doris Ruby. Not Doris – but Billie and Ruby, yes, that goes.'

'There you are then, that'll please Mrs Drake, won't it? By the way, I can't promise that she and I won't rub each other up the wrong way now and again, we're both strong-minded women. But I'll stay as long as you need me. Oh, look – Billie and Elin, hurrying along to meet us. Hello, darlings! I really missed you both.'

'Everything will be better, now *you're* here!' Elin said fervently.

Jenny had been moved into a side room off the main ward. She was still very weepy and it didn't help that her baby took so long over each feed. One session seemed to run into the next; Jenny was exhausted, and frustrated. When the nurse whisked the baby away without saying why, she turned her face to her pillow and dampened it with more tears.

A gentle touch on her shoulder made her aware that a visitor had arrived.

'Jenny, it's me, Mark. I thought I should come to see how my patient is doing.'

She rolled over, rubbed her swollen eyes.

'You know, don't you?'

He sat on the edge of the bed and took hold of her hand.

'About the baby?'

'Yes. I'm being punished, Mark, aren't I? For that day, when . . .'

'Nothing happened,' he said firmly.

'But it could have, and I wanted it to.'

'Oh, Jenny . . . the baby appears to have a congenital heart defect. It's hard to say how she'll be affected by this as she grows. It's not your fault. You must believe me.'

'They say I can go home. My grandma's come to look after me because Elin has to be with her family on Thursday. But the baby stays here for now.'

'The consultant will be along this afternoon, Jenny.' He hesitated. 'I won't come again. I don't think it's wise. Be brave, be positive.'

'I'll try . . .'

Jenny was taken home by ambulance that same evening. Ted carried her upstairs to bed.

'Give us a few minutes alone,' he said gruffly to the family.

Billie opened her mouth to protest, but Elin quickly reminded her that she might put some of the biscuits she had made with help from Mrs Drake on to a plate for her mother.

'And I'll make the tea,' Belle said firmly.

'I'm not an invalid,' Jenny protested, as Ted tucked the blankets round her. Soft cream blankets, satin-edged, their wedding present from Belle. Too fine for everyday. Where were the wool mixture ones from the market? The answer came to her: burned, because she'd been wrapped in them after she gave birth.

'I'm not . . .' she repeated weakly.

'No, but you've had a shock, we both have. We have to think about what the consultant said. The baby – Grandma suggested Ruby, that's Ma's second name, if you agree – isn't strong enough yet to withstand an operation.'

'*Ruby* . . . mm.'

Leave her here, or take her home, you must decide, the doctor had said.

Ted lowered himself on top of the bedclothes, beside her. He was sobbing now.

'Come here,' Jenny whispered. She cradled his head to her breast. *Be brave, Mark had said. I must try, for Ted and Billie's sake. And little Ruby, too. They say a mother's love and mother's milk can work wonders.*

'I'm back, Ted, I'm home. And Ruby soon will be, too. There, I've decided!'

'No more babies, I promise.' He choked. 'We nearly lost you.'

'We'll be careful . . .' Even then, she couldn't quite bring herself to say she loved him, but . . . she'd prove it, in time.

Elin met her other family in the station waiting room. There was Celia, with her fur coat glistening damp in the morning air, and Peggy in a new pink coat, leggings, and bonnet. Charlie sat astride the cases. His grin revealed a gap; he'd lost the first of his baby teeth. A milestone Elin had missed, she thought. He jumped up to hug her tightly.

'I imagine we had a better Christmas than you did.' Celia was glad to relinquish the wriggling Peggy, and to straighten her hat, decidedly askew. 'How're things?'

'Well, baby Ruby is coming home shortly, and Jenny is glad to be there already, particularly now she has our grandma to fuss over her.'

'Mark said he was sorry to miss you, but he had to hurry back to the surgery.'

'He was wonderful, you know, when the baby was born,' Elin told Celia, with a sigh.

'I'm sure he was.' Celia gave her a shrewd glance. 'He's resigned to being single. He intends to dedicate himself to his work. Oh, here's a note from Marian.' The note read:

Change of plan! Jack and I going to spend two days with my parents and we will return at the week-end. You can manage Charlie and Peggy very well without me! It will be easier if they both sleep in your room, I think. Mr Lambert will be home every evening, of course, and Mrs Bunting and Clo during the day.

Please can you check over Charlie's school clothes and make sure they all have names sewn in? (I bought him some bigger vests.) Thank you!

I hope your sister and baby are doing well. I will drop the pram off in Ipswich.

I do look forward to having you back with us.

Marian Lambert

Alone with Mr Lambert in the evenings, Elin thought uneasily.

She asked Celia, 'Are you leaving us when we arrive in London?'

'I'm afraid so. I've used up my holidays now, from last year.'

The children were bathed and in bed; Elin hoped to emulate them later. There was no bathroom in the Ipswich house, the only hot water was from kettles. She'd missed what no longer seemed a luxury, soaking in a steaming tub into which she'd crumbled lavender bath cubes. But first there was dinner to get through with Mr Lambert.

The casserole left in the oven by Mrs Bunting was tasty; Elin couldn't help recalling the gristly hotpot. She dished it up in the kitchen, adding the potatoes. She thought her hand might shake if she served the food at the table, under Mr Lambert's gaze.

Mrs Bunting had laid the table, filled the water jug. There was just bread to cut.

'This is very good,' Mr Lambert said kindly, tucking in. He'd changed, as usual, from his business suit, and donned what Marian dubbed his smoking jacket, in maroon brocade.

Elin cut two pieces of Bakewell tart: golden almond cake, thinly iced, topping shortcrust pastry, spread with, and now oozing, raspberry jam.

'Ah, another Bunting special. I'll make the coffee, my dear, you must be tired after the journey. I hope you sleep well, with the children in your room.'

'Mrs Lambert suggested it . . . I won't have any coffee, Mr Lambert, if you don't mind. I think I'll have my bath now – I've got a bit of a headache,' she invented.

'Leave the dishes. I'll take them to the kitchen. Goodnight then, Elin.'

'Goodnight,' she said, glad to make her escape.

*

Elin had washed her hair. It was growing again, but wasn't yet long enough to put up. She sat by the gas fire in her room, rubbing it into a soft golden fuzz. She was actually nodding off, when the door handle turned. She sat up with a jerk, knowing it must be her employer.

He came in with a tray, which he set down on the bedside table.

'A glass of hot milk, and aspirin. My wife swears by that for a headache.' He looked down at the sleeping children; Charlie in the spare bed and Peggy in her cot. 'They look very angelic, eh? I hope they allow you to have a lie-in tomorrow morning. Don't worry about joining me for breakfast. Now, into bed with you; no darning, or whatever it is you do in the evenings.'

Elin stayed put. She didn't want to cross the room in her nightdress, go past him.

He actually turned back the bedclothes invitingly. 'Oh, come on. I'll tuck you up.'

'No, thank you,' she heard herself say loudly. 'I'm not a child, you know.'

'I'm sorry – I never thought you were . . .'

'Goodnight, Mr Lambert,' she said firmly.

After what seemed a very long moment, he turned and went, without another word.

Before getting in bed, Elin moved the chair and wedged it under the door handle. She must replace it before the children stirred in the morning, she thought. She combed her hair, looking solemnly at her reflection in the dressing-table swing mirror.

Am I imagining it? Surely, he would never – try anything – would he? He's devoted to Marian. But – what if it had been Mark? That too was a disturbing thought.

Belle answered the knock on the door. Jenny was feeding the baby, with Billie close by, watching, while Mrs Drake was rolling pastry on the kitchen table. Wisely, Belle left her to it, where the cooking was concerned. She got to hold the baby more.

A young man stood on the step in a clerical grey suit, hat in hand. He had a faintly foreign look. His lips curled in a spontaneous smile.

'Is Mrs Drake at home, I wonder?'

'Young Mrs Drake? She's busy – with a new baby.' Now why had she said that?

'Her sister then? Elin?'

'Why do you ask?'

'Forgive me. I am Alex, Erminia Buttle's brother. I caught a glimpse of Elin the other day, in town, with a small girl. I wondered if she was working here again in Ipswich?'

'Oh, I've heard of *you*! Come in. I am Elin's grandmother.'

She asked him to wait in the hall while she ascertained whether Jenny was fit to see a visitor.

Jenny tidied herself quickly.

'Yes, bring him in. Ruby's asleep, I'll lay her down.'

'I took my sister and her boys back to relatives in Italy,' Alex said later.

'Didn't that beastly Buttle go after you?' Jenny wondered.

'No. We heard he soon installed another young woman in his house.'

'There will be a divorce, then?'

'No. Erminia may try for an annulment later. She wants nothing from him. He besmirched her name, our family honour. She had no lover. There was no one after her first husband, who was Italian – until she married him, to be a father to her children. Some might say she should have put up with him, it was her duty as his wife; I do not agree.'

'Oh, nor do I. But if he had been kind, she might have grown to love him.'

'Perhaps. Did Elin find more congenial employment?'

'She did indeed,' Belle put in. 'She is treated as one of the family.'

'I am very glad. Now, I have to return to my office. Look, this is my card. Please will you send this to Elin? It will be nice if she gets in touch, but it is right to give her the choice, eh? If she agrees, we can meet again when she is in this area . . .'

'Do come again!' Billie said unexpectedly to him.

He laughed. 'Thank you. You have the same blue eyes as your Aunt Elin!'

'And she's just as cheeky as Elin was at her age,' Belle observed fondly.

TEN

1925

Elin had completed her first year with the Lambert family. It seemed a real landmark to her. Although her worries about her father and his failing business were exacerbated by her awareness of his unfortunate marriage, and the fact she didn't see him very often. She was glad that Jenny and Ted had asked Belle to stay with them indefinitely. Elin knew that they would see she didn't take on too much, while letting her know that her help was appreciated, especially with Ruby, who was making slow but steady progress. *They have a real houseful in Ipswich!* Elin thought.

In the House of Commons, the new government was settling in, and fiery Winston Churchill was the surprising choice for Chancellor of the Exchequer. The bright lights of London still beckoned to many, despite the growing depression, and the Charleston was the latest dancing craze. Fashion decreed short skirts and cloche hats for women; plucked eyebrows and rouge applied artfully to knees as well as to the face. Men sported Oxford bags and ridiculously wide-legged trousers. In Overbridge, as in Southwold, folk were more conservative. As Marian remarked to Elin:

'Celia is the fashionable one in our family! But I'm not too sure about her shingled hair, especially now it's a startling blonde!'

Elin was delighted to be in touch with Alex. Letters went back and forth. She wrote that she looked forward to seeing him at Easter when the family would be in Southwold.

Mrs Lambert says you must come for the day! She approves of you because the senior partner in your firm was at school with her father! I know you won't mind if the little boys are with us. They have been promised a new kite.

You say you have never been to Southwold. Oh, there is so much for you to see! It is my favourite place! I told Erminia all about it . . .

She had taken to heart what Celia had said about Mark. It was time to enjoy herself. *An unattached young man was just* – she smiled at the thought – *what the doctor ordered!*

Marian, the children and Elin were staying in the house on the common for the spring break. Mr Lambert was dealing with an emergency at work. This had been going on for a few weeks already, and several times he had been obliged to attend meetings in the evening and then stay in London overnight with Celia.

'Nothing to worry about,' Marian said, when it was obvious to Elin that there was.

She was worried, too, about her father. She'd written to Richard that she would be in Southwold for two weeks, but had received no word in return.

Still, there was Alex's visit to look forward to, on Easter Saturday.

'How will I know it's him?' Charlie asked, before going on the look-out as usual.

'Well . . .' Elin began, as she wiped Peggy's face after breakfast.

'I believe he's tall, dark and handsome!' Marian put in, laughing. 'And you ought to divest yourself of your pinny, Elin, before he catches you in it. He said nine o'clock, eh? Leave the rest to me! Charlie's ready, of course, so Jack, get your coat and cap on, too. Peggy must stay in her high-chair for the moment.' She looked forward to a quieter day with her daughter, without the lively boys. She was weary after another sleepless night.

A loud noise startled them all. Even as they realised that Alex had arrived on a motorcycle, the engine cut out, and an excited Charlie burst into the kitchen, where Elin, still wearing her pinafore, was packing up the lunchtime sand-wiches in a basket.

'He's here! I told him to come in!'

Elin whirled round, and there was Alex with a haver-sack on his back. He unfastened the chinstrap of a leather motoring helmet with ear flaps.

'I found you then, Elin,' he said.

'Yes . . . you found me,' she agreed, returning his beaming smile.

They cut across the common to the harbour where there was always a lot going on, although the fishing industry was in decline since the end of the war. It was too early in the year for sea-bathing, but they planned to find a sheltered spot on the beach to eat their lunch, and later they would walk along the pier. On the way, Alex told Elin that he was here for the weekend. He'd booked bed and breakfast at a cottage near the front.

'That's nice,' she said, thinking happily that it was rather more than that. Her cape billowed in the stiff breeze and she held on to her hat, which threatened to soar sky-high.

Charlie and Jack darted about but obeyed Elin's strictures to keep in sight.

'A year ago,' Elin recalled, 'my dad was married again.'

'Is that why you haven't gone home for Easter?'

'Well . . .' She couldn't be disloyal to her dad. 'Can't you smell the herring smoking?' She pointed out the blackened smokehouses.

'I do like a fat kipper for my Saturday tea.' He sang to an improvised tune.

'Not tonight, though. Would you care to come to supper? Mrs Lambert said to ask you. We thought you were coming on the little train, of course, and going back to Ipswich this evening, that's why I didn't say before.'

'I kept my new mode of transport a surprise. I thought I might take you out for a spin.'

'Tomorrow? It's my afternoon off. I'm sure Mrs Lambert won't mind.'

'Good,' he said. 'I'd better see where the boys are, don't you think?'

'Watching those children on their skates – see? Not many boats about.' She shivered, and he took her hands in his and rubbed warmth into them. 'Where are your gloves?' he chided. 'Better get moving again.'

They sat on a rug below the promenade, in the lee of the brightly painted wooden beach huts, each quaintly named, which had lately replaced the old fishing shacks.

'Little summer homes – not for sleeping in, of course,' Elin observed, 'but just right for changing in, after swimming, and brewing tea on a spirit stove, or sitting on the veranda in a deckchair, watching the waves. Who needs bathing machines now?'

It felt very natural for Elin to lean against Alex, to allow him to share out the sandwiches and peel the hard-boiled eggs. He poured tea from the flask, and lemonade into the Bakelite beakers Marian had provided for Charlie and Jack.

'*I suppose we look like a family, the four of us, out on a picnic,*' Elin thought dreamily, as people walked by, crunching on a stretch of shingle. She couldn't say that, of course.

'I expect you miss Erminia's boys,' she said instead.

'I hope to visit them in Italy this summer. It would be good if you could come, too. It is much warmer there, and so beautiful with all the olive groves.'

'Oh . . . we always come here for our holidays. Mr Lambert says he had enough of going abroad during the war.'

'I didn't mean you travelling with your family, I meant with me,' he said softly. His arm was round her shoulders now; he gave her a little squeeze.

'Elin, can't we go on the pier yet?' Charlie sounded reproachful. 'And Jack badly wants to *go*, you know . . .'

Elin disengaged herself, scrambled to her feet.

'Come on then, I'll race you there! Alex can pack the basket, roll the rug, and follow us! Catch!' she added, throwing him her hat. 'I don't want to have to chase that!'

They almost cannoned into a crocodile of girls in smart blazers and distinctive white straw hats, from the local St Felix School, promenading with two teachers who looked not much older than their charges. There were cries of: 'Hold your horses', and giggling.

Charlie and Jack dodged the pushchairs and perambulators, intent on reaching the ice-cream seller, with the ice-box attached to his tricycle.

'Let me pay,' Alex offered, catching up at last. 'Eat up, before we go on the pier.'

Marian glanced at Elin's windblown hair, but just remarked: 'You obviously had a good day.'

'Did you?' Elin asked belatedly, hanging up the coats in the hall.

'Peggy obliged by having a snooze this afternoon, so then I prepared our meal. Baked cod and caper sauce. I expect you are all very hungry after a good dose of briny?'

'Oh, we are! That sounds good. Shall I cut the bread and butter?'

'It's all done. Go and rescue your friend from the children.'

'Did Mr Lambert ring?' Elin asked. 'Is he able to get away after all?'

Marian sighed. 'He's at home, thank goodness, but too busy with his paperwork, I'm afraid. Celia kindly offered to give up part of her holiday to help him. Oh dear, Peggy's crying! She's probably taken a tumble. I'll be glad when she's steadier on her feet.'

After supper, Elin and Alex washed up. Marian settled Peggy in her cot and then shooed the boys upstairs for a per-functory wash and thence to bed. When Marian came down, Elin served coffee and the three of them sat in the sitting room and talked for a while.

When Marian looked at her watch, Elin thought she was hinting that it was time for Alex to depart. But as she was about to say so to him, Marian rose from her chair.

'You won't mind if I leave you? I can hardly keep my eyes open. And, Elin, if you're thinking of not taking your afternoon off tomorrow, well, of course you should. The children will be occupied with their Easter eggs and my mother rang earlier to suggest that she and my father should come to tea. She's been busy baking a few nice surprises!'

'If you're sure,' Elin said. 'Thank you.'

It was half-past eight. Marian paused at the door. 'You'll lock up by ten, Elin?'

'Of course I will. Goodnight, Mrs Lambert.'

'Goodnight, both of you. Thank you, Alex, for helping with the children today.'

'It was a pleasure,' he assured her. When Marian went upstairs, he smiled at Elin. 'She is a tactful lady. And very kind. Now come and sit by me!'

'It'll be dark outside,' she said feebly. 'How will you find your way to your digs?'

'The gas-lamps are lit,' he said easily. 'Don't waste time talking. May I kiss you?'

'Yes please,' she whispered, and that was all either of them said for some time. She wasn't afraid that he would take advantage of her, go too far, but equally she was vibrantly aware that she didn't want the excitement and the kissing to stop.

They were startled by unexpected knocking on the front door. Instantly, they sprang apart.

'Marian, are you still up?' a voice called. 'I saw the light in the sitting room.'

'It's Dr Clements, Mrs Lambert's brother,' Elin told Alex.

'Let him in, then!'

She opened the door.

'Mark, we weren't expecting you.'

'Hello, Elin. I decided not to use my key and alarm you even more.'

'Marian's in bed.'

'Oh, I'm sorry. I didn't think it was that late. I was coming tomorrow and then I said to myself, why not tonight? Any chance of a cup of tea and a bite to eat?'

'Of course.' Elin steered him towards the kitchen.

'Have you a visitor?' Mark asked. 'I had to park outside. There's a motorcycle there.'

'Which belongs to me,' Alex said, emerging from the sitting room. 'I was just leaving. I'll see you tomorrow then, Elin, about two?'

'Your haversack,' she reminded him, 'I hung it up with your coat.'

'Aren't you going to introduce me?' Mark asked, quite curtly.

'Oh, Mark, this is my friend Alex, he lives in Ipswich, like you.'

'See your friend out, then, I'll be in the kitchen,' Mark stated.

'I'm sure he guessed,' she whispered to Alex, as he sat astride the motorcycle.

'Guessed what?' he teased.

'You know . . .'

'Kissing isn't a crime, Elin. I rather think I have a rival. He didn't even say good evening or shake my hand. Dr Clements is jealous, I believe.'

She put her arms round his neck, kissed him defiantly.

'Well, the door's open and I rather think he's lingering in the hall, so this will confirm his suspicions!'

As the motorcycle roared off, she went inside the house, but Mark was nowhere to be seen. He'd closed the kitchen door.

He heard, he saw, she thought. *I can't face him again tonight.*

'He's a very nice young man,' Marian said to her brother, after she and the children had waved Elin off on the back of the motorcycle. 'But I hope he goes at a steady pace.'

Mark merely grunted, rustling his newspaper. Marian tweaked it, looked him in the eye. 'I think our dear Elin is smitten. Oh, I don't want to lose her yet!'

'She's too young,' he said.

'She's eighteen now, Mark. She's not a child. I had rather hoped, you know, that despite the disparity in your ages and the fact that you're in the process of divorcing . . .'

'You'd like to keep her in the family, is that it?'

'Is it that obvious?'

'Yes. Stop talking nonsense, Marian. I haven't been a complete hermit these past few months, you know. And before you ask, I don't wish to discuss that! However, I admit I find Elin attractive, although I don't suppose the feeling is returned. Particularly not now.'

'Wait and see. That's all I'm saying!'

'Uncle Mark,' Charlie came to remind him, 'you promised to take Jack and me to fly the kite on the common this afternoon, before Granny and Grandpa come. Elin and Alex said it was too windy yesterday to chance it. I don't see why. Wind is what a kite needs isn't it, to lift it into the sky?'

'Let's take the kite and find out what happens now, shall we? I'm going back to Ipswich tomorrow. We must seize the moment, eh?'

'Just what I was trying to tell you,' Marian said.

Alex stopped the motorcycle by the verge of a newly ploughed field. There were primroses nestling in the shelter of the ditch, and the hedgerows were busy with nesting birds.

'Not so blustery today, but I hope you didn't get too chilly on the bike, Elin?'

'No, I enjoyed the ride round the lanes,' she said, hoping he would think her face was flushed from the slipstream as they sped along, not from being pressed against his back as she hung on tightly clutching him round the waist. A skirt was not the ideal garment for a girl on the pillion seat, and there was a lengthening run in one of her stockings.

'Let's sit here for a bit and talk.' He spread the rug on the bank.

'Last night,' she began hesitantly, 'I don't want you to think that I—'

'I'm sure you don't allow every young man to kiss you the first time he takes you out. It's well over a year since we first met, Elin, and I've thought about you ever since. You and I, it was meant to be, so why waste more time?'

'It's like a dream come true, for me, too, Alex. But . . . I did have feelings for someone else for a while. He wasn't aware of it, anyway, it wasn't possible.'

'Has that dream gone away?' he asked gently.

'I think so.' She looked around. 'You know, we're not very far from my home . . .'

'Shall I take you there?'

Elin shook her head decisively. 'No, it's best if I go on my own, later in the week.'

'You will tell your father about me? I shall write to my sister, she will be glad for us. Erminia and I are close. She came to England first, after our mother died, to join Mario, who works in the asphalt industry here. I followed her when I was fourteen. Erminia is eight years older than me; she was married to her first husband by then, and had her boys. I am now twenty.'

'What will you say in your letter?' she teased.

'That I found you, against the odds, and I'm not letting you disappear this time.'

'And how will you manage that?'

'By declaring my intentions – first to your father and then your employer!'

'I've no intention of marrying before I'm twenty-one! That's three years away. I said to Mrs Lambert that I'd stay with the family at least until Peggy's at school.'

'Did you promise that?'

'Not exactly, she didn't ask that of me, but I made a promise to myself . . .'

'Then I'll make a solemn promise to you, to wait until you're ready. Meanwhile, may I come to see you again before you leave Southwold?'

'I'm sure that will be all right. Say a week on Sunday? I'll have a whole day off.'

They scrambled to their feet. They'd been so absorbed in each other they hadn't noticed the tractor at the far end of the field, now trundling purposefully along the track to the nearby farm gate.

'Time to go,' Alex said regretfully. 'But at least I'll see you again soon.'

ELEVEN

'You should go and see your father, Elin,' Marian told her on Tuesday morning.

Elin decided to walk; it would give her time to think what to say. When she turned into the village street there were a number of folk about, and vehicles parked near the wheelwright's. Pasted to the wall was a large poster saying: 'Auction Today'.

As she stood there, stunned, a lorry drove off, loaded with timber from the yard.

She crossed over, opened the doors to find the floor space in the workshop packed with people. One or two she recognised as locals, the rest were strangers, jostling one another as the auctioneer behind one of the benches called for bids.

'Everything must go!'

'Elin, my dear.' She heard her father's voice. She turned, to see him behind her.

'Dad – why didn't you tell me?'

'I was too ashamed.' He seemed to have shrunk, his shoulders were bowed.

'Oh, Dad!' She embraced him, not caring about the curious, maybe pitying glances. 'Let's go home,' she decided, urging him towards the door. 'Until it's over.'

'The house and furniture will be sold later, too,' Richard told her, as they went inside.

'But why, Dad, why? I can understand business was bad, but the house . . .'

'Debts to honour, Elin. And I have to provide for Frances.'

The silence in the house suddenly struck her.

'Where is she?'

'She packed up; left last week for her brother's. I've already heard from her solicitor.'

They went in the sitting room. Elin made to pull the curtains back.

'Leave them,' Richard said. 'I don't want folk looking in, knocking on the door.'

'I'll make tea.' She felt helpless, but it was something she could do. 'Have you eaten today? I brought you a chocolate cake from the bakery.' Maybe they both needed something sweet to take away the taste of fear in their mouths, she thought.

'Where will you go after it's all over?' she asked later.

'To Ida's. She says I've been good to her since her husband died and the cottage will come to me in due course as she has no family. Your grandma will stay on with Jenny.'

'What will you do?'

'I'll have to find a job. I can't afford to retire. I'm sorry, Elin, there'll be nothing for you.'

'Oh, Dad, I don't need anything! I've got all I need at the Lamberts. I just can't bear to see you sad, that's all . . . but I can't help feeling relieved that Frances has gone.'

'You know, so am I!' Richard admitted. He actually smiled. 'Just us again, Elin, that's good, something to hold on to.'

There was something for Elin to treasure, to remind her of home, after all. Her grandma's wedding china, including the remnants of the bluebird set, was already packed in a box and labelled: 'For Elin'.

'As if she knew this was going to happen,' Elin exclaimed tearfully, when Richard showed her the box. Then, before he could say, she realised that Belle *had* known.

'For your bottom drawer, Mother said. When you do meet the right young man and decide to get married, I hope to be back on my feet and able to provide the wedding feast! But don't be in too much of a hurry, like your sister, will you.'

Elin thought, *it's not a good time to tell him about Alex.*

'Dad, Jenny told me that she isn't your daughter, but you've always treated her as if she was,' she said instead. 'I think that was a wonderful thing to do, especially when you were left with a baby of your own.'

'I loved you both, that wasn't the hard part. It was losing Delia so soon after we married. If it hadn't been for your dear grandma . . .' Tears welled in his eyes. 'And now at her age, now she's a great-grandmother, she's helping to care for a baby again.'

'I hope she'll still be around to advise *me*, when I have children one day!'

'Let's hope so, my dear. Now, shouldn't you be getting back to your family? It's a comfort to me you have a nice home and good people to work for, Elin. You're not to worry about me. I've got my health and strength, and I promise you, all will be well. '

'I nearly forgot to ask you,' Elin exclaimed, as she was about to leave the house. 'Has Luke been in touch?'

Richard shook his head. 'He seems to have vanished into thin air. You know, when we worked together for that short time I had real hopes that he'd turn out well after all.'

'He'd never been loved.' Elin surprised herself with this observation. 'He wasn't as fortunate as Jenny and me.'

She was hurrying along when she became aware of a motor being driven at speed towards her. It screeched to a stop as she scrambled up the steep bank in sudden panic.

'Elin – I'm sorry, I didn't mean to alarm you,' a familiar voice called out. 'I was going too fast! Marian asked me to meet you. Here, let me help you down.'

'Mark! But you left here yesterday!'

'I'll explain as we drive back.' He stretched out his arms to catch her as she lost her footing and slid down the slope towards him. For a few seconds she was pressed against his chest, before he released her. 'You look a bit dazed,' he said with concern.

'I suppose I am,' she admitted, as she climbed into the passenger seat. 'I've had some rather upsetting news.'

'I'm afraid you're about to receive some more. Celia telephoned me at the surgery this morning. There's been . . . an accident. I came to tell Marian myself—'

'I don't understand . . .'

'It concerns my brother-in-law. He has been taken to hospital, gravely injured. Desmond and Celia were at the station as the London train steamed in when he lost his footing, fell on to the railway line. There was nothing anyone could do. Poor Celia, having witnessed it all, is still in shock.'

'How terrible.' Elin's own news did not compare with this. *Desmond*, she thought. *I can only think of him as Mr Lambert.*

They stopped outside the house on the common. There was no Charlie swinging on the gate today. Mark motioned to her not to get out of the car for a moment.

'Elin, there's something I haven't told Marian yet, and nor must you, because it's too awful to contemplate, but Celia thinks it wasn't an accident.'

'I understand, Mark, but, in fact, I just don't know what to say at all.'

'She needs you now, Elin, more than ever,' he said quietly. 'So do the children. She's told the boys, but I don't think they've taken it in yet. Let's go inside.'

The door opened and Marian stood there, white-faced, but composed. Elin ran to her and hugged her tight.

'Oh, Marian,' she murmured, unaware that she had used her employer's first name.

'Thank God we've got *you*,' Marian said.

Elin took care of the packing and prepared lunch, for Marian was being driven home by her brother, together with her parents, whom they were picking up.

'Be good, brave boys, and help with Peggy,' Marian told Jack and Charlie. 'It's best you stay here with Elin. I'll telephone you every day, and Mark will be over to see you after he returns in a day or two.' She hugged the solemn children in turn, then Elin. 'I left the housekeeping purse in the kitchen-table drawer for you, don't worry about spending it all.'

'Goodbye, Elin,' Mark said. As he had done on the evening he'd walked with her on the way home from Clo's, he bent and kissed her cheek. Did he recall what he'd said then? *I do* like you, Elin Odell . . .

She thought, confused, *oh, I do still feel something for him. But what about Alex? Will I have to forget all that now?*

Mark arrived late on Friday afternoon. He'd brought someone with him.

'Clo!' Elin cried in surprise. 'Oh, I'm so thankful to see you!'

It was a subdued Clo, unfamiliar in a neat jacket and skirt, which Marian had provided from her own wardrobe.

'Mrs Lambert said your need was greater than hers, seeing's you've got the children to look after,' she said simply. 'She's got her mum and dad to help her, and my aunt, of course. BP'll be all right with his gran.' But she bit her lip, because she'd never been away from him at night since he was born.

Mark waited until Elin had bathed and put the children to bed before he sat down to talk to her in the sitting room. Clo was still busy clearing up in the kitchen.

Mark had already said he'd be staying with them until after the weekend, when he'd have to return to work.

'It's more bad news I'm afraid,' he began.

'But Marian – Mrs Lambert – was quite cheerful on the telephone.'

'Desmond is still unconscious. He has severe brain damage, spinal and other injuries and is unlikely to survive. Marian feels it's best you all stay on here, with support from Clo.'

'Charlie is due back at school the week after next.' Elin thought that would be a good thing. Charlie, being older, was more upset than Jack about his father's accident.

'My father mentioned it. Don't worry, I'm sure he will see to all that.' He paused. 'Perhaps I shouldn't say this, but we've learned from Celia that Desmond was in considerable financial difficulties, both at work and personally.

Marian is shocked, of course. She suspected something was troubling her husband, but she had no real idea.'

Elin didn't feel she could comment on what Mark had just told her. Instead, she said:

'Clo won't want to leave BP for very long, Mark.'

'I'm sure we could do something about that, tell her not to worry.' He paused. 'What about your young man?'

'My – oh, Alex. I'll write to him and explain that I can't take any time off just now.'

'I'm sorry. Perhaps we are expecting too much of you—'

'Of course not!' she flashed back at him. 'Marian always says I'm one of the family!'

'You always will be, I think,' Mark said quietly.

'Is it all right to join you?' Clo asked diffidently from the doorway.

'Of course it is,' Mark assured her. 'You and Elin, you're in charge here now.'

There was a spare bed in Elin's room for Clo, and Peggy's cot had been in there since her mother left. The boys were in the bedroom next door, so, 'We're all together,' as Elin said. Beyond that was the spare room. The Lamberts' big room was at the end, beyond the bathroom and the attic staircase. Mark, as usual, slept up there under the eaves. This had been his room when he was a boy staying with his aunt.

Clo followed Elin's example; she washed and changed in the privacy of the bathroom at bedtime into a voluminous flannel nightshirt donated by Mrs Bunting. On her return, she saw Elin, propped up in bed, writing a letter to Alex.

'At least you've got a chaperone now, Elin. Not that I think Mr Mark'd ever not behave proper, like.'

'Of course he wouldn't,' Elin said instantly. Best not to tell Clo about the brotherly kiss.

She put down her pencil, giving a smothered sigh. It was obvious that Clo wanted to talk.

'It's been a long day for you, Clo, I expect you want to get off to sleep . . .'

'Keep thinking about BP : . .' There was a break in Clo's voice.

'Of course you do. Mrs Lambert will be the same. But she trusts us to take care of her little ones and we won't let her down, will we.'

'You don't know what it's like till you have one of your own,' Clo said tactlessly.

'I hope to, one day. I'll turn the light out, shall I? 'Night, Clo, I'm glad you're here.'

Clo wasn't able to stay silent for long, even in the dark.

'You still awake, Elin?'

'Mmm.'

'It *hurts* you know, having a baby, especially when you're young and don't know what's happening to you. When it's all over, you're scared, 'cause you don't know how you'll manage – but then you think how lucky you are, if your baby's all right, and how he's yours and that you'll never give him away, like some say you should. Mrs Lambert didn't say that. When she had such a bad time when young Peggy was born, I really felt for her. She doesn't deserve all this upset in her life . . .'

'Say a prayer for her, and Mr Lambert and her family, Clo. I am,' Elin said.

Early next morning, Elin warmed Peggy's bottle, cuddled her close while she drank the milk, then changed her nappy and put her down for another nap.

Clo slumbered on, no doubt exhausted after all the travelling the previous day. Sighing, Elin knew sleep would elude her now. She shaded her light, and decided to rewrite her letter.

Dear Alex,

I have so much to tell you and don't know where to start. I haven't taken it all in yet, myself. It all began when I went to visit my dad on Tuesday. I didn't get a chance to tell him about us because he was in a lot of trouble. His business has failed and he has lost it and soon the house will have to go, too. His new wife has left him, and although he knows that the marriage would never have worked, she intends to have her share of what is left. At least Dad has somewhere to live (with his aunt) and is determined to find other work.

The other news is even more shocking. Mrs Lambert has had to return home, leaving me in charge of the children here, because her husband has been involved in a terrible accident. He's in a very bad way.

You will understand that, as it is not possible for me to see you for the foreseeable future, I feel it is not fair to keep you in suspense, and that I cannot make you any promises regarding our future together.

Please try to understand, and remember that precious time we shared, as I shall.

Your affectionate Elin

If he loves me, Elin thought, *he won't give up easily. He'll be hurt, but I hope he understands.* Then she pulled the covers over her head and wept.

TWELVE

Jenny was collecting medicine for the baby from the surgery. She'd popped along there on her own first thing. Both grandmothers had decreed that she shouldn't take the children out in the rain. Ted's mother had written out a shopping list, and Belle had added an item to the end: Mackenzie's smelling salts, a bottle of which eye-watering crystals she always kept in her bag. It was May, and a dismal day that reminded Jenny of the one earlier last year when she'd taken a tumble, Mark had come along, driven her home and ministered to her.

At her mother-in-law's insistence, she had borrowed her ugly rubber galoshes to protect her shoes; she was also wearing a sou'wester, and a mackintosh cape over her summer dress.

'How is little Ruby?' the dispenser asked, twirling a twist of paper round the bottle.

'She's getting on quite nicely, thank you. Dr Wade says we must continue with the linctus though, to keep her lungs clear.'

As Jenny turned to go, Mark came out from his partner's room. He hurried to the door to open it for her and then followed her out into the street.

'You look bonny, Jenny,' he told her, as she hesitated, wondering what to do.

'Don't be daft – in these squelchy boots, and this awful hat?' she retorted.

'Still fiery, that's good.'

'What's good about it? My grandma always says I'm too quick to answer back.'

'Look, I'm driving to Overbridge in about an hour's time – you've heard about the trouble there from Elin, I presume? I won't ask you up to my flat – but why not get in the car, let me run you into town to a tea shop and I'll tell you the latest news.'

'All right, if you want to.' She knew she sounded ungracious.

Jenny poured tea into their cups, willing her hands not to tremble. They sat at a table for two, not by the window, as Mark had suggested, because she felt guilty at agreeing to come here, and it was possible that someone who knew her might spot her.

'Jenny, my father telephoned me this morning. My sister has been at her husband's hospital bedside all night. It seems he is near the end.'

'I'm sorry . . .' She shook her head as he proffered the plate of fancy cakes.

'I don't know what's going to happen afterwards. A big muddle to sort through.'

'Elin wrote . . . they might have to give up the family home.'

'That's a distinct possibility. Elin's doing a wonderful job with the children in Southwold.'

'She's had to make sacrifices too, you know. Her young man . . .'

'We all appreciate that, Jenny. I imagine he'll wait until things are better.'

'He wrote to Elin that he has decided to go back to Italy to join his sister.'

'Marian will be upset about that when she knows.'

'Oh, you mustn't tell her! That's Elin's business. She was hurt, she thought he was the one, you see.'

'Is that something unique to women?' he asked. 'Falling headlong in love?'

'You know it is,' she said simply.

He sighed and drank his tea. 'If I hurt you, Jenny, I'm sorry.'

'You *were* attracted to me, weren't you?'

'You know it was much more than that. I *had* to draw back, for your sake.'

She hoped her eyes did not betray the pain she felt.

'If . . . when all the trouble in your family is past, and Elin is over Alex, well, you have my blessing. Now, I must go. It seems to have stopped raining and I have to get some shopping. Don't worry about giving me a lift home, I feel like walking.'

She pushed her chair back, left him sitting there. She daren't look back.

When she arrived home, Belle opened the door, took the basket from her, while she took off her damp outer clothes and hung them in the hallway.

'Oh good,' Belle said, 'you didn't forget my smelling salts. Thank you, dearie.' She looked at her granddaughter in sudden concern. 'You look upset, Jenny. What's wrong?'

'I've got a splitting headache, Grandma. Just one of those days.'

'Take a sniff of the salts, then.' Belle held out the bottle.

'I know that remedy of old.' Jenny managed a smile. 'It's not *that* bad. I'll get over it. Where's Billie? I bought her a barley-sugar twist. And I must give Ruby a dose of her medicine, before I forget.'

Marian sat close by her husband, weary beyond words, trying not to move her stiff limbs, to disturb what appeared to be a deep sleep. With her nursing background she was aware that he would probably not wake again. The nurses and the doctor came at intervals, looked grave, then went away after a few whispered words.

It was late evening when, despite her determination not to do so, she succumbed to sleep herself. She struggled awake when a comforting arm encircled her slumped shoulders. Curtains were being drawn round Desmond's bed.

'Marian,' her brother said gently. 'It's over, my dear. It must have been very peaceful and happened minutes before the doctor came with me into the room.'

'Are you sure?'

'Yes. You can see him in a short while. Then I'll take you home. There's nothing we can do tonight.'

She looked at Mark, dry-eyed.

'I know it had to end this way, and later, when I can come to terms with it, I'll be glad, for his sake. But, Mark, I have a dreadful feeling that another nightmare is about to begin.'

Elin had to tell Charlie and Jack, and comfort them. Marian and her family had decided that the boys were too young to attend the funeral. She wrote to Elin:

I will have to stay on here for a time because there is so much to sort out. All I can tell you for sure is that Homeleigh will have to be sold. We will live in the Southwold house from now on. Mark insisted on that. When this place is cleared, some of the furniture will be auctioned, and some sent to Southwold, with our personal effects.

In a few days' time, after the inquest, my parents will return home with Mark. They will bring Clover's little boy with them. I hope she will agree to stay on to help you with the children and the house. I have to let the good Buntings go. I had to give up my job, too, but I will need to seek other employment.

My parents will deal with matters like Charlie's new school – they want to help with this, and are familiar with that nice preparatory school near us. They'll be on hand if you need advice or help at any time. And of course there is dear Mark.

Dear Elin, it is a comfort to know you are coping so well. It is easier just now for me to write, rather than telephone. I'm sure you understand. Tell the children that I love them and will see them soon. I miss them so much. You, too.

Your friend Marian Lambert

Tears smarted in her eyes. Elin thought: *I haven't been able to tell Marian about my dad and all his troubles. They have a lot in common. I feel guilty because I haven't had time to go over to see him and offer him moral support. And Alex – he wasn't so grown-up after all, going away at the first sign of trouble, just like Luke really. They're both boys still, and me, well, sometimes I feel as if I have had too much responsibility put on me too soon.*

Then Peggy pulled at her skirts, as she sat with her head in her hands. Elin picked the little girl up and hugged her tight.

'All right if I push Peggy in the pram to the shops?' said Clo from the doorway. 'We need another loaf of bread. She'll probably go to sleep while we're out. Oh, and the boys are having a scrap in their bedroom and I think you ought to sort it out. Bad news?' She indicated the letter still clutched in Elin's hand.

'You can read it later. I've got no secrets from you, Clo. But I'll tell you the good news now. BP will be with you, soon! Off you go, Peggy, and I'll see what your brothers are up to, eh? Buy a Swiss roll for tea, Clo. We all like that.'

'I'll get the fattest Swiss roll in the shop, to celebrate,' Clo declared. 'With sugar all over it and plenty of jam!'

Elin hurried upstairs to see what the quarrel was about. She discovered Jack lying on his bed, sobbing and drumming his heels, and Charlie, red-faced and cross, pointing accusingly at the jumble his brother had made of his precious clockwork railway, which he had painstakingly set up in the middle of the room. The track had been pulled apart and thrown about; the train and carriages dismantled and overturned.

'He said it was an accident,' Charlie bellowed. 'He said he tripped over it, but he did it on purpose.'

'I didn't! I didn't!' Jack insisted.

'Stop it, right now!' Elin said firmly. She sat Jack up, wiped his eyes and made him blow his nose on her clean handkerchief. 'Charlie, pick up the engine and carriages and put them in the box. Jack, stack the line pieces neatly.

Neither of you deserves to play with the train set today. Then I want you to sit down and tell me why it happened.'

'He—' Charlie began.

'That's enough. Do as I say, please, both of you, and calm down at the same time.'

They have to express their feelings somehow, she thought. They've lost their father and they miss their mother desperately. They don't feel secure any more. I have to help them come to terms with all this, and it's hard, because I miss Marian's guidance . . .

When the tidying-up was done she sat between them on the side of Charlie's bed and drew them close.

'Mummy's been away five weeks now,' Charlie began.

'I know. She's longing to be with you, but there's been so much for her to do since your daddy . . . sadly left you . . . but soon she'll be coming here, because she's decided it's the best place for us to be. You all love Southwold, don't you, and this house, and Daddy did, too, and now it's going to be your home, not just somewhere you come to at holiday time.'

'But most of our things are still at the old house,' Charlie said.

'That's one of the things your mummy has to arrange. We'll make room for them, here.' She paused. 'I want to tell you something. My mother died when I was born, so I never knew her at all. Peggy's so young, too, she won't have memories like you of all the special times you shared with your father. You'll be able to tell her about him, won't you.'

The boys nodded, thinking about it. Then Jack asked: '*You* won't leave us will you?'

'No. I promise. And guess what. When Charlie starts school again, you'll have BP for company, Jack, because he and Clo are going to stay on here as well.'

Jack's expression brightened. 'I like BP!'

'Feel better now? Tell you what, let's go and meet Clo and Peggy – they should be heading back from the shops right now, eh?'

*

'You're going to share our room with us, come and see!' Charlie informed BP importantly.

'Your bed's next to mine,' Jack put in.

'I said he ought to be in the middle,' Charlie insisted.

BP beamed. 'I don't care,' he said, 'as long as I can bounce on it.'

'I'll sort you out,' Clo said robustly. 'Upstairs, all of you!'

Elin was in the kitchen boiling the kettle for tea, while Peggy sat in her high chair, chewing on a hard rusk, when Mark came in, and without comment, opened the kitchen drawer and replenished the contents of the housekeeping purse.

I imagine the money came from his own pocket, Elin thought. Aloud, she said: 'Your parents decided to go straight home?'

'Yes, but they'll be over tomorrow to see the children. Dad wanted to see how the locum was managing. Elin . . .'

'Mmm?'

'While you're on your own for a minute, I have something to tell you. I'm taking over my father's practice. He'll be working with me part-time. He really needs to take life more quietly, particularly after recent events. I'll be moving in here, I hope you don't mind?'

'Why should I mind? It's your home as well as Marian's, isn't it?'

'Marian will explain it to you all later, but I have permission to tell you that she must work to cover the day-to-day expenses. She is also determined that later she'll pay something towards her husband's debts . . . She is going to work in Celia's office, stay with her in the flat during the week, and come home at weekends. It was a difficult decision to make, but she insists it is the only way. I know for a fact that you and Clo have not been paid while all this has been going on – but she promises to make it up to you—'

'She doesn't need to do that!'

'Marian can only do this with help from you, Elin,' he added quietly. 'She trusts you implicitly. And that's why I'll be here, to back you up.'

Elin brought the teapot to the table, poured milk into the cups.

'Sit down and have your tea. Would you like a biscuit?'

'Thank you. You sit down, too. And young Peggy, stop rattling your tray and trying to climb out of your chair – put down that disgusting thing you've been dribbling on, and have a biscuit, before Elin puts the lid firmly back on the tin.'

Peggy grinned and took his offering.

'Ta,' she said loudly. This was something she'd quickly learned from Clo. Marian didn't encourage baby talk.

'Mark,' Elin said, 'you were doing something really worthwhile in Ipswich.'

'I enjoyed the challenge, but . . . don't they say charity begins at home? What about you? This is very different from the post you took on. You're young, you should be carefree and life should be a big adventure.'

'That can wait. I am apprehensive, I must admit. Though when I think how Jenny coped before she had our grandma and her mother-in-law to help her – why can't I? Marian has always been there, even when she was busy with her writing, but now I have to make all the decisions on my own . . .' She broke off, then continued: 'Would it be possible for me to take time off, Mark, while you're here, to visit my father?'

'Of course. I'll take you. Clo can look after the young scallywags for an hour or two, eh? That side of things should be easier now for you, at least.'

The boys came rushing in.

'BP says, where are we going to put the piano when it comes?' Charlie asked.

'Three blind mice, see how they run!' BP and Jack chorused together.

From her chair, Peggy mumbled through a mouthful of biscuit:

'Cut off their tails!'

'They'd better watch out, or I will,' Clo told them, with a broad smile, because she was so happy to have BP with her again.

THIRTEEN

Jenny and Billie were met by Richard at Southwold station. He had to vacate his home in a fortnight's time. He'd written to Jenny that it would mean a great deal to him if she could manage a visit before this, and he hoped Elin would be able to join them now that Mrs Lambert was able to be with her children at weekends.

Ted said they could go, although he'd decreed that Ruby must stay at home.

'It's best she's within reach of our doctor, just in case.'

Jenny didn't dare argue with him, because he'd just heard that workers were being laid off at the mill. This was after they'd been on short time for some weeks. She'd decided not to tell her father until after the weekend. He'd enough to worry about. Anyway, like Elin, she needed a break. It was a pity, she thought, that her grandma had decided not to accompany them, but she understood that Belle didn't wish to see her old home 'all packed up'.

Richard came hurrying along the platform in the bright September sunshine.

'Elin's with him!' Billie shrieked in delight. 'Dr Mark hasn't come,' she added innocently. Then Richard opened the carriage door and helped them alight.

'Still got the pony and trap, that's good,' Jenny said, settling in her seat, with Billie on her lap, no longer a baby, but a sturdy three-and-a-half-year-old in her puff-sleeved dress and round-crowned white hat with upturned brim.

Elin squeezed in beside them.

'Dad needs it to get to work, don't you?'

'Oh, Dad – you've got a job!' Jenny cried. 'That's wonderful!'

'Well, it is, and it isn't.' Richard smiled as they followed the bus full of visitors bound for the local hotel. 'It's cleaning and washing down the yard and outbuildings, you know' he glanced at young Billie – he wouldn't go into gory details in her presence, 'at the big butcher's, in town. And sprinkling sawdust; well, I'm used to that, eh? A job's a job, as they say. At least I can pay my way at Ida's and help her out.'

As they drove past the old wheelwright's, the girls noted the changes, looked at each other, but didn't comment. There was a large new sign:

BOLD BROTHERS.
BICYCLE AND MOTOR REPAIRS.
BICYCLES FOR HOLIDAY HIRE.

Outside there was a gleaming new petrol pump and a glistening rainbow patch of oil on the forecourt.

Ida was waiting for them with the table laid for lunch, and it was hugs all round.

Billie insisted on going upstairs first, to put her little bag and her rag doll on the bed that the three of them were to share.

'I do like this big house,' she said approvingly, which brought sudden tears to her mother's eyes. 'There's room to dance around here.'

'Come on down now.' Jenny cleared her throat: 'Aunt Ida's roast pork smells lovely, doesn't it? She makes really good crackling, like Grandma. I hear she picked the bullaces in the hedge out the back and made a juicy tart for pudding, too.'

'Mummy,' Billie said, as she followed her mother to the bedroom door. 'Why didn't Dr Mark come to the station?'

'Grandad wanted to meet us himself, didn't he. Dr Mark's not family.' *Not yet*, she reminded herself, thinking of Elin, who saw him every day. 'Anyway, Elin said he was driving her friend Clo and her little boy home to see their family. Then he's staying with his cousin in London for the rest of the weekend. Satisfied?'

Billie was at last asleep, but Elin and Jenny conversed in whispers, just in case.

'How is Mrs Lambert now?' Jenny asked.

'Well, she seems so strong, and yet she can't have got over it all, can she? She looks different, Jenny, too. She's had her hair bobbed, and Celia encouraged her to get some new clothes, even though she said she couldn't afford it. She has to look smart, working in London. But I know she can't wait to come home at weekends to be with the children. It'll be good for her to have them to herself this time.'

'I'm glad you've had your friend with you for company, when Mrs Lambert's away.'

'Clo's been very good – she insists on doing all the washing because I have to take Charlie, and now Jack, since the beginning of the month, to and from school. They come home for lunch, too. Clo and I share the housework, but she makes the supper while I'm meeting the boys again in the afternoon, when I take BP and Peggy along with me.'

'It wasn't what you were employed to do, all this, is it?'

'No, and it isn't nearly as much fun. I loved teaching the boys at home, going for walks by the river and feeding the ducks. I didn't even have to make my own bed!'

'I hope Mark makes his,' Jenny said primly, involuntarily recalling the untidy flat over the surgery in Ipswich.

'Oh, he does, after a fashion, but he's very good with the children, and he helps in lots of ways. Yesterday evening he did all the heavy work when he, Clo and I changed the bedrooms around. Marian has moved into our room to be with Peggy, and we have the spare room the other side of the boys' room. The big bedroom is shut up.'

'Elin, I don't like having secrets from you, but you might have been aware ... well ...'

'That you couldn't stop yourself falling for Mark? I guessed, the night Ruby was born.'

'You must think I'm terrible, though, what with Ted, and the children. I didn't ... let them down, that's the truth.'

'I'm glad. You don't have to say any more. Except ... did he feel the same?'

'I believe he did. For a while, anyway, but he'd his divorce to get through. He told me very gently that I was the one with too much to lose.'

'He has his freedom now, Jenny. Marian told me.'

'Don't worry, Elin. He must realise you're the one for him. You're a woman now.'

'He hasn't said anything to me ...'

'Do you want him to?'

'You know I do. I wanted to believe I was in love with Alex. Yet, I told him firmly I couldn't marry him for three years. I know I wouldn't expect Mark to wait that long.'

'Well, now we've sorted all that out, let's get to sleep.'

Jenny actually lay awake for some considerable time. She wondered whether Ruby was missing her. The baby was recently weaned, but still occasionally sought comfort from her mother. When Billie stirred and stretched beside her, Jenny stroked the damp hair off the child's neck.

'I hope *you* find the right person, first time around,' she whispered, then kissed the top of her daughter's head. 'Oh, Billie, I ought to be happy with what I have . . .'

Marian was restless, too, in her unfamiliar single bed. She lay wondering whether the neighbours here were aware of her present circumstances. She had found the sympathetic looks hard to bear from those who lived near Homeleigh. Their name in the local papers and, more briefly, for it was a common occurrence these days, a paragraph or two in the broadsheets, meant that folk were aware of the trouble she was in. The open verdict at the inquest she found hard to accept, but it could have been worse.

She had been naive in the extreme, she realised now. It had all been building up for months. Surely Desmond should have known that she would support him, that she would have been willing to have made economies, to have given up her job which had more status than salary, and to run the house by herself? The job had gone anyway, and the house; now she was determined to work really hard to support her family. *But am I doing the right thing as far as the children are concerned?* she wondered. *Peggy calls for Elin when she's upset, and Charlie found it hard to settle in the local school until Jack joined him there.*

Cutting her hair had been symbolic of her new lifestyle. Desmond had loved her long hair; he'd twined his fingers in it and whispered teasingly that if she ever bowed to fashion, and had her locks shorn, he wouldn't forgive her. Closing the door on their bedroom was important, too.

I have forgiven him, she thought. *Even though my life will never be the same again.*

Elin was back in time to see Marian leave. She'd decided to keep the car, and Elin was glad as they waved her off. It was less tiring than catching trains, she thought.

She stood there, holding Peggy aloft, while the boys perched on the gate, then told them it was time to go inside for bathing and bedtime.

'Oh, can't I wait for Uncle Mark?' Charlie wheedled.

'We don't know when he'll be home, Charlie. He's probably making the most of his weekend off from all of us! Come in, there's a good boy.'

'When is BP coming back?' Jack asked.

'Clo hasn't made her mind up yet. Her mother's been poorly, and she might decide to stay on for a while. We'll manage, won't we?' But her heart sank at the thought of the big Monday wash, and most of the beds to change. She'd leave a note out for Mark, asking if he'd take the boys to school in the morning, she thought. And she'd make him a sandwich with the meat Aunt Ida had cut from the joint and generously shared with her and Jenny.

Later, it seemed strange to have a bedroom to herself for once, for Marian had said to leave Peggy where she was for a night or two, and see how she got on. Elin was pleased to be able to read undisturbed for a while. She had only just turned her lamp out when she heard careful footsteps on the stairs. Mark was home.

He paused briefly outside her door.

'Goodnight, Elin,' he said quietly. 'Thank you for the sustenance – much appreciated. I saw your note – yes, I'll take the boys.' Then he went on along the corridor.

Elin woke with a start next morning. She threw back the bedclothes – it was 7.30 already! Then Charlie opened the door, with Peggy in his arms, and grinned at her.

'We've all overslept, Elin! But I've washed and dressed, and I've told Jack to hurry up in the bathroom. Shall I take Peggy down and put her in her chair? Uncle Mark's up – he called us and told us the time, and said he was cooking breakfast.'

'Oh dear!' Elin was flustered. 'Yes, but be careful with Peggy on the stairs, let her go backwards, it's safer. Tell Uncle Mark I'll be down very shortly – if I can stop Jack messing about with the toothpaste!'

No grapefruit and neatly placed cherry; Mark was frying eggs and bacon. He had the fat too hot, and Elin knew it would take some effort to clean the pan afterwards. The eggs had frizzled edges and were speckled with black and the bacon was crisp and liable to fly off the plate. But the children were enjoying the change from scrambled egg.

'Here you are, Elin,' Mark said cheerfully, wiping his hands on the tea towel tucked round his waist.

'Thank you, this is very good of you,' Elin began, suddenly aware that she had forgotten to brush her hair. What must he think of her?

'More bacon, ta,' Peggy said, sitting there in her pyjamas with egg on the jacket. When they'd departed for school, Elin took Peggy upstairs to bath and dress her. Then she put her down in her cot for her usual nap.

Elin was exhausted after stripping the beds on the first floor, but she stepped over the piles of crumpled linen and made her way resolutely up the stairs. She was bending over Mark's bed, pulling the bottom sheet free from the mattress, when she was unexpectedly lifted off her feet, then turned around.

'Mark!' she gasped. 'Why are you back?'

'Sit down on the bed, and I'll tell you,' he said. 'I asked my father to take morning surgery as I had something important to discuss with you. But first, what d'you plan to do with those sheets and pillowcases?'

She was very aware that he still had one arm firmly around her. She faltered.

'It's a bit late to boil the copper, anyway, Clo's the expert on that; I thought I'd fill the bath with hot water and soap flakes and put the linen in to soak.'

'And what then? You'd be on your knees, washing all that heavy stuff by hand.'

'No, I wouldn't! I'd get in the bath and . . . *tread* it, like they do the grapes in France!'

'And you're the expert on that, I suppose? No, Elin. My sister has never washed a sheet in her life. And I suspect, neither have you. We'll carry all the washing downstairs, fold it neatly and parcel it up for the laundry. The cost is very reasonable, my mother says. She uses the service once a fortnight. The whole lot comes back ironed, what's more.'

'Let me go, Mark; we'd better get on with it then.'

He held her even more tightly.

'Elin, look at me, please.'

All she could think of saying was: 'I still haven't combed my hair,' before he kissed her and took her breath away. She began to shake, not because she was afraid, she realised much later, but because she couldn't help responding to his ardour. Instinctively, they slipped into a more comfortable position, lying together on the bed.

'It would be easy,' he whispered, 'to jump the gun, as they say . . . but, Elin, I'm asking you to marry me first, because I love you, and hope you feel the same way.'

She struggled up.

'I always have,' she sounded almost accusing, 'but you only saw me as . . . a girl, not a grown woman.'

'I thought of you as one of Marian's family, following her lead. I only realised how much you meant to me when I saw you with Alex. I didn't think I could compete with him and his youthful good looks. Marian urged me not to waste any more time.'

'I'm so glad she did! But what about my commitment to Marian and the children? I can't let them down.'

'You don't have to – I've made a commitment to Marian, too, remember? If you agree, we'll marry as soon as it can be arranged, and live here, looking after the children as we do now. When Marian is at home, we'll take time off on our own. It's not ideal, but—'

She put her hand over his mouth.

'Shush. It's already working, isn't it? You'll have to talk to my dad. We'll need his permission, because I won't be twenty-one for another two and a half years!'

'I'll go over there this afternoon, shall I? I hope he won't disapprove of the age difference between us, or the fact that I've been married before. Elin, you won't be disappointed not to have a church wedding, with all the trimmings, will you? It will have to be a civil ceremony, just a quiet affair, special licence and a weekend honeymoon …'

'That sounds perfect! It lets Dad off the hook, doesn't it? Actually he was quite a bit older than my mother, and anyway, he's already met you and likes you! Well, let's be practical. Gather up the linen and we'll see to it downstairs, as you suggested!'

'Can't I have another kiss, first?'

''Course you can,' she said, hugging him. Then she began to giggle. 'Hardly romantic is it, me in an old overall, and you, like your niece, with egg yolk on your shirt!'

As they folded the washing, Mark said, 'I don't really know if I should tell you this, but from what she said to me, I rather think Clo won't be coming back. Her mother's chronic bronchitis is worse. Clo doesn't want to let Marian down, and you too, of course, but—'

'Like you said to me recently, charity begins at home, Mark,' Elin told him.

'Dear Elin Odell, you'll make a wonderful wife, and in time, a good mother – for haven't you plenty of experience in that respect?'

'Let's get young Peggy off to school first, eh?' she suggested, blushing.

I won't say that I know about him and Jenny, she thought. What does it matter now? We have my sister's blessing.

She put her finger firmly on the string as he tied the parcel. 'I'll love you for ever and ever, through thick and thin, Mark,' she said softly. 'That's a promise.'

FOURTEEN

November, 1925

Elin and Mark were married in London at noon on the last Saturday of the month. There were russet and gold chrysanthemums in a plain vase on the registrar's table. These added a welcome touch of colour to the dark wood-panelled room where they sat, flanked by their witnesses. They'd come by car to London with Richard first thing and driven straight here. Richard would return by train to Suffolk later with Celia, who was joining Marian and her family in Southwold. The bride and groom were staying in Celia's flat for the weekend.

I miss my grandma, Elin thought wistfully, *and Jenny and little Billie. I know how disappointed she was not to be my bridesmaid. I suppose I always dreamed I'd wear Grandma's bridal gown on my wedding day, but it was not to be. Celia was so kind though, lending me this elegant velvet costume and her fur stole.*

It was a brief ceremony, very formal, but when Mark slid the wide gold band on her finger and smiled reassuringly at her, that was what really mattered.

Later, when they stood outside, shivering, because it was a raw day, Celia took a few pictures, as Mark's parents had requested, with the box camera that had recorded the years the two of them had spent in Africa.

'The light is bad, but you both look so bright and happy, I'm sure the photographs will come out,' she said optimistically. 'We'll catch a cab – you two go ahead in the car – Mark has a key. You don't need to do a thing, the wedding breakfast awaits you!'

'I can't hold your hand while I'm driving,' Mark told Elin. 'I must keep my eyes on the road. Let's hope we have time to snatch a kiss before the others arrive.'

'Plenty of time for that, after they've left; I'm more interested in what's on the table – breakfast seems like hours and hours ago!' she teased.

'It was,' he said ruefully. 'Elin, I can't help thinking you deserved a better day than this. Your father reminded me, when we talked, how young you are. Perhaps we should have waited, as he suggested, until you were nineteen next spring. We could have married on a sunny day in Suffolk with all your family, and mine, there.'

'Shush. That doesn't always work out, as my dear dad found to his cost.'

'Like me . . .'

'Ah,' she said positively, 'but this time you've married the right girl.'

'I know that,' he said softly.

They both knew it would be a short one, before returning to their ready-made family.

There was a large iced fruit cake in the centre of the table, with a card propped against it.

'A wedding present from Mr and Mrs Bunting!' Elin exclaimed. 'Thank goodness they have both found work again. I was worrying about them. Look at this, Mark; dear BP drew the picture on the card, and Clo sends her love.'

'I see we're depicted as Mr and Mrs Bunny Rabbit!'

'You've got holes in your top hat for your ears to come through.' She giggled.

They heard the slamming of cab doors from the road outside.

'Come here . . . we've got two minutes before the door bursts open and the others join us . . .'

The covers were taken from the dishes to reveal carved meats, bowls of salad, tiny potatoes, a golden glazed pork pie with curly-edged crust and freshly made mayonnaise.

'Tuck in!' Celia advised them, handing Richard the bottle-opener. 'Save some champagne for the toast!' She glanced at her watch. 'Just over an hour before we have to catch the train. I asked the cab driver to call back.'

'I could have run you to the station in the car,' Mark reminded her.

'I know that, but aren't you and your wife going out on the town? There's so much for Elin to see on her first real visit to London. Did you book a show for tonight?'

'I have to admit, I'm afraid not.'

'Oh, *I*'ve got plans for the rest of the day,' Elin told them. They all smiled at that.

It seemed no time at all before Celia and Richard had to say goodbye, and there were hugs all round.

'Thank you,' Elin whispered in Celia's ear. 'For helping to make this a wonderful day. And for letting us stay here.'

'Well, you'll be back to normal all too soon, won't you. Good luck, my dear.'

Richard kissed his daughter.

'I'll see you both soon. I'm really glad you'll be near me.' To Mark, he said, 'You're a very lucky chap.'

'I know that,' Mark replied quietly, gripping his new father-in-law's hand.

Elin watched through the window and waved as Celia and Richard stepped in the cab. As she let the net curtain fall back into place, Mark's arms encircled her from behind, and turned her to face him, like that day not so long ago when he'd asked her to marry him.

'What next?' His voice was muffled as his lips caressed the top of her head.

'I must get changed, because I can't go downtown dressed like this.'

'*Down*town? *Out* on the town, Celia suggested. D'you really want to venture out on such an afternoon? I can think of better things to do.'

'Oh, I'm sure you can,' she said ingenuously. 'But I'd like to go down to the river, to see the Thames barges, maybe even the ones which sail to Ipswich. It stopped me being utterly miserable at the Buttles', the sight of those barges silhouetted against the evening sky . . .'

'It might be too foggy for that later on. But if that's what you want, let's go.'

Elin dressed warmly, wearing the red jumper her grandma had made for her the Christmas before she joined Marian's family at Southwold, topped with her cape, with the collar turned up. She pulled her woollen cap well down over her ears. She tucked her arm within Mark's as they walked along in the gathering gloom, expelling their breath in cloudy puffs.

They stood on the embankment and gazed down over the great river. Cars passed slowly by them, headlights like golden orbs. A bus, full of passengers returning home from work, ground gears noisily, leaving a lingering smell of petrol to add to the pungent aromas from the Thames. These Elin was familiar with; of oil, fresh paint, coal and mud, the sulphurous air. She was mesmerised by the activity on the water. Great ships, seemingly on a sure collision course, but steering clear, of course; barges and the boom of the foghorns. Then she spotted a sail or two, which made her grip Mark's hand in excitement.

'Look, Mark! Are they the grain-carriers for Ipswich?'

He smiled at her. 'Perhaps. You're shivering in this wind. Time for more exploring?'

Elin nodded. 'We don't have to go back to the motor yet, do we? You can see so much more if you walk. I've got my sensible shoes on!'

'Come on then,' he said, 'before the fog blots it all out.'

They wandered around for some time, and on their return to the parked motor, found a coffee stall set up at the street corner. There was the mouth-watering smell of frying sausages, of strong coffee, served in thick white cups. They stood to one side as other eager patrons crowded round the stall. There was the sudden flare of matches as crumpled Woodbines were lit, and loud, excited voices. Elin licked her greasy fingers.

'Mmm. That tasted good. I could do with more milk in the coffee, though.' She grimaced as she took a draught from her cup.

'Drink up,' Mark advised. 'Let's leave the night workers to it, eh? Plenty more food to eat up, back at the flat.'

He made the fire up, on their return.

'Don't want to go to bed yet, do you?'

'No, I'm still hungry. We can't let the feast go to waste.'

Later, she did fall asleep in the big chair, her stockinged feet on the fender. Mark leaned over her, woke her with a kiss.

'You go in the bathroom first and then warm the bed up, eh? I'll tidy up in here, and be along later,' he said tactfully.

Elin unwrapped a present from Celia, left on the coverlet. She knew what it was, because Celia had mentioned it casually earlier, but the little note brought tears to her eyes.

It's new, I never had the chance to wear it. You will cherish this as I have, I know.

With my love,

Your friend, Celia

Sheer silk, she thought, running the material through her fingers. Bridal white, sleeveless, cut on the bias, the cross-over bodice fastened with a single pearl button. She slipped it over her head, smoothed the nightgown over her hips. She regarded herself solemnly in the long, swinging cheval mirror. The light behind her made the garment see-through.

'More the night for flannel and bed socks,' she murmured aloud ruefully. She turned and climbed into the bed: 'Three-quarter size, not quite a double,' Celia had said, 'but I guess you won't mind that.' Elin turned the lamp low, and pulled the sheet up under her chin. She drifted off to sleep again; it had been an eventful day . . .

'Elin, darling,' Mark whispered urgently in her ear.

She stretched, yawned, then nestled against him, suddenly vibrantly aware of his hands sliding down her silk-clad shoulders, his fingers hesitating over the little button.

'Mark...' She pushed the small pearl through the buttonhole herself. 'Look, I'm sure you can tell I'm nervous, but then you are, too, aren't you? It's the most natural thing in the world, and I want it to happen, because, well, I love you.'

'I only thought – you're so young, Elin, and—'

'Have I made you happy today? D'you love me?'

'Yes! You know I do. Believe me!' His arms tightened round her, his lips caressed, warmed her bare skin.

'Then show me just how much,' she said softly, as she thrilled to his touch.

Jenny lay awake thinking of the two of them together. Ted was out at a workers' meeting. Sitting round a glowing brazier, she thought, with other worried men, seemingly oblivious of the fact that they would be better off at home with their families, with the warmth and support offered there. They were more fortunate than some. They had help with the rent of their little house from her grandma and Ted's mother.

Ruby coughed, shifted restlessly in her cot in the corner of the bedroom. Jenny didn't have to worry about Billie, who shared a room with Belle. That was something. They had to be constantly vigilant with the baby, especially in inclement weather.

Jenny heard the front door close, and his mother's call: 'Is that you, Ted?' Then his uneven tread up the stairs. This meant that he'd had a drink or two after the meeting.

Abstemious Ted! And to spend money on beer when they had to be so careful with the pennies now . . . She turned over, away from the door, pretending to be asleep.

It was no use. She felt his hot breath, smelled it, as he nuzzled the back of her neck.

'I know you're awake, Jenny. Thinking of *him*, are you? Of how it could have been, if the two of you—'

She rolled over, facing him.

'Shut up!' she whispered fiercely. 'Have your way with me, I don't care – I was never unfaithful to you, except in my mind. I've tried to forget, I really have, you mustn't taunt me like this!'

'I'm sorry,' he wept later, when he was sober. 'Forgive me, Jenny, please.'

'I'm your wife, aren't I?' was all she said. Not bitterly, but with resignation.

'Breakfast in bed, I didn't expect this.' Elin smiled happily. She sat up as requested as Mark plumped an extra pillow behind her. Then he moved the tray from the bedside table to rest on her knees. 'Grapefruit,' she exclaimed, 'we always had it at Homeleigh. I'm glad you remembered.' She tucked the napkin round her neck. She mustn't drip juice on the silken bodice, now demurely buttoned up.

'I wanted to spoil you today, because all too soon you'll be looking after the children, Marian and me running the house, just as if nothing has changed.'

'Oh, but it has!' She dug her spoon into the fruit. He hadn't thought to cut round the sections with a knife. She wouldn't say, of course.

'Shift along a little, didn't you notice it was breakfast for two?' As she obliged, he asked: 'What are your plans for the morning – more exploring, before we go home?'

'What's the weather like?'

'Cold and damp.'

'Then let's stay right where we are. It's, um, cosy under the covers.'

'You never beat about the bush, that's something I've always admired about you. So long as you don't fall asleep on me again,' he said fondly, 'it's a wonderful idea.'

*

'Come upstairs, you two – tell me if you approve,' Marian said to Elin after all the hugging and congratulations were over. Charlie and Jack spread a pack of cards all over the sitting-room floor and now, with some interference from Peggy, muddling them up, they invited their uncle to have first pick in the game of 'pairs'.

'Now you know I'll like what you've done, if Elin does, and you can see I'm hemmed in by the children . . .' Mark didn't look as if he minded at all.

'It's a pity Celia had to leave before you arrived, she was the inspiration behind this.' Marian opened the bedroom door, the one that had been closed since the spring.

'I thought . . . Mark would just move in with me,' Elin faltered. 'Dad told me he'd be bringing over Grandma's brass bed while we were away, as she wanted us to have it because it had to be stored in the loft at Aunt Ida's . . .'

'This room is meant for two,' Marian said. 'Richard kindly came over and shifted the big bed in here. The other one he dismantled and put away.' She paused, then: 'My aunt had rather spartan tastes, but I didn't think you'd mind the other bedroom furniture. At least it's not from . . . Homeleigh. That was all sold, of course.

'Celia put up the new curtains and cleared the dressing table. We took the liberty of setting out your favourite things, like your trinket box, see?'

Marian was pale-faced, her eyes betrayed her weariness but she was smiling.

'I didn't expect . . .' Elin said slowly.

'I know you didn't. It was the least I could do. You need somewhere you can be private, be like normal newlyweds.' She paused. 'Everything will be all right, won't it?'

'It already is. Thank you for this. I really don't know what to say.'

'I'll go and rescue Mark, send him up, then you can unpack and get changed.'

When Marian had gone, Elin looked around properly. The bed was made up with the best linen, she saw, taken from the trunk where it was stored wrapped in tissue paper. New pillows, filled with duck down, were Belle's wedding gift.

Elin unbuttoned her dress, slipped it over her head. She took off her court shoes with a sigh of relief, then she padded on her stockinged feet to the fitted wardrobe cupboard, opened the doors. Her clothes were hanging to one side; Mark's to the other. He had very few possessions, she already knew that. Perhaps it was a good thing, she thought, no memories of his first marriage. She looked up. On the top shelf were her two hats, the one Marian had bought her when she started work here, and the one she'd worn to her father's wedding. In a corner she glimpsed a bag. Puzzled, she pulled it out.

She turned the somewhat crumpled straw hat in her hands. She recognised it immediately. Jenny's straw boater with the jaunty bunch of cherries. Why did Mark have it – why had he kept it? she wondered. Should she – *could* she – ask him?

Footsteps sounded along the corridor. Hastily, she stuffed the hat back in the bag, pushed it to the back of the shelf, closed the cupboard doors. He came in, looked around.

'Isn't this splendid!' Then he noticed the petticoat. 'Oh, Elin, stay just as you are, darling . . .' There was no mistaking his meaning.

'We must join the family . . .' she said unconvincingly, rubbing goose-pimpled arms.

He removed his jacket, put it on the chair. 'Take your time, Marian said.' He drew her, unresisting, towards the bed. 'Let's slip under the eiderdown, you'll soon warm up.'

In her new-found maturity, Elin realised he'd been starved of what she herself had said so naively was 'the most natural thing in the world'. To her delight, she'd discovered this to be true. Their new life together was all that mattered now, not past loves and longings.

PART TWO

1931

FIFTEEN

It was Elin's twenty-fourth birthday. Breakfast in bed; Mark had insisted. She didn't need to worry about seeing to the children, because Clo had returned to them some time ago after her mother died, and life here had been easier since then. Marian's two boys were now at the grammar school and left for Lowestoft just after 8 a.m. BP would be bound to join them there in due course, his proud mother thought. Meanwhile, he kept an eye on Peggy, now a frisky seven-year-old, as they walked to school.

Elin smoothed out the torn wrapping paper that littered the bed. How lucky she was to have had presents from all the family, even if Peggy *had* burst into their room with her offering just after dawn. The post had been brought to her at the same time as the scrambled egg on toast. There was a lovely, shiny card from Marian with an excited message inside:

Dear Elin,
This is your day, make the most of it!

Present on Saturday – I can hardly believe I'm coming home for good just in time for the children's Easter hols!

Best love,
Marian

When Marian had first imparted this welcome news last weekend, for a brief moment Elin imagined that she and Mark would be able to set up home on their own. Nearby, of course, for Marian would still need their moral support. However, when Marian said she'd written to the local hospital, had been accepted on the strength of her past experience, but this would involve shift work, Elin knew that things would remain more or less the same.

'It's time to leave London,' Marian had said. 'Although we're told the country is recovering from the depression, it certainly doesn't seem that way to Celia and me. The General Strike was a terrible thing, though people pulled together like they did in the war. I've managed to pay something towards my debts; now I can resume my nursing career.'

Elin picked up Jenny's card, signed by her, Ted and Billie. Jenny had suffered so much over the past two years, she thought. First, the loss of her younger daughter, even though this was not unexpected, and then, just a few months ago, their dear Grandma had passed away in her sleep. There was no present from Jenny, but a colourful, homemade bookmark from her niece; Ted was still on the dole. Jenny worked at the fish and chip shop in the evenings, to help out. This was still a good cheap meal for folk living on the bread-line. Her boss sent her home with a bagful of scraps, fished from the fryer. Billie enjoyed those frizzled bits. Fortunately Ted's mother was there to look after the rising-ten-year-old, because Ted spent most nights in the pub, commiserating with his mates.

Elin wiped her eyes, thinking this was her first birthday without a message from Belle. The service had been held in their church; they had brought Belle home. She'd not seen her sister since. Jenny had been a pale ghost of herself then, thin and shabby in her borrowed black clothes. Elin had looked away when Jenny clung to Mark, sobbing on his shoulder. *She still has feelings for him*, she'd realised. *Poor Jenny. I'm so fortunate.*

'I hope you didn't mind my comforting the poor girl,' Mark had said quietly later to Elin. 'She hasn't recovered from losing Ruby yet, and her husband seems to have given up.'

'Not crying on your birthday, surely?' She heard Mark's concerned voice. He was dressed ready for the surgery. He sat on the edge of the bed and took hold of her hand. 'Think how young you still are, darling, compared to me, eh?'

'You're not old,' she said fiercely. 'Thirty-seven isn't old.'

'No. Getting on to start a family though, don't you think?'

'Don't you think I've been hoping for that as much as you have, Mark?'

'Perhaps we should have had a baby earlier; oh, I know we agreed that we'd wait until Peggy was at school, but she's been there a while now, and when Clo came back to help you, I thought—'

'It's not for want of trying!' She wept afresh.

'Hey, you can't say that hasn't been enjoyable!' He tried to make her smile.

'Give me a hug, tell me you love me, on my birthday.'

'I love you, Elin.' He held her close, stroked her hair. 'Glad you've grown your hair; no fearsome Marcel waves for you. Don't worry, it'll happen soon. We know there's no reason why not. Now, have a good day, and mind you wear my present tonight.'

'I will,' she promised. The sapphire ring had been a lovely surprise.

'Time you had an engagement ring, having missed out earlier,' he said softly.

'Off you go – try not to be late, we're planning a special meal, and Dad's coming too, after he finishes work.'

They were enjoying their seafood platter and green salad with crusty bread and farmhouse butter, when there was an unexpected knock on the door.

'Late post?' Elin conjectured.

'I'll go!' Charlie offered. He still liked to be the first to greet visitors.

It was indeed someone with a small package in his hand, and a heavy bag slung over one shoulder. He was a bearded man, wearing a seaman's jersey with trousers tucked into boots.

'Charlie? I don't expect you remember me. May I speak to Elin, please?'

'Elin!' Charlie called, not knowing what to say.

'Aren't you going to ask me in?' The stranger smiled.

'We-ell ...' Charlie was saved by the arrival of Elin and Mark.

Elin knew him immediately, despite the bushy beard.

'Luke! Come in, do.'

'Thank you. I hear it's your birthday – anyway, this is for you. Good evening, Mark.'

'Good evening. Yes; don't stand there on the step, Luke, come inside.'

Clo fetched another plate and cutlery and they made room for Luke at the table, next to his stepfather. Richard shook his hand emotionally.

'Thought you'd gone for good, boy. You never kept in touch.'

'Ma made it clear she'd be glad to see the back of me.'

'I didn't share her view. You worked hard for me, I appreciated that.'

'I went to the docks, got talking to some seamen there. Before I could think twice, I was on board a ship and the lowest member of the crew. I've been with the same out-fit ever since, worked my way up, and been to Australia twice. I'm on long leave. I suppose I got to thinking I had a family of sorts, and I ought to look 'em up. I got a shock when I found the business had been sold, and new people in the house. I went along to Ida's and she told me Ma had left you in the lurch years ago. She said you were seeing Elin tonight as it was her birthday. Married! I could hardly believe it. Ida said to come over here.' He looked across the table at Elin, sitting by her husband. 'I already had a present for you, a gift from overseas. That was a bit of luck!'

'Thank you,' she replied simply. 'I'll open it after we've eaten.'

The boys had been silent for too long; they were eager to ask Luke about his travels.

'Are you ever seasick?' asked Jack. 'D'you really roll about on deck?'

'Wasn't your beard very hot in Australia?' BP wanted to know.

'Did you see kangaroos close up?' from Charlie.

Luke grinned. 'Seasick? Always, until I got my sea legs. I was clean-shaven in Australia. Not only did I see kangaroos, I saw koala bears and kookaburras, I dived off the coast of Queensland, had a trip to the outback, and encountered crocs and the odd shark at times. But mostly I was in port, overseeing the loading and unloading of cargo.'

Clo brought in the birthday cake, candles ablaze.

'If you boys can stop asking questions for a few minutes, we can sing happy birthday, and Elin must blow the candles out before the wax drips on the icing.'

'Elin, you haven't introduced me to your friend yet,' Luke told her.

'This is Clover; we met at the Lamberts' in Overbridge.' Elin hoped Aunt Ida had put him in the picture, regarding events there. She added: 'Clo is BP's mother.'

'You look far too young for that,' Luke exclaimed to Clo. 'But I can see the resemblance now – he's handsome like his mum!'

Clo had certainly changed in looks, if not in her spirited outlook on life. Her skinny frame had filled out, her face was rounder, she'd lost that pinched look; her once greasy locks hung in a shining bob. She wore her smart clothes with confidence. These had been purchased from the inestimable Denny's because, as Marian said: 'Good things are worth the extra money, because they last.' Elin still wore her cherished cape each winter. Unfortunately the store had been burned down last year, but was about to be rebuilt.

Clo blushed at the compliment.

'Better blow *now*, Elin, or else . . .' she commanded.

They watched as Elin obliged, then Mark gave her a hug and a kiss before they all crowded round to watch her cut the cake, and to collect their slices.

'Where are you staying tonight?' Richard asked Luke later. 'I'm afraid there isn't room at Ida's, but I could give you a lift somewhere.'

'You can stay with us, there's a spare bed in the attic, we'd be pleased to have you,' Mark offered unexpectedly.

Elin was unwrapping her gift. 'An opal brooch. Oh, Luke, you shouldn't have . . .'

'I gave you a brooch for your seventeenth birthday – remember? It was only a cheap one, rather crude as I recall. You deserved better.'

'Oh, I've still got it; thank you for this, it's very nice.' She felt guilty because she'd not cared for the other brooch and had never worn it. For some reason, she felt compelled to display the sparkling ring worn above her wedding band. 'I'm well off for jewels now – Dad gave me this necklace, and the beautiful sapphire ring is from Mark.'

'What about playing a game? It's a party, isn't it?' Peggy made herself heard at last.

'Almost your bedtime, Peg. Still, we'll grant you a birthday dispensation,' Mark said.

'What's that?'

'Allowing you a little leeway.'

'What's that?'

'You get to choose while Charlie and I wash up, after Jack and BP clear the table.'

After shooing the children off to bed, Clo went up to the attic room to tidy it for their guest.

'This is very good of you, thank you,' Luke said from the doorway. 'I think I'll turn in now, too. Richard is just leaving.' He gave an exaggerated yawn. 'It's been a long day. We docked at dawn.' He looked around for some-where to put his bag.

'Here,' Clo said, taking it from him and placing it on a chest in the corner. The bag was heavy, and clanked as she set it down. She thought: there's a bottle or two wrapped in his spare clothes . . . he hasn't changed much, then, from what Elin told me about him. I reckon he's wanting a drink more than an early night.

She'd better go, she realised, as he pulled his jersey and singlet over his head revealing his muscular torso. Elin had described him as a callow youth.

He moved between her and the door, leaning on it.

'Now a goodnight kiss from a pretty girl would be just the ticket.'

'I'll scream, they'll come running and boot you out,' Clo said loudly.

He grinned. 'It was worth a try. Don't forget Peggy's game of consequences – and the paper you read out: "Luke met Clo at the party". That must be a good sign—'

'Of what? Please let me out. Goodnight, Mr Goldsmith. Breakfast at eight.'

He gave a mock bow, opened the door.

'And the consequence was, "They were made for each other",' he said to her retreating back.

Clo pretended not to hear, but went quickly down the stairs. She encountered Elin outside Peggy's room.

'She went out like a light, after all the excitement . . . what's wrong, Clo? Luke didn't try – did he?'

Clo nodded. 'Don't make a fuss. Nothing happened. I saw to that.'

'I really thought he'd changed – I'm sorry.'

'I'm glad it wasn't you. Mark might have punched him!'

'He'd certainly have regretted asking Luke to stay here overnight! Shall I tell him?'

'No. I'm just glad you told me, you know, about Luke, after your dad's wedding. I feel sorry for him, actually, I can't think why.' *And I can't think why*, she thought, *I nearly let him grab me. I haven't felt like that since my young Greek waiter, and look what that led to. Not that I regret having BP, but the romance didn't last any time at all.*

'I don't suppose Luke remembers that; he was too inebriated at the time.'

'What are you girls chatting about?' Mark called from their bedroom. 'Time for an early night all round for the grown-ups, after all that excitement, I reckon!'

A little later, in bed, Elin wound her arms round her husband's neck, gave him a lingering kiss.

'Thank you, Mark, for my wonderful present, for making this a special day.' She paused. 'You weren't jealous of Luke, were you, years ago – like you were of Alex?'

'Don't be daft. Alex was a virile young man, he spelled danger to me, but I liked him; Luke isn't your type. I know how soft-hearted you are, that's why I asked him to stay.'

'Not for long, though. I'll suggest he looks up his mother. They must still have feelings for each other.'

'That's enough about him. Let's concentrate on us . . .'

Luke left after breakfast next morning.

'I'm going to visit Ma,' he said, as if he'd guessed what Elin was going to say. 'Tell Richard I'll let him know how it went before I go back to sea. Thanks for everything. I'll see you again.' He looked at Clo.

Clo discovered the empty rum bottle under his bed. As he had, she wrapped it up, within the folds of the discarded sheet. She smuggled it downstairs to hide the evidence in the dustbin, because she hoped to see him again, too.

Marian was home, and it was a time of adjustment for them all. Elin had to remind the children: 'Ask your mother' when they ran to her with a request. Clo wasn't sure whether she should revert to her original status. Elin's role as governess was no longer necessary, but as Marian's sister-in-law, now she really was one of the family.

It was Marian who eventually brought the subject up. She sat with her feet up, still in her uniform, one evening after a hard day at the hospital. Elin was waiting up for her and Mark, who had been called out on a maternity case.

'You must eat something,' Elin urged. 'How about some buttered toast?'

'I suppose I can manage that – thank you, Elin. What would I do without you? You run this household so efficiently.' Marian sounded tired and defeated.

Elin sat down opposite Marian. 'I'm sorry, Marian, I never intended to take over from you, and I couldn't have managed, if you hadn't taught me how to – I just tried—'

'I know, my dear. I should have stayed at home and looked after my family myself. After about six months I realised I had made a mistake. Oh, the children were happy, you and Mark were married and I was so glad about that, but it wasn't fair to expect you to put off having a family of your own for that length of time. I missed out on all the usual motherly things: looking after the children when they were ill, marvelling at Peggy's crayon pictures when she came home from school; it was you she wanted when she tumbled down and grazed her knees, she didn't spend the time with me that the other two did, before their father died. That really hurts.'

'You'd like to give up work?' Elin asked tentatively.

'I can't. I must support my family.'

'Look, we ought to have talked this over when you were first home. Clo worries that she's a burden, though I tell her we can't do without her. She runs the house – us – just like Mrs Bunting used to, but I've never forgotten what Mr Lambert said the day you interviewed me, that *you* were "in charge of all matters domestic". We'd all be happy if it could be like that again. Why don't you settle for working part-time, as you did in the old days?'

'D'you think we could manage? And you, how do you see the future, Elin?'

Elin's face was suddenly rosy. 'I'm – not sure yet – but I'm hoping, that Mark and I will be parents around Christmas time. I haven't said anything to him yet.'

'Oh, Elin, I'm delighted for you! You *must* tell him right away – tonight when he comes in. Promise me! I'll express my surprise, when you both impart the good news.'

It was past midnight when Elin, curled up on the sofa, woke from a doze. Mark came into the room, where the gaslight was turned low, and looked down at her.

'You should have gone to bed,' he reproved her.

'I waited up specially. Cup of tea?'

He sat down heavily beside her.

'I'd love one.' He rasped his fingers over his chin. 'Why does a man's beard seem to grow apace in the early hours, I wonder?'

'I suppose you don't notice it when you're asleep. Give me your coat, and I'll be back before you know it, for the kettle's been brought to the boil several times.'

'I might go to bed.' He stumbled back on his feet. 'I delivered twins unexpectedly tonight, both boys.'

'All's well?' she asked. 'I'll bring the tea upstairs, then.'

'All's well,' he repeated.

He sipped the hot tea as she slipped off her dressing gown then joined him in bed.

'Did you have a good day?'

'Yes, the usual sort. Marian was in late, too, but we talked about things at last. She's decided to work part-time in future. I'm sure we can manage. After all, we share the bills, and Clo's wages. I could have something else to occupy my time . . .'

'Why don't you take the opportunity to relax, instead of taking on more work?'

'Oh, but this is something I've always wanted to do – to be a mother myself.'

His cup rattled in the saucer as he set it down.

'Did you say what I thought you did?'

'You're not very observant, Doctor! I'm two weeks overdue. What's your opinion?' She hugged him round the waist, waiting.

'When did it happen?' He sounded dazed. 'When will it be?'

'How about my birthday, a month ago?' she teased. 'Next Christmas, I hope.'

'Darling, that's wonderful! How shall we celebrate?'

'Let's think about that tomorrow, Mark. We should both sleep well tonight.'

SIXTEEN

The children were enjoying the long summer days. The three boys – Charlie, Jack and BP – were old enough, Marian considered, to be trusted to be out and about on their bicycles, to be self-reliant like the youngsters, many from deprived city areas, in the Duke of York's boys' camp set up on the common for the first time this August bank holiday.

They took packed lunches, fishing rods and bait, a ball to kick around and a towel in case they had a dip in the sea.

'Not if the red flag is flying, mind,' Marian cautioned them.

The boys invariably arrived home late each afternoon with midge bites and scratches on their bare legs, rips in their drill shorts if they'd crawled through a hedge, and with the plaintive cry: 'We're starving!'

Peggy didn't like being excluded from the fun, but she'd been promised a week away with her mother, staying with Celia, visiting the museums and Madame Tussauds. She was very like her father in many ways, more serious than her brothers.

'Why don't you ask your sister and her little girl to stay – they can have our beds,' Marian suggested to Elin one evening.

Elin had the mending basket on her lap. She couldn't sit and do nothing. Soon she might start on the baby's layette, she thought. It would be nice to handle soft, fine wool, not the thick grey sort she used for darning the heels of Mark's hand-knitted socks. This particular pair had been made by Belle, her last birthday present to him. Grandma, she thought, how she would have loved to hear about the baby.

'It's not an easy journey now the little train is no longer running; anyway, I don't think Jenny could afford to come – she'd be too proud to say.'

'I could help out there,' Mark put in. 'I'd like to see Ned Wade before he and his wife emigrate to New Zealand in September; afterwards, I could collect Jenny and Billie from Ipswich, and Jenny wouldn't feel it was charity.'

'We're off in three days, you'll need to get a letter in the post tomorrow,' Marian reminded her. 'Suggest they stay on a couple of days after we get back, then Peggy can enjoy Billie's company. I'll drive them back home.'

'But you'll need your beds back,' Elin reminded her. 'We'll be a full house then.'

'There's the attic room, and a camp bed somewhere around.'

'I suppose so . . .' Elin snipped a new length of wool, rethreaded her needle.

Later, after Marian and Clo had gone to bed, she went into the kitchen to fill the water carafe, and to nibble on a couple of dry cream cracker biscuits. Mark followed her out.

'Still feeling queasy?' he asked, concerned.

'It's improving, as you said it would, but these help.'

'You didn't sound too enthusiastic about having Jenny and Billie to stay.'

'I haven't told Jenny yet about the baby, you see,' she admitted.

'Elin, dear, you're almost half-term. She'll be happy for you, I'm sure.'

'I know. It's just that it'll bring it back to her, having Ruby, at Christmas, too, and later on, losing her. I can't bear to upset her. Poor Jenny, she's been so unlucky, and I—'

'Some would say *you*'ve had a lot heaped on your shoulders these past years, too.'

'But now things are better, aren't they, and we've so much to look forward to.'

'We certainly have. Here, pass the tray. We'll make sure Jenny has a good time, eh?'

Jenny pleaded with Ted to let her go with good grace.

'We don't want Mark to realise we haven't been getting on too well lately, do we. I still have some pride even if you haven't.'

'As long as you remember he's married to your sister,' he warned her.

Mrs Drake took Billie out shopping and bought her a pair of sandals to wear.

'You shouldn't have spent your pension on her,' Jenny worried.

'She's got the toes out in those cheap canvas shoes,' her mother-in-law said.

'At least I won't have to worry about Ted getting enough to eat; I'm grateful to you for all you do to help us out.'

'Can't let that child suffer,' Mrs Drake said gruffly.

She got on better with Ted's wife now that Jenny's grandma was gone. Mrs Drake would never admit it, but she was actually on Jenny's side. Ted had been a dutiful son in the past, but latterly, he had lost his mother's respect. Drink had been his father's weakness, too; *blood will out*, she thought, compressing her lips into a thin line.

Billie waited on the doorstep, ready to call: 'He's here, Mum!' through the open door. She wiggled her toes in the comfortable leather sandals. It was nice not to have to wear socks in this hot weather. Her mother had spent yesterday evening letting down the frock she wore, and neatly sewing a false hem to the back so that her stitches coincided with the ridge left by the old one. Gran had trimmed her hair and put a new ribbon round her summer hat. Billie intended to discard the hat as soon as they had driven out of sight.

The motor drew up outside the house. Billie duly shrieked, and Jenny came out, carrying a small case and a couple of bulging carrier bags. She'd given Ted a hasty peck on the cheek, but he'd stayed sitting at the kitchen table.

'Remember what I said,' he grunted merely. Mrs Drake, however, waved them goodbye.

'Hello, you two, nice to see you. Hope I didn't keep you hanging around too long.' Mark opened the rear door of the car. 'In the back, Billie; Jenny, in the front seat.'

'Open your window,' Billie insisted, 'or I'll be sick; you feel every bump back here.'

'Take no notice of her,' Jenny told Mark. 'She likes all the attention.'

'How are you?' Mark asked as they drove along. 'You look much better.'

'All those chips. But working there takes my mind off things, as well.'

'That's good,' he said.

That was the end of their conversation.

Elin had spent the morning wondering what to wear. She hadn't mentioned her pregnancy in the letter she sent Jenny. Clo observed that she'd changed her clothes twice already.

'You don't show much, honest. You're getting all hot and bothered; put on that white blouse Mrs Lambert gave you, 'cause it's on the big side, and wear it outside your skirt. Then no one will see your elastic waistband extension!'

'That'll soon be stretched to the limit, too.' Elin sighed ruefully.

'Anyway, she'll see what's what, and then you'll have to say.' Clo looked thoughtfully at Elin. 'You're not worrying about what'll happen when the baby comes, are you? Not with a doctor and a nurse in the family!'

'I can't help thinking about little Ruby . . .'

'I know. We need to make this a happy time for Jenny and Billie, eh?'

Elin nodded. 'I'm being nosy now, did you have another letter from Luke today?'

'I was going to say, but you kept going off. Yes, he's coming back any day now. His last trip he says. He wants to settle down, get a job and that. Having had a flea in his ear from his old mother, he says we're the nearest to family he's got.'

'*We*?' Elin grinned. 'Can he change his ways, though?'

'I'll see to that,' Clo asserted, not realising what this implied.

Elin needn't have worried about Jenny's reaction; her sister took one look at her then flung her arms round her and hugged her tight.

'Oh, Elin, how wonderful! You're going to make me an auntie at last!'

'What are you whispering about?' Billie asked. 'Where are the boys?'

'Oh, they'll be back when they get hungry! Elin's having a baby, Billie!'

'Anyone can see that,' Billie said, which made them all laugh. '*I'm* hungry now!' she added hopefully.

'We've had our lunch, but don't worry, we saved some for you!' Clo told her.

'You go out and enjoy yourselves,' Clo told them the next day. 'Before the weather changes. That's what I told them scallywags before they biked off.'

'What about you, Clo?' Elin asked.

'There's a job or two I been saving up, when I've got a bit of peace and quiet.'

'Why couldn't I go with the boys?' Billie demanded.

'You haven't got a bike for one thing, and goodness knows what those lads get up to.' Elin smiled at her niece. 'We'll probably meet up with them on the pier later. We'll get lunch out, Clo, then why don't you join us on the sand this afternoon – by the beach huts?'

'I might,' Clo said, 'but don't count on it. It depends.' *It depends*, she thought, *on whether I have a visitor or not.*

When they'd gone, Clo whizzed around with the carpet sweeper downstairs, then decided to make a cake for tea. There was still half a jar of the raspberry jam she'd made, she thought; a nice soft sponge, split, with the jam spread thickly inside, and the top sprinkled with icing sugar. Ginger snaps: the boys liked those in their lunch box. She spiced those up with stem ginger from what Marian called the oriental jar, renewed each Christmas.

She hastily rubbed her floury hands on her apron, then whipped that off when she heard the cheery tattoo on the front door.

'Baking? What a welcome back!' Luke sniffed appreciatively. 'Where's the reception committee?'

'Only me at home today.' Clo was unexpectedly overcome with shyness.

'Oh, well, then . . .' He closed the door, and gave her a bear hug in the hall.

Clo extricated herself at last, firmly pushed him away. 'Cup of tea?'

'What about a piece of cake?'

'Still in the oven. You'll spoil your lunch.'

'Oh, what have we got?'

'Lucky for you, I put two chops in just now – couldn't waste the hot oven. You could have telephoned, you know. When did you leave the docks?'

'This morning. Had to go to the shipping office and sign off, first. I'm homeless and jobless now.' But he didn't sound worried.

'We might be able to put you up for a couple of days. Elin's sister and her daughter are staying now, while Peggy and her mum are in London. But when they're back—'

'I'll get digs before then,' he assured her. 'The attic, is it?'

She nodded. 'I should ask Elin first if it's all right.'

'You know it is. Come on then – tea it is.'

As they sat in the kitchen drinking the hot tea, she said: 'I know about your past, Luke.'

'About me getting a girl in the family way, I suppose.'

'Yes. Though Elin said you was young and foolish at the time – like me, I s'pose.'

'I didn't stand up to my responsibilities though, like you,' he said quietly.

'Oh, I never thought of parting with my baby! I had to grow up quick, I tell you.'

'Whereas I went on making more mistakes, and drank too much, like a fool.'

'You're sober today,' she realised.

'Did some hard thinking after I left you. I hope you've forgiven my cheek that night . . .'

'You'll have to prove you've changed,' she said primly.

'I will. The minute I met you, Clover, I just knew, you see, you were the one.'

'I'll mind your shoes and things, while you two have a paddle, before the rain comes,' Elin offered. She rested her back against a groyne, on the slippery top of which Billie was now walking precariously.

Though clouds hung ominously low, and there was a cold wind off the sea, the beach was milling with holiday-makers: children bounding down the open wooden steps from the beach huts, and deckchairs galore.

'I'd rather go swimming,' Billie said hopefully. 'Flounder, rather!'

'Not after what you've just eaten,' her mother said. 'You'd sink.'

They held hands as they ran down to the sea, squealing as the water rushed over their feet, the shingle shifted and they almost lost their balance.

Elin watched them idly. It was good to see Jenny laughing and having fun with her daughter. They'd hiked their skirts up, but they were already damp from the spray. She wished Jenny would let her hair down, literally, too. Those ugly, plaited 'earphones', she thought. When she mentioned it, Jenny had said wryly: 'Ted doesn't like me to look alluring in the fish and chip shop. Anyway, my hair gets all oily from the frying. I didn't get a chance to wash it before we came.'

Clo's voice made Elin start.

'Found you at last! You aren't where you said you'd be. See, Luke's here!'

They were also holding hands unselfconsciously. *They've clicked!* thought Elin.

'Hello, Elin – Clover told me your good news – congratulations,' Luke said.

They plumped down beside Elin.

'You two look as if you've news of your own,' she observed, grinning.

Clo blushed. 'Oh, it's too soon for that – but—'

'I'm hopeful!' Luke put in. 'I've got to prove myself first, she says, and I will.'

At mid-afternoon they were joined by the boys, who'd spotted them from the esplanade as they wheeled their bikes along.

'We looked for you on the pier,' Charlie said reproach-fully.

'Any grub left?' BP asked.

Elin rummaged in the bag, found half a packet of biscuits.

'Tide's on the turn, why don't you have a swim?' she asked.

'Not warm enough today.' Jack shivered exaggeratedly.

'Whatever is *that*?' Luke gazed upwards into the sky at a giant silvery object.

'*Get down!*' Jenny's cry startled them, but they reacted instinctively by flattening themselves on the beach. 'It's – it's a *Zeppelin* – can you believe it?'

Elin looked at her incredulously. She was too young to remember the terrifying Zeppelin raid on Southwold in the great war.

'An airship, you mean?'

'Yes! It's flying so low – it could crash – they go up in flames, you know!'

'It's passed over us now, can't get any higher, I reckon, because of the clouds,' Luke said. He stood up. 'Come on, forget it – you can read all about it in the papers tomorrow.

Let's make for the amusement arcade! I've got a pocketful of pennies!'

'Stop shaking like that, Mum.' Billie was embarrassed. But she pulled her mother to her feet and gave her arm a comforting squeeze as they climbed the steps to the cliff path.

Mark, Clo and Luke took the children to the cinema for the early evening performance of an Eddie Cantor film. It was Mark's idea; he came in from work and after greeting their unexpected visitor, added casually: 'Who fancies going to the pictures, then?'

To Elin he whispered, as he kissed her goodbye: 'I thought you and Jenny might appreciate a couple of hours by yourselves.'

Dear Mark, she thought now, he knows me – us – so well. Jenny, who'd taken the opportunity for a bath and hair wash, sat on the footstool below the sofa so that Elin could tease the tangles out with her brush.

'We take after our mother for our hair!' Jenny exclaimed, after an 'ouch!' or two.

'I wish we had a photograph of her.' Elin sounded wistful.

'I'm sure Dad has one tucked away, maybe a wedding picture; I'll ask.'

'There, you can get a comb through it now, I think.'

Jenny got up, sat next to her sister, with a sigh of relief.

'Tie your hair back with a bow, like you used to, Jenny.'

'Getting too old for that.'

'Nonsense; you're only thirty.'

'I wish . . . I wish I was young again, still at home with Dad and Grandma and you.'

'But then you wouldn't have Billie, would you? And I wouldn't have Mark!'

Jenny's bottom lip quivered. 'If only we could stay here with you, Elin. I don't want to go back to Ted. I know that sounds awful, but it's true.'

'Oh, Jenny dear, if only you could. But the house is bursting at the seams, now.'

'I know. Tell Mark to send a telegram directly when the baby's here and I'll come for the day as soon as I can.'

'Don't worry – you and Dad will be the first to know!'

The time for confidences was almost over; they heard excited voices as the cinema party approached the front door.

'It was a really funny picture!' Billie enthused. 'You and Elin ought to see it, Mum.'

'Guess what?' BP butted in, sensing that Billie was going to tell the story there and then, when he'd something important of his own to impart, overheard in the cinema. 'That old Zeppelin only just skimmed the lighthouse tower! Apparently it was on a flight all round the country and had to come down low here or it would have been caught in the clouds! I was the only one of us to really see it, the rest of you were lying doggo!'

'So were you,' Billie pointed out.

'Sandwiches in the kitchen,' Elin said. 'Then have a wash, and off to bed.'

'Had a good old chinwag?' Mark asked, after the young ones had departed, and Luke and Clo lingered in the kitchen, ostensibly washing up.

'Yes . . .' Elin yawned. 'Oh, excuse me, but I'm ready for my bed, too.'

'All that fresh air today,' Jenny said. 'I might stay down here for a bit; Billie won't be asleep yet. Goodnight, Elin – thanks for being such a good listener.'

Elin kissed her. 'You'll be up later, Mark?'

'Mmm. I still feel wide-eyed – Eddie Cantor has that effect, I find!'

Mark sat on the sofa beside Jenny, keeping a space between them.

'I saw you wiping your eyes, Jenny. Care to confide in me, too?'

She turned to face him, eyes brimming again.

'It's a long story – Elin will tell you.'

'That's just it, she won't. She's so loyal; you must know that.'

'I – can't bear the thought of going back to Ted . . .'

'Things are that bad?' he asked, concerned.

She nodded. He moved closer, enfolded her in his strong arms.

'Oh, Jenny . . .' was all he said, his voice muffled with his lips against her hair.

'I still love you,' she whispered.

He released her immediately then. After a long moment, he said gruffly: 'Never forget how much we care for you, Elin and I.'

'I know.'

Clo and Luke sat on the hard kitchen chairs and chatted of this and that.

'You won't want to give your job up, I know, when we're together,' he told her.

'I could still come in every day, as I used to do.'

'How did you manage then – with a baby to care for?'

'My mum looked after BP. Well, not as I'd have liked, I'm afraid. She'd had a hard life and I s'pose she was worn out when he come along. She had two fierce old hounds, but he was a fearless child and those grumpy old dogs never went for him.'

'I think he and I get on well.'

'Good. 'Cause if you didn't I wouldn't consider you.'

'Consider me for what?' Luke asked boldly.

'As a husband. Nothing other than that, Luke.'

'I never thought of myself as the marrying kind . . .'

'Well then, you'd better start thinking that way, eh?'

'I'll try. How about tucking me in tonight?'

'You are trying, I can see!'

But she didn't say she wouldn't.

'Is Jenny all right?' Elin asked carefully, as she snuggled up to Mark in bed.

'Jenny . . . It means a lot to her, being here with you.'

It was an answer, but not a complete one, she thought.

SEVENTEEN

Peggy was delighted to see Billie when she and Marian returned on the Friday afternoon.

'How long can you stay?' she demanded.

'Mum says she must get back to work soon; anyway, before we know it, it'll be time to go back to school. Mark's taking us home this Sunday. What did you do in London?'

Billie fidgeted while Peggy unpacked at her mother's bidding. Being a tidy child, she sorted out her clothes into piles, whereas Billie would have upended the case and emptied the contents on to the bed.

'We went to the National Gallery, where people talk in whispers, or stand for ages just contemplating, as Mummy says. Some of the pictures are amazing; they must have taken years to paint. Lots of chubby cherubs and ladies with *drapes*, as Mummy put it.'

'Did you go to see the waxworks?'

'Yes, but Mummy thought I was too young for the Chamber of Horrors. Too realistic, she said.'

'Well, did you go to the zoo?'

'I'm afraid not. You need a fine day for that, Aunt Celia told us, or you'll have to eat your sandwiches in the monkey house!'

'Oh, that sounds fun! Do hurry up.'

'Let me just do my hair first.' Peggy combed her immaculate black bob. 'Yours could do with a tidy-up, too.'

'Not much point,' Billie said cheerfully. 'I've inherited the family bird's nest. Mum or Gran grab a brush and pin me down occasionally but when I complain they threaten to take me to the barber for a short back and sides. Not that I'd care, if they did!'

'We're not at all alike, are we, but I do like you; you make me laugh!'

Downstairs, Marian and Jenny were looking on while Elin unwrapped Celia's generous gift of baby clothes. Clo had her coat on, and was obviously about to go out.

'If you see the boys, tell them they might have been here to greet their old mother!' Marian reminded her ruefully.

'Can't we go with you, Clo?' Billie asked.

'Sorry, not this time.'

'Where are you off to?'

'I'll tell you later,' she said mysteriously, and departed.

Clo hurried across the common. *Another rainy August afternoon! Not summery at all*, she thought.

'Be there at three-thirty sharp,' Luke had said. 'We stop for tea in the office then. I promised to be back by four. I told my boss I must have your approval.'

He'd got the job at the ship chandler's the day after he arrived in Southwold, on the strength of a testimonial from Richard and his connection with the sea. The pay was reasonable, and he enjoyed taking his turn in the shop, meeting customers.

He'd also been fortunate, it seemed, in finding somewhere to live, again due to Richard, who was well respected in the area. Thanks to his new resolve, he hadn't blued his last pay packet from the shipping company, so could manage the rent 'up front'.

Clo saw him waiting on the corner of the cobbled Victorian terrace; ran the last few yards, splashing her stockings with mud and hoping her umbrella wouldn't blow inside out.

'Look above the lintel – see the date and that smiling, painted-plaster face? That must be a good sign,' Luke said, opening the door of the third cottage along the narrow street, with a key. 'Two up, two down, a bit neglected, but the rent's cheap, and when we're married we'll make a real home of it.' There, he'd said it: committed himself.

'We can whitewash the walls' Clo was glowing 'and it's convenient for everything – not too far from Mrs Lambert's, or your shop, and BP will be all right later on for the bus to his new school. Can't see the sea from here, but I can smell it . . .'

'Not too near the brewery?' he asked.

'No, I'm used to that smell, too. I love to see the horses pulling the dray. Mrs Lambert's offered us some furniture, including the old piano for BP, and a double bed.'

'Well, it's good of her – though I mean to buy us a new bed, as soon as I can afford it.'

She gave him a quick kiss. *No curtains up at the windows*, she thought, blushing.

'You really want to marry me, Luke? I bet your mother won't approve – her son marrying a working-class girl from a poor home, who don't always speak proper and—'

'I told you; I knew right away when I saw you, Clover, you were the one.'

'You were *sweet* though,' she said carefully, 'on Elin at one time, weren't you? You gave her that pretty brooch when you come back . . .'

'Ah, but I intend to buy *you* a ring! She was always nice to me, so was her father, I have real respect for them both. But I was aware that Elin was sweet, as you put it, on Mark, from the beginning.'

'That's all right then. What's the time?'

'Time we left here, but now I've got your approval, I hope to move in this weekend.'

'Can I tell the others when I get back?'

'They appear to know already,' he teased her, 'about the wedding.'

'Oh – what I said about the furniture? You don't mind, do you?'

'This is the best thing that's ever happened to me,' he said as he closed the door.

Elin hugged her sister.

'Oh, I've enjoyed your visit! Remember me to Ted and his mother.'

'Mind you don't do too much,' Jenny said, giving Elin's tummy a gentle pat.

'You, too!'

'I wish you weren't going, Billie.' Peggy sighed.

'You must come again, Billie,' Marian told her, 'in the spring. I have a feeling that the Christmas holiday will be too busy here!'

Mark put the luggage in the car.

'Coming, you two?'

'Wait!' Clo called from the hallway. 'Something for your tea!' She held out a bag.

'Thanks! Say goodbye to BP for me.' Billie ran to fetch her offering. 'I thought he'd have been here to see us off.'

'He must be still helping to unload the furniture with Mr Odell at Luke's,' Clo said. She was anxious to join them, but wouldn't say so.

Jenny heard the rustle of the bag in the back of the motor as they drove along.

'Leave a few buns for when we get home, Billie, eh? How can you be hungry after that big Sunday dinner?'

'I'm a growing girl,' Billie mumbled with her mouth full. Then she settled down for a nap, to pass the journey away.

After a while, Mark said quietly, 'I hope things will improve for you at home, Jenny.'

'I'm going to make a real effort, and I pray he will, too. I should have realised that he was grieving as much as me for little Ruby. I turned away from him, then. We had a good marriage in the early days. He resents me working when he can't get a job, but we need the money.'

'That's not right. Elin and I have worked together throughout our marriage. We're very happy, Jenny, especially now. I love her so much.'

'That means the world to me . . .'

For a moment he took his hand from the wheel and covered hers, clenched in her lap.

'I'll never forget though, what *we* almost had together.'

'You don't regret it?'

'No. We didn't betray anyone else; that's important. Well, you'd better wake Billie, because you're almost home. I won't come in.'

Home, Jenny thought, as the front door opened and Ted stood there, spruced up and smiling. He took the case from her hands.

'Good to have you back,' he blurted out. He was nervous, she could tell. Maybe he'd worried that they wouldn't return.

She put her hands on his shoulders; the case was between them but she leaned forward and kissed him on the lips. She felt his sudden, sharp intake of breath. She stepped back smartly as he put the baggage down.

'You nearly dropped that on my toes!' she exclaimed, but she was smiling, too.

'Come here,' he said huskily, hugging her close. 'I missed you, Jenny.'

'Let me pass,' came Billie's plaintive voice. 'Why are you two being so soppy?'

Then they were all laughing, and Ted walked with Jenny, keeping his arm firmly round her waist, calling out to his mother in the kitchen:

'They're here, Mum – Jenny's back!'

'Haven't you done enough today?' Marian surprised Clo in the kitchen, cleaning the top of the cooker. It was just after ten o'clock in the evening.

'Oh, Mrs Lambert – I couldn't sleep, thinking of Luke on his own in a strange place.'

Marian smiled, took the washing cloth from Clo's hands.

'Sit down. I'll make us a hot drink, eh? Clo, I'm surprised at myself, saying this, but, he doesn't have to be on his own, does he? You could move in and get things really straight before the wedding next month; BP can stay with us until after that; after all, you'll be coming in every day, won't you. That way he won't get unsettled before he goes back to school.'

'If you're sure . . . Luke's not very domesticated, and—'

'And he needs you. Now. I understand. So will BP, he's an easy-going chap.'

'There are two bedrooms.' Clo sipped her tea. 'But only one bed, so far.'

'Clo, dear, I'm not as strait-laced as you think.'

'I was . . . going to make him wait, Mrs Lambert.'

'Make the most of your time together, my dear. I thought my husband and I had years ahead of us, so I concentrated on the children more than him. He kept his own problems to himself. If I'd known, well, that dreadful thing . . . might not have happened, then.'

Mark popped his head round the door.

'Tea? You didn't offer me a cup!'

'I didn't realise you were still up and about, too,' Marian retorted. 'Well, I'll pour you one and you can sit down here with me while Clo quickly packs a bag. Then, if you wouldn't mind escorting her to Luke's place, and hurrying back, we can all get a good night's sleep!'

'Thanks,' Clo said sheepishly, shooting off. 'See you at seven-thirty tomorrow!'

'I gather, dear sister,' Mark said, 'that you gave her the same advice you gave me.'

'Not quite; but I'm very hopeful that their story will also have a happy outcome.'

'You didn't say the more usual "happy ending",' he mused.

'I know that's not always possible,' she said softly.

'I must tell Elin where I'm going; don't wait up, Marian.' He paused. 'I just wish the outcome could have been different for you.'

'You helped me get through, all of you. Where would I be without my family?'

There was still a light glimmering behind the hastily put up curtains at the top of the house. Mark said a quick goodbye and left Clo to knock on the door. He would watch from the corner to make sure she went inside before going on his way.

'I wondered who on earth it could be,' Luke said, dazzling Clo with his torch.

She shaded her eyes with her hand. 'Aren't you going to let me in?'

'Of course. You surprised me, that's all. Is something wrong?'

'No, Luke. I hope you'll think it's right . . . I didn't like the thought of you being by yourself, that's all, and Mrs Lambert agreed. BP's staying put until after the wedding. We . . . we'll have time now to get to know one another proper. That's important.'

'Only one bed,' he said. 'D'you want me to take the old sofa?'

'I want us to be together. We've an early start tomorrow, so let's go upstairs.'

At dawn, she grimaced ruefully as she washed in cold water in the basin on the washstand. No home comforts here, she mused. Not even a rug on the floorboards; but as she recalled the night spent in his arms, a smile spread across her face. She turned to see her lover regarding her with the same expression. He held out his arms invitingly.

'Time for one last cuddle, surely?'

'I ought to cook your breakfast,' she said unconvincingly. 'I can have mine at . . .' she just stopped herself from saying 'home' and said instead: 'there.'

'I can get something to eat from the bakery – please, Clover . . .'

She was in her chemise, so it'd only take a moment to get dressed, she thought.

Later, while he was washing, she slipped her dress over her head, unrolled her stockings, and addressed his back.

'Luke, there's something I should've said. I hope it's not too late, after . . . I'm not sure I want another baby. I thought BP was all I needed, especially as I've been treated like one of the Lamberts these last few years.'

He turned, rubbing his neck with the towel.

'It wouldn't be fair on the lad either, I reckon, at his age. As you say, maybe we'll find last night decided things for us; if not, I promise to take care of it, in the future. I don't mind either way!'

'As long as *you* don't mind,' she said awkwardly. 'I won't either. I'll have to go! As we haven't got a gas stove here yet, you must come along after work for supper with the family, then we'll return here and get busy with the whitewash! We must have it looking nice before your mother sees the house.'

'My mother? When d'you think we'll see *her*?'

'At the wedding, I hope. We've only got one parent between us, and Richard, your stepfather, of course – we'll ask him to give me away. And Mark can be your best man, and Peggy my bridesmaid – I'm glad we're getting hitched in the chapel in the high street. I've been going quite regular since that open-air service I got caught up in last summer. It was singing "For those in peril on the sea" what did it. I didn't know *you* then, of course.'

Luke gave a mock groan. 'Now I know I'm really getting married at last!'

At Luke's request, Richard booked a room for Frances in the hotel. He hadn't seen her since their separation and communication between them had ceased after the settlement. However, he'd enquired after her welfare through her solicitor from time to time. The letter advising Luke that she would attend his wedding had been sent to her son, of course.

'She will arrive on the Friday afternoon before the wedding on Saturday. She hasn't mentioned meeting Clover or me before the service, but she does ask for you to call at the hotel to see her that evening after eight o'clock,' Luke told Richard.

'That makes me feel apprehensive,' Richard said. 'I wonder what she wants?'

'To apologise perhaps for the unhappiness she caused you?'

'I doubt that, but I'll go, of course.'

When he arrived home from work on Friday, Richard spent some time getting ready for the meeting. He shaved, oiled his hair and changed into the suit he had worn for both his weddings. It was already pressed ready for tomorrow.

'If you don't mind, I'll have my supper when I come back,' he told Ida.

'You're feeling nervous, boy?' She tweaked at his tie.

He nodded ruefully. 'I expect she'll see a change in me.'

'We're all older, and some of us feel it,' she said, rubbing her rheumatic hands. 'Good luck, anyway.'

The clerk at the desk had been watching out for him.

'Mrs Odell wishes to see you in her room, sir. Up the stairs, second on the right.'

Frances opened the door immediately to his knock.

'Good evening, Richard. I'm glad you could come.'

'How are you, Frances?' he asked politely as he followed her into the room.

'Take a good look at me, and I'm sure you'll see.'

They faced each other under the bright centre light. The shock of seeing her so thin and obviously ill made his heart pound.

There was a table in the corner, with the remains of a meal, hardly touched. She motioned him to sit down on one of the chairs.

'Luke saw you six months ago – he didn't say you were – like this.'

'It was early days then. I was aware of it, of course, because of my nursing training. I didn't want Luke to know; I was angry at what was happening to me, and I didn't want his sympathy. We've never been close – which he probably blames on me.'

'He wanted you at his wedding, and was pleased you decided to come.'

'I imagine he also feels apprehensive,' she said shrewdly. 'Wonders what I might do, or say, to upset the bride. Is she from a good family, d'you know?'

'You must judge for yourself. She's a hard-working girl, with plenty of spirit, and she's determined Luke will be a reformed character from now on. Are you aware that Clover has a son? Before you ask, she wasn't married to his father. Unlike my Delia, she was able to keep her baby with her. Delia was so happy when Jenny could come to us.'

'Did Delia ever think about the feelings of the foster mother who had cared for that child for four years – did she tell you who she was?'

'I . . . don't understand . . .'

'Then she obviously said nothing. When Delia knew she was pregnant, she confided in me. We'd first met when she arrived at my boarding school. She was only six years old. As a prefect I took her under my wing. I wouldn't say we were close; the age difference was too great, but the headmistress impressed on me that Delia was vulnerable, having recently lost both parents. I hadn't seen or heard of her for some years when she arrived at my hospital as a probationer.

'The man concerned transferred to a senior post at another hospital before she knew she was pregnant. Because he was married, we decided not to tell him. I came up with a solution to her dilemma. I was over thirty, about to be married myself, moving with my husband to his new parish. He knew of a place where she could stay when her condition became obvious to the hospital, until her baby was born. It was agreed that we would foster the child for an indefinite period, that Delia would return to her nursing career, and that she would pay towards the baby's keep. My husband's parish was not a wealthy living. It seemed a good solution. I have never been sentimental, I did not envisage finding it difficult to give the baby up when the time came.'

'This is difficult to take in, Frances . . .'

'I realise that. When Delia met you and told me that Jenny would be living with her after you were married, I made things as awkward as I could. What changed the situation was the unexpected: I became pregnant myself. My husband urged me to let the child I thought of as my own daughter go to her real mother. Reluctantly, I agreed. Because of all the unpleasantness, I guessed that Delia would not keep in contact.'

'To think that she didn't share her troubles with me.' Richard showed his anguish. Then a thought struck him. 'Is that why you decided to move to Langford, to look us up, all those years later?'

'Yes. I was shocked when I discovered that Delia had died only three years after your marriage. I felt cheated: if I had known I would have tried to get Jenny back . . . I had to face the fact that she was grown up, married and had a child of her own.'

'So you decided to take your revenge on me instead – was that it?'

She sighed. He saw then that her hands were shaking, as she wiped sudden beads of sweat from her brow. He noted the dark rings under her eyes, the unhealthy pallor of her skin, the way she clutched at her stomach, obviously in discomfort.

'I don't expect you to forgive me, Richard. But I owed you an explanation.'

'You're tired; I can see this has all been too much for you. I must go. You ought to get some proper rest before tomorrow. Frances . . .'

'Yes?' She rose with difficulty, ignoring his proffered hand.

'I won't tell Jenny; there's no point. Or Luke. Just promise me you'll play your part tomorrow in making it a happy day, for him and Clover. And, Frances, I'm glad you want to make your peace with me; if I can do anything to help you, you only have to say.'

'You're a good, decent man, Richard Odell. Thank you. Goodnight.'

He hesitated briefly, then inclined his head to kiss her cheek.

'You'll soon be free,' she whispered. 'I *can* promise you that.'

EIGHTEEN

The wedding morning dawned, and although there was an autumnal mist first thing, the sun broke through well before eleven, the time of the service.

Marian came downstairs at seven intending to cook breakfast, only to find Clo, who had stayed the night with them, already in the kitchen.

'Oh, Clo,' she sighed. 'I was going to bring you breakfast in bed this morning – then I meant to ensure the bathroom was free so that you could have a leisurely bath, and then you would have plenty of time to get ready.'

Clo wore her apron over her dressing gown, her hair concealed by a chiffon scarf.

'I was too excited to stay in bed, Mrs Lambert. I've done the grapefruit and I was just going to whisk the eggs ready for scrambling – the boys are sure to be down shortly.'

As if on cue, BP came into the kitchen in his pyjamas, rubbing sleepy eyes.

'What time is it? What's for breakfast – wedding cake?'

'Oh, you! The usual. Where are your slippers and dressing gown?' Clo scolded fondly, giving him an unexpected hug.

'Aw, Mum,' he protested.

'Out of the kitchen, both of you!' Marian told them. 'Clo, have your bath now, before those boys take all the hot water. BP, you can keep the boys and Peggy upstairs until you hear the call, eh?'

Mark appeared soon after they had departed. He was dressed, and something about his drawn expression alerted his sister.

'Anything wrong, Mark?'

'Been awake most of the night. Elin was restless and uncomfortable.'

'Not – the baby, surely?'

'She's not in labour, thank goodness. She overdid things yesterday. Still a couple of months to go. She must be persuaded to take things more quietly from now on.'

'Difficult today, eh? Best say nothing to Clo, I think, don't you?'

Mark nodded. 'I've told Elin to stay put until an hour before the ceremony. She says she can't face breakfast yet. I'll ask the family not to disturb her, eh?'

However, Clo was already knocking tentatively on Elin's bedroom door, having heard Mark's tread down the stairs.

'Elin, can I come in for a minute?' She went in, to find her friend still lying in bed. 'Oh, sorry – you weren't asleep I hope?'

'No. Mark won't let me get up yet. Look, don't stand there, come and sit on the bed. I'm so glad you came. How're you feeling now the day is here?'

'Happy, of course, but nervous, too. Mainly because Luke's mother will be there!'

'Clo, have a look in my handkerchief drawer in the dressing table; there's something I want you to have – yes, that tissue-wrapped parcel on the top. Open it and see if you like what's inside. Celia gave it to me on *my* wedding day – she never had the chance to wear it herself and I only wore it the once . . .'

Clo held the white silk nightdress up against her.

'It's lovely, Elin – are you sure you want to part with it?'

'I think it's something special to pass on to another bride. I hope you'll do that, too.'

'Oh, I'm sure I will! Thank you – I can't wait to put it on tonight – although' she smiled at the thought 'it won't take long to slip it off again!' She bent over Elin and kissed her forehead. 'You rest up, dearie, and I'll soak in a nice hot bath!'

'I'm glad you're not about to desert us, Clo . . .'

'I'll never do that! Like you, I feel like one of the family now.'

Clover was driven to her wedding by Richard in the pony and trap on a typical late October morning, cold but crisp, with shimmering pale sunlight and smoke curling from every chimney. Folk out shopping in the high street paused to wave, seeing the white ribbons plaited in the pony's mane and the bride holding on to her little cloche hat, which matched her woollen dress and jacket, the mauve-pink of clover, chosen to please Luke.

They entered the chapel to be joined by young Peggy in blue velvet with a white muff. Clo was reassured by the sight of the groom and best man turning their heads to watch them coming up the aisle. The front pews were occupied by family and friends and she was relieved to see that Luke's mother had not insisted on sitting in solitary splendour, but had Richard's aunt beside her. Clo gave her son a special smile as he sat, solemn-faced, alongside Charlie and Jack.

'Sing up . . .' she whispered in passing. She was very proud of his treble voice and perfect pitch.

The music from the harmonium swelled, then faded away as the minister warmly welcomed them all to the union of Luke James Goldsmith and Clover Annie Butt.

Then Luke squeezed her hand and murmured in her ear, 'I love you, Clover.'

She wasn't nervous any more. *Family, friends and flowers*, she thought; *what more can I ask for?*

A few snapshots were taken, including one of the pony and trap.

'Her final outing, dear old girl,' Richard said ruefully. 'She's retiring and going out to grass; I've bought a bike!'

They'd made an appointment for a formal studio photograph later that week. As Frances wouldn't be there then, Mark took a picture of the bride and groom flanked on either side by Luke's mother and Richard. Together for once, but still apart.

Mark was keeping an anxious eye on Elin, and as soon as he could he made his way to her and suggested he take her home.

'I haven't had a chance to throw any confetti yet,' she said stubbornly.

'Peggy will love to do the honours for you,' he said firmly.

She gave in more easily than he had expected. 'Well, I suppose I can put the kettle on,' she said. They were having the reception at home; Marian had arranged it all.

Mark signalled to Marian. 'Can you come?' he mouthed. She'd travelled the short distance to the chapel in his car.

She understood. Frances was expecting her taxi. She could bring Ida and Peggy, and the boys could walk back, she decided. Richard, of course, would drive Clo and Luke, now surrounded by Clo's friends from the chapel, who'd been waiting to congratulate them.

The boys didn't walk, they ran, arriving breathless at the house as Mark parked the car. He gave them a distracted wave, then he helped Elin alight, and took her indoors.

Marian waited in the hall, to brief them.

'The excitement's been a bit much for Elin. Mark insists she rests in her room before lunch. Now, don't you go worrying Clo about this, BP. The last thing Elin wants is to spoil her special day. You boys can greet the guests and make sure they are comfortable in the sitting room – entertain them while I make coffee to warm them up, eh?'

Upstairs, Mark eased off Elin's shoes.

'Why didn't you tell me your ankles were swollen?' he exclaimed. He straightened up, looking concerned. 'Make yourself comfortable on the bed; then I'll take your blood pressure. How d'you feel?'

'I don't know . . . head hurts,' she said in a small voice. 'I can't be ill today, I *can't* . . .'

'Relax, darling. You're just tired, I expect. No wonder, after last night.' There was a telephone extension in their room. He'd ring his father, he thought, to ask his advice.

BP took the request to entertain the guests literally. He hadn't played the piano, which had belonged to Marian's aunt, in the sitting room before – his practising had been on the old Homeleigh instrument, now installed in his new home.

He lifted the lid cautiously, and settled himself on the stool. He was the only one of the four children to have continued with his music after Elin had taught them the rudiments. A teacher at school had kindly offered free lessons to reward his enthusiasm.

Something suitable for the occasion, BP decided, unaware that he was being observed by Luke's mother. The sheet music was no longer fashionable. He selected 'Drink to Me Only With Thine Eyes', performing with such verve, that all conversation ceased.

'Let me turn the pages for you!' Peggy cried, rushing to the piano.

There was polite clapping, and then Marian came in with the coffee.

'Don't be embarrassed, Clover,' Frances said to Clo. 'The boy has an obvious talent, which should be nurtured. You intend to change his name, I presume? Goldsmith would be more suited to a performer on the concert platform than Butt.'

The gentle squeeze of Luke's arm encircling her waist told Clo not to rise to this slight. He answered for his wife.

'Don't forget Dame Clara Butt, the famous singer, Ma. We think *Robert* should make up his own mind on that.'

'Don't go off. We haven't talked yet.'

Clo sat between the two of them on the sofa. She was glad she had taken a moment or two on her return to sleek her hair behind her ears with the sparkling paste clips that Celia had sent her for the 'something borrowed'. 'But I want you to keep them, of course!' she'd said.

'Would you care for a piece of shortbread, Mrs Goldsmith?' Charlie asked politely.

'No, thank you,' she said dismissively. 'It'll spoil my lunch.'

'It won't hurt, surely,' Luke said to her. 'You've obviously lost weight, Ma.'

'Nonsense! Look.' She produced an embossed envelope from her handbag. 'I asked Richard where you were spending your honeymoon weekend, and he said, at your little house. I gather you're not straight there, yet. I have taken the liberty of booking you in at my hotel for two nights – don't worry, I shall be early to bed and off by midday tomorrow, so I won't be playing gooseberry. I have already settled the bill.'

'I don't know what to say,' Luke began.

'Then don't say it. Call it my wedding present to you both.'

'Thank you,' Clo said simply on behalf of them both. On an impulse, she turned to kiss her new mother-in-law.

Frances took out her handkerchief as if to dab her cheek, but wiped her eyes instead.

'Look after him, Clover. He won't believe it, but, too late, I realise what he means to me.'

'You're not well,' Clo realised, discerning the pallor beneath the rouge.

'Ma?' Luke queried sharply.

'Not well,' Frances repeated. 'Nothing to worry about, though.'

Elin appeared in time for the meal, apologising for having changed out of her wedding finery into one of her loose smocks, with slippers on her feet.

'I got over-excited, I guess.' Marian noted the hectic flush on her cheeks, the way Mark hovered round her, putting cushions behind her back when she sat at the table.

'What's up?' she asked him, as they fetched the covered dishes from the kitchen.

'I've asked Dad to pop over when the guests have departed and Clover and Luke have gone to the hotel – did you hear about that? I'd like you both to take a look at Elin and tell me what you think. Her blood pressure is far too high.'

'She may have to go into hospital—'

'I think that's a distinct possibility. But you know Elin, she's determined not to upset the party. Or her father after he's made it up with Frances at last.'

'Turkey and all the trimmings!' Clo cried in delight. 'And it's not even Christmas!' She looked at Marian. 'How did you manage to do all this without me knowing?'

'Courtesy of the bakery! But the cake, naturally, is a Bunting special – and there's a telegram from your aunt and uncle for the best man to read when we have the toasts.'

'Well, I'm just going to say, before you all tuck in,' Luke put in, 'this is the best day of our lives, and all of you have helped to make it so!'

'I shall eat in my room, so I'll say goodnight now.' Frances dismissed them at her door.

'We'll see you in the morning,' Luke said.

'Not too early I hope.' There was a touch of the old acerbity.

Luke patted her shoulder. 'Goodnight, Ma.'

'Goodnight, Mrs Goldsmith,' Clo echoed. As they walked along the thick-carpeted corridor, she said, 'Couldn't we do the same? After the wedding lunch, just a sandwich would do me, Luke. That dining room looked rather grand and the other guests . . .'

'Distinctly po-faced. Can I order half a bottle of wine?'

'Why not! You've been so good. You deserve it today.'

Later, Clo stood in front of the dressing-table mirror, regarding herself in the white gown. She thought: *it looks too elegant for me. I'd have chosen something more . . . frilly, um, what's the word? Feminine. But I guess Luke will approve.*

He undressed in the bathroom. The old-fashioned hotel had that effect. No impropriety here, he mused ruefully. Now he came up quietly behind her and she suddenly saw his reflection over her shoulder.

'You look beautiful, Clover,' he said huskily. His hands slid round the sensuous silk to cup her breasts; his lips caressed the back of her bare neck. She shivered with delicious anticipation.

'It's a nice, soft bed,' she murmured. 'Let's pretend it's the first time, Luke.'

'First time as Mr and Mrs Goldsmith.'

'I do like the sound of that . . .'

*

Elin was reminded of the journey she had made with Mark to the hospital on the night Jenny had given birth. Only then she had cradled little Ruby in her arms, and fortunately none of them had known that new life would be such a short one. Now she prayed that their baby would not be born before time.

'Not far, thank goodness,' Mark said, as they parked outside the cottage hospital. 'Marian made sure they had a bed for you. You'll see her on Monday morning.'

'I thought you said I was just going to be here overnight ...'

'Darling, this is the best place for you, while they make a few tests.'

An hour later, he kissed her goodbye, and, already sedated, she allowed her heavy eyelids to close, so she did not see him go.

The bedclothes were firmly tucked around her in that high, narrow bed; a single lamp cast a pool of light on the desk in the corner of the small room where the night nurse sat.

In the morning Elin was woken to be helped on to a bedpan, then a young nurse gently washed her face and hands with a soft flannel and pleasantly warm water, as if she was a child. Sleep soon claimed her again after a mere mouthful of breakfast.

She was hardly aware of what happened at intervals during the rest of the day. She protested faintly at the momentary pain in her earlobe, as a sample of her blood dripped into a little dish. She tried to concentrate when asked to keep the thermometer under her tongue. At intervals she was supported and urged to sip water. Injections were given or a cuff tightened round her arm as her blood pressure was taken. She slept during the doctor's morning round, and throughout the afternoon when Mark sat patiently beside her.

Sunday was such a blur, it was a shock to come to suddenly sometime during the following morning. She struggled to sit up, but her limbs felt like cotton wool. Her eyes focused gradually on flowers in a vase on the bedside table; on a covered jug of water, then her gaze shifted sideways and she saw Marian, in her uniform, smiling at her.

'You're back with us then,' she said simply.

'Where?'

'You're in our little hospital, Mark brought you here on Saturday night.'

'The baby?'

'Still where he should be. The sedatives worked well. You'll be all right, don't worry.'

'When can I come home?'

'Not yet, I'm afraid. Bed rest, quiet – doctor's orders.'

'Clo – oh dear.'

'Clo and Luke are blissfully unaware of all this. They came home this morning; Luke was due back at work today and Clo is coming to us this afternoon. Mark will put her in the picture then. He got the children off to school. Nothing for you to worry about. Make the most of your time off! Richard will be in to see you after work.'

'Mark?'

'Still at morning surgery. He'll be along here shortly. He's allowed to visit when he likes, at the nurse's discretion. That's me, at the moment!'

'That's all right, then.' Elin slid back under the covers. She was sleepy again.

Marian tucked her in. 'You're in the best place,' she whispered fondly.

Clo had been busy preparing BP's room. He'd decided to stay where he was during the week in term-time and come home at weekends. It was an arrangement they were all happy with. She'd see her son mornings and afternoons.

She didn't expect Luke again until supper, but he arrived unexpectedly at lunchtime.

'I missed you!' he said. 'A cheese sandwich and a cuppa would be nice.'

'If you don't mind the smuts on my face from the fire, you can give me a kiss.'

'Just a quick one. I thought we ought to open the letter Ma left for us. She said to wait until we were at home.'

She'd tucked it behind the clock, Elin and Mark's wedding present, on the mantelpiece.

Luke read it aloud as she poured the tea.

Dear Luke and Clover,

Thank you for inviting me to your wedding. I did not wish to spoil your day by telling you that my indisposition is more serious than I said. I have a growth in my stomach. Nothing can be done. You will probably hear from your uncle soon.

I am glad to have met you, Clover, and to know that you are happy and settled at last, Luke. There should be something coming your way to ensure your future comfort. However, you will appreciate that I owe a debt to Richard, which must be paid – albeit not fully, of course. I regret my attitude to him and realise that I was hardly a loving mother to you.

Please forgive me, then I can go in peace.

With my love to you both – look after that clever boy, Your mother

Clo put down the teapot and went to him as he sat at the kitchen table, silent and stunned now.

'She's a brave woman, Luke. I didn't expect to, but I took to her, you know.'

'I'm glad,' he said. 'And if there's enough, we'll put some aside for BP's future.'

NINETEEN

Elin was still languishing in the hospital a month later, despite her pleas to be allowed home.

'Is it because of what happened to Jenny?' she asked Mark one afternoon.

He hesitated. 'The baby's doing well. This is a precaution, Elin, because of your family history. I asked Richard about your mother, and it seems probable that she had the same problems as you have, before you were born.'

'You mean . . ?'

'No, I don't. Childbirth is not so hazardous as it was then. Bed rest is essential in your case. Try to be patient, darling.'

'Oh, I am! But Marian looks so tired, and you do too, and I worry about that.'

'We've all expected rather too much of you over the years. You were very young to take on all that responsibility when Marian lost her husband. When you come home with the baby, I'm positive you'll soon be your usual energetic self.'

'I can't possibly stay here another month!'

'I hope you'll be allowed a weekend in the family fold before that. But you'll be having the baby in hospital, Elin, we can't risk a home birth.'

'I'd guessed that,' she told him dolefully.

'I've an idea how to cheer you up,' he said, plumping up her pillows behind her. 'But don't ask me, because I'm not saying.'

The following Saturday afternoon, wrapped in rugs, Elin was wheeled in a bath chair to the car. She blinked in the harsh November light as Mark carefully deposited her in the back. She suddenly realised that the front passenger seat was occupied.

'Jenny!' she cried joyfully, as her sister turned to smile at her.

'Mark picked me up earlier,' Jenny said.

'It's wonderful to see you! But what about your job, it's your busiest evening, isn't it?'

'Ted's taken over from me! The owner needed a full-time assistant, I said I couldn't manage it, but I suggested Ted. Now he's doing the lot; gutting the fish, peeling spuds and chopping the chips, frying and helping to serve customers, too.

'Billie sends her love; she wanted to come today, but we thought it might be too much for you. She's more exuberant than Marian's lot! Ted's mum is in charge.'

'Ted didn't mind about you, then?' Elin asked, as the car moved off.

'No. Since he's working again, and I'm not, he's a lot happier, thank goodness. Oh, Elin, I've been fretting at not being able to spend a day or two with you. You're about to celebrate your wedding anniversary, aren't you, so this seems a good time.'

'Six years ago – I can't quite believe it,' Elin said, as they drew up at their house.

There was Charlie, unfamiliar in his first pair of long trousers and the close-cropped hair decreed by his school. But the grin was the same, although he no longer greeted visitors with a hug. The front door opened and the whole family was revealed: Richard, Marian, trying to hold Peggy back, Jack and BP. Behind were Clo and Luke.

'I don't think actually that Billie would have made much difference,' Mark said wryly.

Jenny got out with her bag, and Mark supported Elin as they followed her up the path.

'One at a time,' Mark warned them. 'Let me get Elin settled in the warm, first.'

It was crumpets for tea, toasted by the boys, and spread with butter by Peggy.

'I feel like royalty, being waited on, hand and foot,' Elin said softly. She looked over at her father and her sister. 'Remember how dear Grandma enjoyed tea by the fire?'

Her father cleared his throat. Mark gave him a little nod.

'I'd best get this news over with, Elin. Frances passed away a week ago. I had to attend the funeral, with Luke, that's why you didn't see me for a few days.'

'Oh, Dad – Luke, I'm sorry.' Elin didn't know what else to say.

'She made sure that . . . things will be easier for me, and Luke and Clo.'

'That's good.'

There was an awkward silence. Then Clo cut the fruit-cake into slices.

'Twelve pieces – that's one over – who's having that?' Peggy asked hopefully.

'The one who brushes up the crumbs,' Marian said. 'Then you and the boys can go in the other room to listen to the wireless. Elin's had enough chatter for one day.'

Later, when Marian was chivvying her offspring to bed, Clo, Luke and BP said goodbye and departed for their own home. Richard kissed his daughters and said it was time he left, too. That left Elin, Mark and Jenny by themselves.

'Your bag is still in the hall, I'll take it up to your room,' he told Jenny.

'He's giving us a few minutes on our own,' Elin observed.

'I know. He's so kind. He must be longing to get you to himself.'

'I'll take up most of the bed. I'm *huge*, Jenny!'

'You'll soon have a nice flat tummy again. Have you got any names in mind?'

'Not really. It ... didn't seem wise, I suppose, with things as they are.'

'Mark is confident all will be well.'

'I want to believe him, Jenny.'

'Maybe I shouldn't say – but I will. I don't regret having Ruby, Elin, despite the pain of losing her. Now that is easing, I accept that was how it had to be.'

'Are things better between you and Ted?'

'Much. I still feel wary because of how he misjudged me . . . you know . . . but I can't really blame him for that. Billie is the reason we've tried to put the past behind us, of course.'

'She's growing up.'

'Too quickly. Make the most of those precious baby days, Elin.'

'I'll try.' She yawned. 'Oh dear, I just keep dropping off!'

'Have a snooze. I'll be upstairs.'

Jenny passed Marian on the stairs.

'Realised we hadn't made your bed up! Mark's doing it. You're in Clo's old room.'

'Thanks,' Jenny replied. 'Elin's having a nap, by the way.'

'Then I'll tiptoe in, and quietly tackle the mending. I miss her help with that!'

Mark was just pulling up the blankets over the fresh sheets.

'Did you see Marian?' he asked.

'Yes, she explained. Thanks, Mark – I can finish it off.'

'We'll do it together,' he said. He tossed her the clean pillowcases.

When they'd finished their task, they sat on the edge of the bed, talking.

'Elin will be all right, won't she?' Jenny asked anxiously.

'I haven't told her yet, but the consultant believes a caesarean is advisable soon. Her blood pressure may soar out of control if she is allowed to go on to her due date.'

Jenny reached impulsively for his hand, squeezed it briefly.

'Oh, Mark . . . look, I shouldn't say this . . .'

'But you will, eh?'

'Don't you think it's time you and Elin set up home on your own?'

'Has Elin said as much, to you? We made a commitment to Marian, even before we married. Elin has always been so involved with Marian's children.'

'They're growing up, Mark,' Jenny said gently. 'They're becoming independent, even young Peggy. Clo made the right decision, to move out with Luke, even though she's still very involved with the family here, and wouldn't change that. I know you and Elin would be the same. You need time, and space, to concentrate on each other now, your own family. No, Elin hasn't said anything to me. Please think about it, that's all I ask.'

'I will, I promise. Though it's not the moment to discuss it with her. Thank you, Jenny.'

'What for? Interfering?'

'Caring about Elin and me,' he said simply. He rose. 'Time to go, I think.'

Elin stirred as he bent over her on the sofa.

'Did I drop off?'

'You did. Aren't you going to make room for me beside you?'

'Of course. I'm longing for a cuddle. That's if you can get your arm round me!'

In the corner of the room, Marian stuffed the mending back into the basket.

They didn't notice I was here, she thought ruefully. *But, that's as it should be. Time to make myself scarce.*

In her room, Jenny, reflecting, absently smoothed the eiderdown where they'd sat.

Marian drove Jenny back to Ipswich on Sunday after lunch; Peggy went along to see Billie. The boys took themselves off to spend the afternoon with BP. Clo would give them tea.

Elin and Mark made the most of the precious hour or so together until it was time for them to return to the hospital.

'Elin, there's something I ought to tell you. You won't have to wait much longer for the baby to be born. Your doctor intends to perform a caesarean some time next week. You and the baby will be home in good time to celebrate Christmas.'

'I . . . don't understand. Can't I have the baby naturally?'

'It's not that. The main concern is for you. The baby should be fine.'

'Do I have any choice?' she asked. 'Could I say "no"?'

'You could, but . . .'

'It would be such a relief to get it all over,' she said in a small voice.

'Yes, it would. Of course, it will take longer to recover, as you'll be all stitched up.'

'But then, as I always say,' she tried to joke, 'I have my own doctor and nurse to look after me at home! Fetch down the case of baby things, Mark. We'd better make sure we've got everything we need.'

'I'll be there with you, I promise you.' He wanted her to know that.

Billie was in school; Ted had already left to make ready for the lunchtime frying after his usual Monday off. Mrs Drake was taking her turn behind the tea urn at the Tuesday wives' meeting in the chapel hall down the road. So Jenny was on her own when she heard the second post arrive.

Just one: a bill, she thought, turning it over in her hands. A large manila envelope, with her name and address typed on it. Inside was a short letter, from a solicitors' office in Berkshire, to the effect that they were enclosing a sealed letter as requested by their late client, Mrs Frances Odell (formerly Goldsmith, née Burton).

Jenny made herself a strong cup of tea before opening that. A further slip of paper fluttered on to the table and she left that for the moment.

My dear Jenny,

I explained a few well-overdue facts to your father when we met recently at Luke's wedding. His immediate reaction was to say he felt he could not pass on certain matters concerning you. However, in view of the fact that these secrets could go with me to my grave and might never be revealed, I am taking it upon myself to write to you because I feel you have a right to know.

You will be aware that I knew your mother before she married. You were not even three years old at this time, so you probably have no recall of the time you were fostered before she could care for you herself. It may come as a shock to you to know that I was your foster-mother. Delia and I had been nursing colleagues: she confided in me when she became pregnant. Initially, I refused to give you up. Then the unexpected happened, I discovered that I was expecting a baby myself – Luke. The acrimonious struggle between your mother and myself meant that she refused to have any further contact with me.

I could never shake off my hurt and resentment towards her. I admit that my marriage to Richard much later was a form of revenge. It was too late for me to attempt a reconciliation with you.

This is not to advise you of a windfall, I apologise for that. I have to think of your father, and my son, first. But, in these last few weeks, quite by chance, I have seen your real father's name in the newspaper. He has retired from his post at a London hospital, and is recently widowed. It appears that he and his wife were childless. I have been able to ascertain his address and telephone number for you.

Although he never knew officially of your existence, I am sure he must have suspected what his liaison with your mother could have led to. Because he has no family ties, it would seem to me that, should you wish it, you could get in touch – you could show him this letter, signed by me, as verification.

Goodbye, Jenny – I'm sorry that we did not get the chance to become close again.

Frances

Feeling dazed, Jenny retrieved the slip of paper. Montague Hadleigh, she read, then the address blurred before her eyes.

She came to, wondering what on earth had happened. She was slumped at the kitchen table, the paper still gripped in her hand. *Norwich*, she thought. *I could get there by train . . . First, while I'm here by myself, I must write the most important letter of my life.*

Mark was staying with Elin overnight in the hospital. He had a camp bed close beside her. The operation was scheduled for the following morning, Wednesday, and sleep eluded him, thinking about it. Elin had been given something to relax her, and he was glad that she was not lying awake, too. His eyes eventually closed around 2 a.m., but barely fifteen minutes later, he suddenly jerked awake, wondering for a moment where he was.

The nurse put her finger to her lips.

'Just making sure all's well, Dr Clements. I'm sorry I disturbed you,' she whispered.

His eyes followed the flickering of her torch to the door, then she was gone, continuing on her round.

'Mark?' Elin murmured uncertainly.

He flung the bedclothes aside, leaned over her anxiously. 'What is it, Elin?'

'Just a niggle, it's gone now, don't worry.'

'Where?'

'My back, I think . . . I don't really know. Let me get back to sleep.'

He felt her brow; it was damp, but cool.

'All right, now?'

'All right,' she repeated.

He kissed her on the cheek. 'Goodnight, then.'

He slept again until almost five, then stretched his cramped limbs.

'Mark?' Elin's voice again. She was half-sitting up.

'Sorry – do you need the commode? Let me turn the lamp up.' He reached for his dressing gown, took a while to locate his slippers.

By the time he had his arm round her back to help her out, he felt her body stiffen and heard her gasp.

'Elin!' he said in disbelief. 'How long has this been going on?'

'Since . . . when I said, in the night . . .'

'Why didn't you call me?'

She couldn't answer, being in the grip of a further contraction.

Then she said weakly, 'I thought . . . if you knew . . . you'd ring the bell, and I'd be taken off for the op then, not later . . .'

'I think it's too late for that now, darling. But I'll have to call for help, I'm afraid. Ease back, and I'll see how far advanced you are.'

Everything happened so fast after that. Elin was carried away on a tide of what seemed like unrelenting pain; she struggled in vain as a mask was held over her nose and then she succumbed to oblivion.

She came to lying on a high bed, in a different place, under a bright light. The pain was gone, indeed she felt numb, as if her body was detached from her. Realisation came suddenly, and she cried out. Her eyes barely focused on a huddle of white-coated people beyond the bed. One of them moved swiftly towards her.

'Elin – it's all over, thank God. The baby's here.'

'Mark – I thought I could do it – on my own.'

'But you did! Or almost. No operation, just a couple of stitches, Elin. You had some ether to ease the pain, then the baby was helped out. All's well! We have a daughter, darling. She's on the small side, but perfect. Would you like to see her now?'

'Please . . .'

A nurse brought the baby to her, tucked her under the blanket close to her mother.

'What are you going to call her?'

'You can choose, Elin, I don't mind,' Mark said tenderly.

The name came to her instantly.

'Bluebell,' she said, looking with awe at the crumpled little red face, the oily dark hair. 'The "belle", because of Grandma. She's no beauty yet, but I don't mind!'

Relieved laughter rippled round the room.

'Bluebells in November?' From an amused nurse.

'When are we going home?' Elin asked hopefully.

'As soon as you're fit enough. Make the most of your enforced rest. Well, I must go and phone Marian so she can spread the good news. I'll see you two back in your room.'

Our baby, Elin thought. *I've had plenty of experience with children, of course, but like Clo once said, 'You don't know what it's like till you have one of your own.'*

TWENTY

'Ten days to Christmas – we'll never be ready.' Elin didn't sound too concerned, as she waved goodbye to the hospital staff from the car, then held out her arms for the baby. Mark wrapped them around with a blanket.

'Comfortable? Then we're off.'

'We're going in the wrong direction,' Elin told him.

'No, we're not. You'll see. Got a call to make first . . .'

'Oh, Mark, I don't feel like it today; I have to say I'll be likely to pipe my eye when all the family are crowding round. It could all be too much. Silly, I know.'

'Not silly at all. Understandable. Plenty of time for visitors in a day or two.'

They'd driven through Southwold now, turned away from the sea and were travelling along country lanes. Only the odd leaf or two trembled on the tree branches, but here and there was a bush of glossy holly, bright with exquisite scarlet berries. There were small patches of ice glinting on the grass edging the footpath. It was mid-morning, a school day, so there were just a couple of women hurrying to the local shops, toddlers tagging along.

'Oh, I know where we're going!' Elin exclaimed. 'To your parents' house!'

'You don't mind?' he asked tentatively.

'Of course not, it's time they met Bluebell! But we won't stay too long, will we?'

'Just as long as you want to,' he said mysteriously. 'Right, here we are.'

Mark's mother opened the door, obviously dressed to go out.

'Here you are, then! Come in out of the cold.'

Then Dr Clements appeared, buttoning his overcoat.

'Welcome home, all of you!' He looked at Mark. 'I gather you haven't told her yet?'

'Told me what? You're just off somewhere, aren't you – Mark should have made sure you'd be in. I'm sorry—'

'Go in by the fire, my dear, and between us we'll explain.'

It was a small house, with cosy, low-ceilinged rooms. The surgery was in an attached building, rather as Elin recalled her father's old house, alongside his business premises.

'You were earlier than we expected.' Mrs Clements divested herself of hat and coat. 'Still, now I have a chance to hold the baby! May I?'

'Of course you can. This is your grandma, Bluebell.'

'Shall I begin the explanations?' Mark's father asked his son.

'Go ahead, Dad.'

'Mark mentioned he thought it was high time you set up home on your own. You have a family of your own to consider now. I told him I'd been thinking of finally retiring and was hoping he would want to take the practice over. With that in mind, I said, he'd need to live on the job. We talked it over with Marian, and she came up with the ideal solution. Mother and I are moving into the house on the common, and should be very comfortable there; we'll be involved with the children, but only as much as we want to be, Marian says. I must say we are looking forward to seeing more of them, though; we missed out on our own children's growing up, you see, due to being overseas.'

'I hope you won't mind living with our old-fashioned furnishings, Elin, for the time being. We've taken what we'd like to keep, and the rest can be replaced when you want to,' Mark's mother added. 'I hope you'll be as happy here as we've been.'

'Say something, Elin – please don't feel I went behind your back,' Mark pleaded.

'I . . . wasn't expecting this, that's all, Mark,' said Elin, very quietly.

'There's more,' Mark admitted. 'If you agree, Mother and Dad have decided to sign this all over to us. In return, we would give them our half-share in Marian's place. I just wanted us to have a home of our own – I thought you deserved that more than anyone.'

'We ought to go, Mark,' Dr Clements said. 'You need to discuss this in private.'

When his parents had departed, Mark came back into the living room, to find Elin nursing the baby. She looked up at him, and he saw the tears in her eyes. He dropped to his knees in front of her.

'Darling, I should have waited until you felt capable of coping with all this—'

'Yes, you should. You always say we're equal partners, don't you. But, Mark, I'm crying because I'm happy; you've done the right thing, you really have. When I can take it all in, I'll love being here, just us, I know it. Bluebell and I, we won't have to share you.'

'And I won't have to share you, either.' He rose. 'More coal on the fire, I think, then let's see what Mother's left for our lunch! Did I ever tell you how much I love you, Elin?'

'Yes. But I don't mind how often you say it. Nor does the baby!' She turned Bluebell against her shoulder, gently rubbed her back. 'I haven't forgotten how to do this, see; it seems ages since Peggy was almost as tiny—'

'And you came into our lives and stayed there,' he said.

When Jenny received an answer to her letter, she agonised for a couple of days over whether she should tell Ted. Eventually, she waited until he came home from his late shift at the chip shop, after her mother-in-law and Billie were in bed. After all, she reasoned with herself, I told him the truth about my birth before we got married.

They talked in whispers while she massaged his back. He suffered pain in his shoulders after a long stint with the potato-slicing machine, pulling the handle down and forcing the chips through the blades to drop into the bucket of cold, salted water.

'You should have told me this before, when you received the first letter.'

'I know. But I felt I must write to . . . this person, right away.'

'Supposing he had reacted differently – denied any connection?'

'Well, he hardly seems overjoyed. Just agrees to see me and that this Friday will be convenient. He says which train to catch, that I will be met at the station. Please say you don't mind me going, Ted, because I intend to do so, anyway.'

He rolled over on to his side, turned off the bedside lamp.

'I can't stop you, then, can I? Be careful, that's all I ask. Goodnight, Jenny.'

'Ted . . .' She snuggled up to him, relieved at his reaction.

'Not tonight. I'm far too tired,' he said dismissively.

She lay awake for ages, wondering how Friday's meeting would go.

'You look like your daddy, don't you, Blue?' Clo, visiting Elin on her afternoon off, was enjoying her role as honorary aunt. 'She's got his nose, see?'

'Not quite! The usual baby blob, I think. Her looks are improving though, and she's got blue eyes to justify her name! Like BP, she's got a namesake to live up to, so she may be a belle eventually, eh?'

'I can tell you like living here, Elin. You don't miss all the space?'

'No. That was ideal for a big family, as we'd become, but this is perfect for us. I can manage everything myself, though I miss seeing you every day, of course.'

'I feel exactly the same about our cottage. Luke and I – it's working out so well.'

'What about BP?'

Clo hesitated. 'Well, him and Luke are already good pals, but he told me he doesn't want to call him Dad, because he isn't. I suppose I was a bit hurt he decided to stay on with the other boys during the week, but Luke says he can understand that; Charlie and Jack, he's spent half his life with them, after all.'

'Maybe he felt, you know, a little embarrassed about you and Luke sharing a bed – children are funny like that.'

'I must admit I thought that, too.' Clo's cheeks went bright pink as she bent over the baby and gave little Bluebell a kiss. 'Babies smell so nice, don't they?'

'Not giving you any ideas, is she?'

'No. Luke and me, we decided it wouldn't be fair on BP. And I wouldn't like to go through all that again, would you?'

'Mark says *he* wouldn't! He might change his mind later on, I suppose.'

'I'm glad we're all going to be together for Christmas Day in Southwold, anyway.'

'So am I,' Elin agreed. She held out her arms for her baby. 'She's snuffling. That means she's hungry!' She unbuttoned her blouse. No need to be coy, with Clo.

'Does she wake you up a lot in the night?'

'Much the same as every newborn baby,' Elin said ruefully. 'But following Marian's example, we have her crib by our bed. Mark turns the gas fire on, and makes sure we're warm enough while she's nursing. Then he insists I dive back under the covers, and he changes her nappy. Doctors made good dads, it seems!'

*

Jenny sat on the train, which was packed with middle-class women with fox-fur tippets, obviously going to Norwich for last-minute Christmas shopping. She felt conspicuous, with her bushy hair in an old-fashioned knot in the nape of her neck, and her lack of powder and paint. She'd brushed her navy overcoat well, but it was wearing thin; she'd taken the precious silk stockings Mark had sent her years ago from their hiding place in the chest of drawers, and polished her shoes to a good shine. The little felt hat had come from a jumble sale; with its crumpled net removed it looked quite smart with a band of blue petersham fastened in a jaunty bow. Mrs Drake hadn't questioned her as to where she was going. Jenny suspected that Ted might have told her something. Anyway, she'd offered to lend her daughter-in-law her chapel-going gloves. *At least I have a good dress under the coat,* Jenny mused. *It may be old, but Elin took great care of it, and since I shortened the hem and replaced the collar and cuffs, the blue dress Marian bought for her when she was sixteen still looks smart.*

She clicked open her handbag, checking that her ticket was tucked in her purse. Almost there. She took a deep breath. 'Don't let him talk down to you,' Ted had warned her. 'You've nothing to be ashamed of. *He* let your mother down, after all.'

She followed the other passengers out on to the platform, her ticket was scrutinised and the return half returned to her. Beyond the barrier she tried not to panic when no one approached her immediately.

'Jenny Drake?' She hadn't expected her chauffeur to be young, in a camel overcoat and soft hat. At her nod, he added: 'Follow me. The car is over there. Not far to go.'

They drove, not speaking, slowly along to the outskirts of the city, but Jenny was feeling too apprehensive to appreciate the impressive buildings they passed. The car moved smoothly down a side road, drew up outside a mews. There were tubs with neatly trimmed small trees at intervals outside the block of converted apartments.

Jenny's companion pressed a buzzer on the door, then inserted a key in the lock.

'Follow me,' he said again. No 'please', which made Jenny bristle. He opened the first inner door.

'Miss Drake,' he announced, ushering her in.

A man stood with his back to her, obviously winding a clock on the mantelpiece. He finished his task, put the glass back in place, then turned to scrutinise Jenny.

'Ah . . .Would you like coffee? You look cold.' He rang a bell. 'Sit here, would you. Arthur, take her coat, then return; I want you to take a note of what is said.'

Jenny found her voice.

'Dr Hadleigh, I presume? We haven't been introduced.' She mustn't let him intimidate her, she thought resolutely.

'Address him as *Mr* Hadleigh,' Arthur murmured smugly, as he went out.

'And I am *Mrs* Drake,' she responded smartly, before he closed the door.

Mr Hadleigh positioned his chair opposite, looked at her long and hard.

'Well, I can see the likeness to your late mother. So I have no reason to believe you are not her daughter . . . ah, the maid with the coffee. Leave the trolley: we will serve ourselves. Lunch at one-thirty today.'

'Is the young lady staying for that, sir?'

'I'm not sure. Mr Jamieson will let you know a little later. Oh good, here you are, Arthur. Sit over there with your notebook.'

Jenny, in turn, took in every detail of Mr Hadleigh's appearance. She surmised that he must be sixty, of an age with Richard, but he looked younger. He had a good head of silvery hair, plump, smoothly shaven cheeks and a high colour, indicating a love of rich food and good wine. His clothes were obviously expensively tailored, and she noted the thick gold watch chain across his plum-coloured waistcoat, strained across his middle.

'Now, tell me, Mrs Drake – what exactly do you expect of me?'

'I was hoping you would be pleased to see me, that's all.'

'You believe yourself to be my long-lost daughter, is that it?'

'I have good reason to believe that. I have a letter—'

'Pass that to Arthur. It could be a forgery.'

'I hardly think so. It was forwarded to me by the writer's solicitors after her death. No, I am not handing this over to your Mr Jamieson. He might destroy it, or refuse to give it back to me. Would you like me to read you the relevant parts?'

'That won't be necessary.' Mr Hadleigh sounded amused. 'You are obviously your mother's daughter; she could get on her high horse, as I recall. I am not denying that I knew your mother when she was a young nurse, but I am not confirming that we had an adulterous relationship, either. She had to blame her predicament on someone, that is understandable; it was convenient that I had moved on, could not contest her claim.'

'My mother kept your identity secret – she asked nothing of you! She only confided in a colleague, an older nurse, then Frances Burton, but about to be married to the Reverend Goldsmith. She was the writer of this letter. Mrs Goldsmith looked after me for a while, until my mother married. As I said, when I wrote to you, my mother died when my sister was born. I was then six years old.'

'So, in effect, you were then without either a mother or a father.'

'That's not true! I had the best of fathers, despite there being no blood tie between us. His own mother, our grandmother, cared for my sister and me.'

'Is your father, as you call him, still alive?'

'He is. I love him dearly.'

'Then why the interest in finding your real father? You have a husband, possibly a family—'

'We have a daughter. She's ten years old. I had another child, she . . . sadly died when she was very young.'

'From what cause may I ask?'

'We were told, a congenital heart defect; something we were not aware of in our family. Why do you want to know?' Jenny demanded.

'This could be the evidence you are looking for,' he said drily. 'Such a condition runs in my family. I lost two siblings in a similar fashion. It is the reason my wife and I decided not to have children ourselves.'

'Then surely it was unfair of you to seduce my mother as you did!'

He was angry now. 'How dare you assume that! I only admit that your mother imagined she was in love with me, that she encouraged me—'

Jenny got up. 'You can stop taking notes right now, Mr Jamieson! I am leaving. Please fetch my coat.'

Mr Hadleigh rose too. 'You are departing without that which you came for?'

'And what do you imagine that was?' She snatched her coat, and put it on.

'Money, of course. You planned to blackmail me; ruin my impeccable reputation.'

'How dare you! I expected nothing of you – wanted nothing, except to see the man who fathered me – I even thought you might be glad to see me. Goodbye, Mr Hadleigh!'

Jenny hurried away from the house. She hoped to find a bus stop nearby in the main road, so that she could catch a bus to the station, otherwise she faced a long walk.

A car cruised alongside, but she stared resolutely ahead.

'I have been told to give you a lift,' Arthur Jamieson called through the open window.

'No, thank you.' *I can be polite*, she thought, *even if they can't*.

'Wait a minute – I didn't expect to be, but I'm on your side. My uncle was obnoxious.'

'Your uncle?' She stopped in her tracks.

'Yes. I had a vested interest in the outcome of your discussion. Look, get in. Please.'

The Daimler moved away from the kerb, turned the corner of the road.

'I have something for you.' He indicated a package he had removed from the seat before she sat down, which he had placed on the window shelf.

'I don't want it!' she said mutinously. 'Especially if it's money. That would only prove him right.'

'He had it ready, of course, just in case things turned ugly. But it would have been given with conditions, threats of legal action, I suspect. See what he scribbled hastily on the front, before I dashed after you?'

Jenny didn't touch the packet, just looked.

'No strings attached,' she read aloud.

'Exactly. This is a gift, because he couldn't help admiring you. "Tell her," he said, "I wish things could be different. But they can't. I won't see her again. Regard this as a stroke of luck, the sort which has obviously evaded her until now." '

When he saw her into an empty carriage on the train, he took the package from his pocket, thrust it on her lap.

'Take it. Good luck!'

As the train chugged along, Jenny opened the package with trembling hands. A thick wad of five-pound notes! She wouldn't – couldn't – count it now. As she pushed it into her handbag, she remembered what she had tucked away at the bottom of the bag for sentimental reasons, after her beloved grandmother died. *I never go anywhere without this*, she seemed to hear Belle say.

Jenny uncorked the little bottle, sniffed the smelling salts, long and hard. It made her splutter, but at least she had a good excuse for the tears that spilled down her cheeks.

That night, lying in bed, she watched as Ted counted the money out on the counterpane.

'Five hundred pounds. A small fortune,' he said at last.

'Put it away,' she said. 'I wish I could send it back.'

'You deserve it,' Ted insisted.

'Frances can rest in peace now.'

'And so can we.'

TWENTY-ONE

August, 1933

The news filtering through from Europe was unsettling, particularly from Germany, but the front page headlines of today's *Daily Mirror* were 'GREAT CRICKET SENSATION'. Half a page was devoted to the retirement of D.R. Jardine, who had captained England against Australia. After details of Mr Jardine's illustrious career, there was the simple observation that he had adopted the fast-leg tactics, which had caused the 'body-line' controversy.

The other main story, with captioned photographs, told of the Duke of York's visit to the annual boys' camp at Southwold where, as usual, he spent the night under canvas. The duke was pictured in his bathing costume, being offered a biscuit after his morning dip. But the recent sweltering weather was over, it appeared, which relieved those returning to work after the bank holiday.

Elin took the bus into Southwold on Wednesday morning; she enjoyed the weekly outing and so did Bluebell, now a lively toddler, who would be two in November.

She'd done a little shopping and now sat on a bench overlooking the beach, drinking a cup of tea bought from the nearby refreshment booth, and trying to read the paper she'd bought, while Bluebell drummed her heels in her pushchair and licked her ice-cream cornet.

A finger poked the newspaper and startled her. Marian stood in front of her, smiling.

'What a nice surprise to see you! Both in blue, too. I do like you in that dress, such a nice shape. Bosoms are fashionable again, which is good news for you and me!

'I've just come off duty – fancied a breath of briny before going home! The beach is swarming with boys – though the Duke of York left earlier this morning, I understand. Our boys have been looking on enviously and wishing they could join in the fun.'

'Read all about it, before I use the *Mirror* to mop up the spills of ice-cream.'

'Nice to make the headlines *here*, eh? But what's this? "100 BACHELORS FLY ATLANTIC IN ONE HOP." '

'Missed that! What does it say?'

'Gist is Italian pilots in a plane armada; greeted by excited girls strewing flowers in their path. Oh, something much more serious – "GERMANY TO CURB NAZIS" '

'And a jolly good thing, too. Have you heard from Peggy and Billie yet, I wonder?' The girls were spending a week with Celia. She'd collected them from Marian's and they'd travelled by the new motor-coach from Southwold to London.

276

'Not from them, but Celia rang yesterday evening to say she was soaking her poor old feet after they'd dragged her around all the sights! She does enjoy their visits, though.'

'Me got icey-cream,' Bluebell put in, batting the *Mirror* with the sticky remains.

'Time to walk to the bus stop; sit still, Blue, and let me give you a lick and a promise, or they won't let us on the bus.' Elin glanced at her watch. 'Mark will be in for his lunch directly we get back.'

'I still miss you, you know,' Marian said, as she folded the crumpled paper. 'My parents are early to bed, some-times before the boys, and then it seems an empty evening on my own. We used to have some good chats over the nightly chores, didn't we.'

'Oh, Marian – d'you feel as if we deserted you?'

'Of course not. You and Mark, it all turned out for you, as I hoped.'

'Maybe you'll get married again. That's *my* hope.'

'I wouldn't even consider it until the children are fully off hand.'

They embraced then went their separate ways, hurrying as it began to rain.

'You must be soaked!' Mark exclaimed, as they dashed up the front path.

'Cooled me down nicely! Don't fuss! The pushchair hood kept Blue dry.' Elin grinned as Mark unstrapped Bluebell and carried her indoors. 'Salad for lunch; I laid the table.'

'How would you like to accompany me to Ipswich on Friday?' he asked. 'I've that lecture at the hospital to attend, but I could leave you with Jenny for the day. I'm sure my mother would love to look after Blue, and Marian would be around later.'

'I don't need to think twice about that! She's becoming a right little pickle, though, aren't you, darling?'

'Just like you were, I gather from Richard.'

'Me tired . . .' Bluebell yawned, pushing her plate away.

'All that fresh air,' Elin told her, lifting her from the high chair. 'Upstairs for your nap!'

'Let's follow suit; forget the washing-up, and make the most of my free afternoon! See, it *was* a good idea of mine to move Blue into the other bedroom.' Elin had demurred at first, but Mark had said wryly that they all needed a proper night's sleep.

'Oh, *you!' I should have changed out of this damp, clinging dress*, she thought, *it's given him other ideas!*

'Can't stop! Have a good time, you girls,' Mark called out to Jenny, as she and Elin hugged each other on the doorstep.

'We will!' they chorused. 'You needn't hurry back.'

'Five o'clock, all right?'

They nodded; waved him off.

'I like your new front door, it's very smart,' Elin told her sister as they went indoors.

'Well, we decided to take the plunge; accept the land-lord's offer to sell the place to us. You know how cautious

Ted is, he insisted we wait before we spent any of our wind-fall. Three hundred pounds! I never thought we'd own our own house . . . oh, here's Gran.'

Mrs Drake had obviously overheard this exchange.

'Well, I expect you'll be glad if I go down the shops, so you can gossip,' she said.

'Have a cup of tea with us first,' Elin put in quickly. 'It's nice to see you, Mrs Drake. We'll be going out later, won't we, Jenny?'

'Don't worry about lunch, Gran – we'll probably eat out,' Jenny said.

'Ted's at work?' Elin enquired, sitting down at the kitchen table.

'Yes.' Jenny poured the tea. 'Lot to do on Friday, being payday. We did think of taking a little corner shop, but the only ones doing well nowadays are the tobacconists.'

Her mother-in-law's lips pursed again.

'Be content with what you've got, Jenny.'

'Oh, I am! And I'm grateful, Gran, for all you've done to help us out since you came here, you know.'

'I don't mean to be fault-finding,' Mrs Drake said unexpectedly. 'I'm getting old, Jenny, and infirm, and it's hard to take.'

'I know, I do understand,' Jenny said softly.

When Mrs Drake had gone out, they rinsed the cups, and began to plan their day.

'Let's go to town, to the shops, then finish up at that nice little tea shop. They do a light lunch, don't they?'

'Mmm . . .' Jenny hadn't been there since she left Mark that day, when she'd given him and Elin her blessing, and walked away, broken-hearted. Now, she linked arms with her sister and added: 'Like old times, just you and me, isn't it? Mind you, you must bring young Blue to see me soon. No additions to the family planned yet?'

'Mark's changed his mind; he says he would like more babies, being a late starter in that respect! I'm the one holding back, I suppose. I'm enjoying what seems like a second honeymoon, now we can relax more – no children bursting in on us – you know what I mean.'

'That's wonderful, but is it really because of what you went through last time, Elin?'

Elin gave a little shake of the head.

'I don't think about that. I'm very well now, and not rushing around as I was then, despite Marian, Mark and Clo trying to stop me, so I'm optimistic it wouldn't be like that again . . .'

'I should have said, what happened with my darling Ruby – well, that problem came from my real father's side of the family – nothing to worry about as far as you're concerned.'

'You didn't hear from him again?'

'No, and I'm not likely to. Oh, look, a sale of summer clothes! I suppose they're making room for the winter collection, despite the warm weather, and it being August!'

'Come on then – let's make a hole in the housekeeping money!'

Some time later they emerged tousled but triumphant from the dress shop, each clutching a large carrier bag.

'Real silk stockings, too – what a snip! Not worn silk since my wedding day. How about you?'

'I've only ever had one pair. I kept them for ages before I wore them, the day I visited Mr Hadleigh, actually, and of course I laddered them. Just as well; Ted wouldn't have approved, if he'd known.'

'Mark's always encouraging me to buy pretty things, but with a dribbling baby, well, you have to be practical, don't you.'

'I wish Ted was more romantic,' Jenny remarked wistfully.

'Maybe that sophisticated black frock will do the trick. Half price! It's a wonder we didn't tear it into two, when we spotted it at the same time!' Elin joked.

' "Spotted" is the reason it was so cheap! I reckon someone brought it back and changed it. It smells of perfume, too and needs dry cleaning – but it's still gorgeous!' Jenny was already realising she'd made a mistake, but couldn't upset Elin, who'd urged her to buy the frock. Black crêpe, with a silver belt and lamé butterfly on one shoulder; just right for a night out, but not to the local flicks, she thought ruefully.

The tea shop was not as they recalled. The furnishings were shabby, the tables no longer laid with linen, but with grubby cork mats. Jenny looked critically at the cutlery.

'Just a cup of coffee, eh?' Elin mouthed at her, as the waitress came up.

They drank the weak brown liquid and left as quickly as they could.

'Shall we go back to yours, Jenny? We could buy some fish and chips from Ted's place – then I'd get a chance to say hello to him. We'll get some for Mrs Drake, too.'

'Good idea! Let's catch the bus!'

Ted was preoccupied with the deep-fryer, but he rallied and selected three large pieces of skate.

'Nice, crispy batter,' Elin approved. 'We were supposed to be having a light lunch, so go a little easy on the chips!'

He eyed the dress-shop bags.

'Been buying up the town?'

'All in the sale,' Elin said quickly. She hoped Jenny wouldn't get into trouble.

'See you tonight,' he told Jenny. 'I'm glad you called in, Elin. You look well.'

'I am, and I'm always happy to be with Jenny, of course.'

Mrs Drake was pleased to see them, and to unwrap the newspaper parcels.

'Keep the papers,' Jenny giggled, 'I always like to read them, despite the grease.'

They smoothed them after they'd eaten, and entertained Mrs Drake with past news.

'Sir Malcolm Campbell set up a new world speed record in *Bluebird* in Florida . . .'

'The obituaries – oh, Jenny, look at this.' Elin pointed.

Jenny's eyes took in the headline: 'MONTAGUE HADLEIGH', and beneath it the words: 'Montague Hadleigh, the eminent surgeon suffered a fatal heart attack . . .'

Jenny took the paper in trembling hands. She took in that the funeral had come and gone, by the date.

'That's that, then,' was all she said.

In London, Billie and Peggy had been shopping, too. They were going home the following day, so it was present-buying time for their families.

'I'm penniless!' Billie said blithely, pleased with her souvenirs. 'But then, I always am. Mum says I spend my pocket money before I get it.'

'I save half of mine,' Peggy said virtuously.

'Saving's not much fun! What d'you think, Celia?'

Celia was trying to remove some sticky cakes from their box, for tea.

'After pandering to your sweet tooth all week, I need to go back to work to earn more!'

She smiled at them, to show she didn't mind. She'd miss them, she thought. Their mothers thought she was kind, taking on two girls coming up to adolescence; Billie was twelve and Peggy was ten. But she loved having them to stay. Celia was almost forty; she'd accepted that she was now unlikely to marry and have children of her own. She'd never met a man who could match up to her late fiancé.

'Eat up, then baths and bed – we have to make an early start, remember,' she said.

She was startled when Billie gave her an unexpected hug.

'When I grow up, I'm going to work in London, and I'll live with you, Celia!'

'I look forward to that,' she managed, with a lump in her throat.

The letter arrived in October:

Dear Mrs Drake,

This is to inform you that my uncle, the late Mr Montague Hadleigh, stipulated that after his death I should contact you with regard to a certain matter. I would be grateful if you could call at the mews address one day soon. Please advise a date and time of arrival. I will, of course, meet you from the train.

Yours sincerely,
Arthur Jamieson

This time, she didn't keep the letter to herself, but showed it to Ted when he came in from work that evening.

'What do you think it means?' he demanded.

'I don't know. May I go?'

'You must do as you think best. It could be to your advantage.'

'*Our* advantage,' she corrected him.

'Monday would be a good day; I'd be here for Ma. She finds Billie a bit of a handful.'

'Billie's growing up, that's all. Gran's not used to dealing with girls, you being an only.'

'She's a strong-willed child. Wonder where that comes from?'

'Me, I suppose?' she flashed back. Then she took a deep breath. 'At least I know who my father was now, even if I didn't take to him.'

'Let's hope he took to you, then,' Ted said. There was no mistaking his meaning.

'Where did you get that outfit from?' Ted asked on Monday morning.

'I bought it in a sale, the day Elin was here – remember?'

'You look very smart,' he said grudgingly, regarding her in the black dress. 'But maybe bare arms aren't suitable on this occasion.'

She slipped on an angora wool cardigan, another bargain buy.

'Is that better?'

He pulled her to him, held her tight.

'I don't mean to be grumpy, it's just that, you mean so much to me, and I can't help it, I don't like the thought of other men ogling you.'

'This cousin – I suppose that's what he is – must be several years younger than me. When we met, it was obvious he regarded me as an interloper. Probably still does!' Jenny kissed him. 'I'll back in time for tea. Cheerio, Ted.'

*

'I nearly walked past you,' Arthur Jamieson said. 'You look different.'

Jenny felt much more confident than the first time they'd met. The dress made all the difference, she thought. Also she'd taken the plunge, had her hair cut; not too short, or Ted would have complained, but swinging in a bob to her shoulders. The little black beret suited her. She'd applied lipstick in the train. Ted wouldn't have stood for that.

Mr Jamieson was attentive today. He saw her into her seat in the car, and opened the door to hand her out when they arrived at the mews house.

'I hope it wasn't a shock for you,' he asked, as they drank their coffee, 'To learn after the event, that Mr Hadleigh had died?'

'I read it in the *Telegraph*,' she said primly.

'You will appreciate that, ah, you could not have attended the service. All his former colleagues and so on . . .'

'I understand. You don't need to make excuses, Mr Jamieson.'

'Arthur. And you are Jenny, of course.'

'Well, Arthur, will you please tell me why I am here?'

'I think . . .' he hesitated, looked apologetic. 'I should say that my uncle did not change his will. That would have meant certain, ah, things being made public. I am the main heir, as was expected. However, he indicated that it was up to me whether I decided to pass on some of my good fortune to a "deserving cause".

'As before, this is an unofficial payment. I hope you will accept this, because I am sure it was what my uncle desired, to make amends.'

He rose, unlocked the bureau in the corner, and withdrew a parcel.

'Again, as the amount is in notes, I prefer to hand it over to you personally.'

'I . . . don't know what to say . . .'

'Then don't say anything. Now, there's one more thing: would you like to choose an item from my aunt's jewel box? I shall auction the rest, along with other valuables, before I move into the house.'

'You're not married?' Jenny asked.

'I am engaged. My uncle approved my choice. I can afford to marry on *my* terms now. I wanted to get this business out of the way before that.'

'If I accept the jewellery, it will be for my daughter; his granddaughter.'

He nodded. 'Shall we take a look now? Or later, after lunch?'

'Right away; d'you mind? This has all been – a shock. I'd like to go home shortly.' *I must leave*, she thought, *before*

I break down and cry. 'Don't worry,' she added, 'you can forget I ever existed now, just as your uncle did for all those years.'

Arthur cleared his throat noisily. 'I know he regretted that, the moment he saw you. I won't forget you, Jenny. In fact . . . if we had met in different circumstances . . . well, I have to admit I find you attractive. By the way, I discovered this photograph in the bureau. It must be your mother; the likeness is so striking. Would you like to have it?'

Jenny took the picture mounted on card. The corners were curled, as if it had been often handled. She saw a young woman in a nurse's uniform, with curly hair tucked under a cap, and expressive eyes, long-lashed. She studied it for a long moment in silence.

'I can understand why my uncle desired her, threw caution to the wind . . .'

'Will you fetch the box now, please? There is a train just after midday.'

'Don't worry,' he said ruefully, 'I can see you're not in the least interested in me. Mad about your husband, I suppose?'

'That's as it should be,' she asserted. But she thought, *not as it is.*

She arrived home to find Ted thoroughly upset.

'Thank God you're back!' he babbled. 'Ma collapsed, shortly after you left – she's been taken to hospital.'

'What's wrong, Ted?' She gripped his shoulders. He was shaking and sweating.

'Doctor said a stroke. Her face was all lopsided; she couldn't speak, Jenny. They don't know if she'll get over it. I had to leave her, because of Billie coming home from school. I can return to the hospital now you're here . . .'

'I'm so sorry,' she said, meaning it. 'I'd better pack you a bag for her – I'll do it right away. If you have to stay there overnight, I'll let the chip-shop people know, and I could help out there for a few days while Billie's in school.'

He turned back, as he was about to leave.

'What happened to you?'

'Another package, a final payment, you could say. I'll leave it unopened until we can open it together. But I have a bracelet for Billie – I'll have to tell a fib about that, eh? Give Gran my love, and tell her I'll visit as soon as I can.'

When he'd gone, she busied herself finding a suitable frame, removing a faded print, fitting in her mother's photograph. She stood it on the sideboard, next to pictures of Richard and Belle.

'Mother, father and grandmother,' she said aloud. 'My family.'

TWENTY-TWO

Elin received the telegram telling her that Ted's mother had passed away some six months later. Mrs Drake had lingered on, but never recovered from the effects of the stroke. Jenny had nursed her devotedly at home.

Elin thought immediately: *as one life goes, another comes into being.* In early May there would be a new member of the family.

The pregnancy hadn't been planned, but they were both happy about it. This time, all appeared to be well. There were only three weeks to go. Clo came over to help out one day each week and Elin looked forward to seeing her. It was a great help, and quite like old times. Blue adored Clo and followed her around with her toy carpet sweeper, or stood on a stool at the sink and washed her dolls' clothes in soapy water.

'Put your feet up, Elin, while you've got the chance!' Clo declared, bringing a footstool into the kitchen, so that Elin could rest but join in the endless chatter.

'Jenny is planning their first real holiday since she and Ted married; Billie says she wants to go somewhere where the sea's warmer than it is here in the east!'

'I know. Little monkey wrote to BP and invited him to go with them, this summer! I don't suppose her mum and dad knew a thing about it.'

'I imagine BP was rather alarmed at the prospect. Thirteen-year-old girls are more mature than boys of the same age. Also, she seems to have cast Peggy off . . .'

'That's a shame. They were such good pals, weren't they.'

'Billie's always had a rebellious streak. Peggy will catch up eventually!'

Blue was rolling out pastry with a heavy hand, and a thump here and there. Now she requested the cutters and produced rather off-colour pastry cases for jam tarts.

'Pass me the gooseberry jam please, Clo. I'll do that bit.' As Blue opened her mouth to protest, Elin added: 'You're in enough of a mess already. More flour on you than on the pastry, Blue. You can lick the spoon after-wards, eh?'

When Clo declared it time for a break, they went out into the garden and sat on a bench to enjoy the warmth of a perfect April day. Blue didn't sit still for long, but went round the flowerbeds with her little watering can.

'I wonder what she'll think of the baby,' Elin mused. 'At two and a half she can't really comprehend what it's all about.'

'She's quite an independent little soul already,' Clo assured her. 'By the way, Mrs Lambert suggests I spend a couple of weeks over here with you after the baby arrives.

She doesn't really need me to work so many hours now-adays. Her mother helps out. Luke says we can afford now for me to retire! But I carry on more for love than money.'

'I know you do! Haven't you reconsidered having another baby, Clo?'

Clo shook her head. 'No. Luke *needs* me, you see. I have to be a mother as well as a wife to him. Oh, he's fond of BP, got ambitions for him, but it suits him, the boy being at Mrs Lambert's in the week, and only with us at weekends. That's a sacrifice I had to make when we got married, but I do see him every day, don't I. Charlie and Jack think of him as another brother. He don't need us to come up with one!'

'Where d'you get all your wisdom?' Elin marvelled.

Mark came out into the garden to find them.

'Jam tarts for lunch, I see!' he joked. Then he added: 'Just had a call from Mother. Apparently you're to expect visitors this afternoon, Elin, about three o'clock. She said it would be a big surprise, but, she was sure, a pleasant one. I'll be out on house calls after lunch, but I'll try to get back before tea.'

'Pity we decided on smoked haddock today, though it's quick and easy to do,' Clo said, dishing it up with a perfect poached egg apiece. 'The smell of fish hangs about, doesn't it?'

'Well, when you live close to the sea it does anyway, cooked or not,' Elin answered. 'We'll entertain 'em in the garden; put the deckchairs out.'

The knock on the door came as the clock struck the hour.

'Shall I go?' Clo asked.

'No – I will. Hold Blue back till they're inside!'

It was rather an anti-climax. There was a car parked in the lane outside the cottage gate, and a tall youth standing back politely, cap in hand. They stared at each other for a long moment. Then the visitor enquired hesitantly:

'Are you Elin?'

He's not from this country, she thought, aware of a marked accent. She nodded.

'Should I know you?' she asked.

He nodded in return and smiled: 'You really have no idea who I am?'

The dark eyes gave her a sudden clue. 'One of *Erminia*'s boys?'

'Bruno. You helped us to climb the barricade! Bertie is in the car. Our uncle drove us. It is our first visit back here. We promised our mother we would see you, if we could.'

'Oh, Bruno! I've never forgotten you! Tell the others, come in!'

'Hello,' the boys' uncle said, bringing up the rear.

'Alex – it's good to see you again!'

'I may kiss you, I hope, for old times' sake?'

'Of course you can!' She knew Mark wouldn't object to the continental greeting.

'We're sitting in the garden!' Clo called, ushering the boys out there.

Elin and Alex sat side by side, and she looked down ruefully at the sagging canvas on her chair.

'All this weight! I must look so different to you, Alex.'

'Your face is as beautiful as I recall,' he said gallantly. 'Pregnancy brings a special bloom. I should know. My wife and me, we have already three children.'

'You're married too – oh, I'm so glad!'

'You imagined I would be languishing for love?'

'Well . . . you married an Italian girl?'

'Yes, of course. She also is expecting another baby; it is early days for her. She stayed home with Erminia. She decided the boys were too young to travel on their own – can you believe they are sixteen and fourteen years? This despite the fact that I came over here by myself at Bertie's age. Erminia still thinks her sons are children. She worries so.'

'Is she well? You must give me her address – I'll write.'

'After her marriage to Buttle was annulled, which took a considerable time, she married another older man, a good one this time, a widower with his own olive groves. He has been a proper father to her boys. Yes, she is well, and very plump because she enjoys her food very much. She sends her love.'

'Did you continue with your law studies?' she asked.

'Yes, after a long break. My brother-in-law insisted. He paid my fees. As I said, he is a good man. My family and I, we live in town now. But our country is under a new order, like Germany. The fascists are everywhere. We keep our politics to ourselves.'

Bluebell had been enjoying a game with the boys on the lawn. They were indulgent with her, allowing her to kick the beach ball when she shrieked excitedly: 'My turn!'

'I talked to Mrs Lambert; it seems life is better for her family now. She said they came through it all, with the support of you and your husband.'

'Not just us, Alex. Clover was always there for all of us.'

'Talking about me?' Clo, who'd been busy in the kitchen some time, now re-emerged.

'What have you been up to, Clo?' Elin smiled.

'Knocked up a fruitcake for tea, we'll have to eat it hot, but I know Mark enjoys it like that, and a few scones. Mark's just arrived back – he says he'll see you in a minute, when he's changed! I laid the table in the dining room. Coming in?'

'If Alex will kindly help me to heave myself up – yes! Thanks for doing all that, Clo.'

Elin had forgone her afternoon rest, so she was glad when Mark proved to be an attentive host. He and Alex chatted like old friends.

'If you are staying with your relatives in Suffolk for two weeks, you must come over again before you go back to Italy, Alex.'

'I will certainly hope to do so. If I can borrow my brother's car again.'

It was time for them to leave. Elin was suddenly tearful and hugging the bashful boys.

'I must go, too,' Clo realised. 'My husband will wonder where I am.'

'We can give you a lift to your house,' Alex offered.

'I need an early night,' Elin told Mark, as the car drove off, 'after all that excitement.'

'I'll see to Blue. Then I'll bring you some supper on a tray, eh?'

'That hot cake's given me indigestion – I couldn't eat another thing, Mark.'

When he came upstairs around eleven, he found Elin wide awake.

'What's up, darling? Too much excitement?'

'No . . . just feel restless, that's all.'

'Baby?' he said sharply.

'I'm not sure. Could be . . .' She grimaced with an obvious spasm.

He pulled back the bedclothes, and took in the situation immediately.

'Oh, Elin – why didn't you say? I'll have to ring the hospital – ask Marian to collect Blue – don't get dressed, just put on your dressing gown!'

'I'm staying right here! My blood pressure is about normal – you just said so! Yes, ring Marian but ask her to come and help, please. We can manage, can't we?'

'It looks as if we'll have to! Stay put then, and I'll get everything ready after I've phoned. But be prepared for a trip to the hospital afterwards anyway, for the baby's sake.'

Just before three in the morning, after an easy labour, Elin's little son was born.

'I can't believe it,' Elin murmured happily.

'Nor can we,' Mark said with feeling.

'Now we're going to wrap you both up,' Marian said, 'because the hospital has a bed all ready for you, and Mark needn't worry about Blue, because I'm here, and she obviously didn't hear a thing, in her room.'

'Is it really necessary?'

'Not so much for you, but for the baby's sake. He's a little premature, after all. Don't worry, you'll be home again before you know it. I'll ring Dad around seven, Mark, and ask him to take the morning surgery. The boys can get themselves off to school, and Clo and Mother will see to Peggy . . . What are you going to call the baby?'

'I haven't the faintest idea,' Mark told his sister. 'I'm in shock, too! Elin?'

'I'd thought of Primrose, to go with Bluebell,' she yawned.

'Well, think again!' Mark said, as, on cue, they heard Blue's early morning call.

*

Clo was there when Elin and Mark brought the baby home ten days later. They'd stayed in hospital for longer than she'd hoped to because the baby developed jaundice. Mark reassured her this was quite common with a second baby particularly one which had arrived before time. After this early setback, little Dickie, named for his grandfather, Richard William, was now making steady progress.

'Oh, you darling!' Clo held out her arms for him. 'Blue wants a kiss from Mummy.'

Blue's face crumpled; she wound her arms tightly round her mother's neck and gave little hiccuppy sobs.

'Hey, you're making my collar all damp! I gather you missed me, then? Let's sit down and have a cuddle, and Clo can tuck Dickie in his crib, until he decides it's his turn . . .'

'*My* mummy!' Blue asserted, refusing to let Elin go.

'We've a present for you; let me look in my bag and you can have it.'

Still sniffing, Blue tore the paper from the cellophane-topped box.

'Aren't you going to take the baby doll out?'

'Is it a boy?' She looked suspiciously at the doll's romper suit.

Elin thought quickly. 'It can be a boy or a girl. You choose!'

'A girl, Mummy.' The top was off the box now.

'Well, that's good. Now we've got two babies, a boy and a girl, and I know your baby will be less trouble than Dickie! She'll sleep through the night, for one thing.'

'What are you going to call her?' Mark asked.

'Primmerose,' Blue said promptly, busy divesting the doll of her clothes.

'Oh, you knew something I didn't, eh? Your mother was going to spring the name on me. Going to give Primmerose a bath, are you?'

'No. I just seeing she's all there.'

'Good idea. Well, come with me to find another present. Your grandpa Richard's been busy, carving a little cradle for her.'

Elin sighed, and wiped her eyes.

'I feel exhausted after that,' she admitted to Clo.

'Well, you don't have to do anything apart from feed the baby, Elin, while I'm here. I'll stay over this one night, but' – she hesitated, then confided – 'I don't like to leave Luke by himself in the evenings you see . . . I s'pose I think he might be tempted . . .'

'Surely not! He adores you, Clo!'

'Oh, I don't mean he'd, well you know, *stray* – but I smelled drink on his breath the other day – he said they'd had a small celebration at work, it being the boss's birthday like, but it worried me, 'cause that's the first time since he promised me . . .'

'You have to trust him, Clo. Three years; that's a good sign, isn't it?'

It was Clo's turn now to dab her eyes with the hem of her apron.

'Clo dear, go home tonight. You must put Luke first. Mark can cope here.'

'What would I do without you?' Clo asked huskily.

'Or us, without you?'

Alex and his nephews called as promised, at the end of their holiday. They'd squeezed two extra passengers in the car.

'Mark's idea!' Jenny beamed. She whispered in Elin's ear. 'The minute Billie set eyes on Bruno, she insisted on coming too. Fortunately it's Saturday; no school!'

Billie spared the new baby a quick glance.

'More fun at Blue's age,' she decreed. 'Bruno and Bertie have been telling me all about Italy. It sounds just the place for a holiday. Though Dad's set on the Isle of Wight.' The boys smartly followed her and Blue into the garden, vying for her attention. Billie was blithely aware of the effect she had on them, with her long shapely legs revealed by a short skirt.

'Tea for four then,' Mark said, counting heads. 'Elin, Jenny, Alex and me. But first, I'll turn the garden tap off, before Blue spots it's connected to the hose.'

'I'll put the kettle on,' Jenny offered.

Elin couldn't help noticing that both Mark and Alex cast appreciative glances at Jenny, in her smart black dress, with bangles on her bare, upper arms. *She looks like the younger sister today*, she thought, with a pang. *I'm still fat, wearing a sensible button-through dress because it's easier to nurse the baby, my hair's a mess, and that bloom Alex*

*mentioned before has been replaced by dark circles under
my eyes from lack of sleep . . .*

Then Dickie began to cry. Elin scooped him up from
the Moses basket, made her excuses and went into the sitting room. The others stayed in the living room, with the
French windows open to the garden.

After a while, Mark came in with two cups of tea. He
put Elin's down on the little table, and sat with her while
she finished feeding the baby. Then he reminded her:

'Drink your tea. I've had mine. I'll put Dickie back in
the basket, now he's replete.'

'What about the guests?'

'Jenny had a bright idea. They are taking Blue with them
and going in the car to the beach for an hour. I said you'd
be feeling better by then – all right?'

'What d'you mean,' she demanded, 'feeling better? I
never said—'

'Darling, you didn't have to. Time for both you and
Dickie to have a sleep, I think.'

When he came back from settling the baby, Elin already
had her eyes closed.

He carefully fastened her buttons, put a cushion under
her head.

'Thank you for staying with me,' she whispered drows-
ily. 'But you should have gone with the others. It's a lovely
afternoon for the beach.'

'Nothing I like better than being with you,' he said,
smoothing her hair off her forehead.

She thought, *I know he means it, but . . . why did he look at Jenny like that, earlier?*

'We should have realised you're not up to visitors yet,' he added solicitously.

'I'm not up to much at all,' she sighed.

'Your body's telling you, you need to rest, Elin darling. So, jolly well obey it!'

Billie waded recklessly out to sea, and despite tucking her skirt up at the waist, the hem was soon wet from the lapping water. She anticipated that Bruno would follow her.

As she turned to see if she was right, a bigger wave smacked her back, swept her off her feet; she floundered, shouting for help, only to be hauled up by Bertie, not Bruno.

'Can't you swim?' He was obviously amused. 'Not that you needed to.'

'Oh, go away – I can manage! Stop laughing at me, will you?'

She trod across the shingle strip and snatched at her sandals.

'*Mum!*' she yelled.

Bertie waited while she struggled to push her wet feet into her sandy footwear.

'Bruno told me to assist you, as I am wearing shorts, while he is in long trousers.'

Jenny was sitting against the breakwater, worrying about creasing her best dress. She hadn't even noticed that

Billie had gone. Indeed, it was a relief. She really was at a trying age. Alex and Bruno were nearby, helping Blue build a sandcastle.

'Mum!' came the clarion call again. 'I need that towel you're sitting on!'

'Silly girl,' Blue observed. 'All wet, Auntie!'

'I can see that,' Jenny said, exasperated with Billie. She threw the towel to Bruno, he passed it to his brother, who draped it clumsily round Billie's shaking shoulders.

'Time to go back?' Alex asked, trying to keep a straight face.

Blue suddenly jumped gleefully on the castle and demolished it.

'Why did you do that?' Bruno looked quite upset.

'Because she wants your attention,' Jenny told him. 'Rather like her big cousin!'

'Erminia will be happy we saw you,' Alex told Elin later, as goodbyes were said. 'We mustn't lose touch again.'

Billie was still sulking, particularly as she'd been forced to change into one of Elin's old skirts, which came halfway down her calves.

'I'll come by myself next time,' Jenny said with a sly look at her daughter, as Billie followed the others out to the car. Mark, holding on to Blue, was seeing them off.

Elin embraced her. 'I'd like that. When I'm feeling myself again.'

'You will. I hope that doesn't take you as long as it did me.'

'You look wonderful, Jenny. I'm so glad all's well with you and Ted, despite your grumpy daughter!'

'She'll grow out of it. We did, after all. The future's looking brighter . . .'

'Even with all this talk of another war? Marian worries about her boys' future.'

'Let's pray it never happens. Take care of your lovely babies.'

'I will. 'Bye, Jenny dear.'

'Give my love to Dad, sorry I couldn't see him this time, eh?'

'Mum! Hurry up. We're waiting to go,' Billie said from the doorway. 'You'll have to sit between me and that stupid Bertie in the back. Bruno bagged the front seat.'

'Have a nice journey,' Elin wished her sister, with a smile.

'We won't come in, if you don't mind,' Alex told Jenny, when they arrived at her house. Bruno wound down the car window.

'Billie – I have something to say to you.'

'What?' she said ungraciously. But she went to the window anyway.

'I hope we'll meet again one day, that's all.'

'I thought you didn't like me . . .'

'Oh yes, I do, Billie Drake. Goodbye!'

TWENTY-THREE

1935

In May, the celebrations to mark the Silver Jubilee began. On a Saturday afternoon, Elin and Marian, with Blue, Peggy and Billie, joined Celia among the vast crowd lining the route of a royal procession in West London. The girls were ushered to the front with all the other youngsters, where the solid presence of the bobbies positioned by the Belisha beacons reassured parents. Streamers fluttered from windows of tall buildings; people leaned perilously over balconies. Cheering was deafening as the ceremonial coach went by, with King George and Queen Mary seeming rather overwhelmed at their reception.

The capital was floodlit after dark. Westminster Abbey, St Paul's Cathedral, the National Gallery were major attractions; they couldn't get to see them all, but the family went along to marvel at the magical illumination of Admiralty Arch.

'Fairyland!' was the excited response of three-and-a-half-year-old Blue.

The Thames played its part; the training ship *President* was festooned with strings of lights; its tall masts glowing as they appeared to finger the sky.

Lights were switched on all over the country; the wireless, now a fixture in most homes, crackled with excited commentary; there were street parties, music and impromptu dancing. The colonies, too, celebrated in style.

'Oh, I *do* love London!' Billie exclaimed later, as she and Peggy pulled out Celia's new bed settee, purchased from Barker's in Kensington High Street. 'I'm glad we're not sharing a bed with fidgety Blue, like Elin and your mum. We can talk all night if we want to.'

'I hope you won't want to,' Celia remarked mildly, looking in to see if they were comfortable in the sitting room. 'Blue takes after her cousin, as far as fidgeting goes.'

'I wish the boys could've been here, 'specially BP.' Billie retained a soft spot for him.

'Where on earth could we put 'em? I've promised they can visit soon. Goodnight, girls.'

''Night, Celia,' they chorused.

Clo felt uneasy. She should have accompanied Luke as he'd urged her to, to see Southwold celebrating the Jubilee, she thought. There was plenty going on in the town tonight – it was really lit up. But she was tired having looked after young Dickie most of the day while Mark was busy with emergency calls. There had been a spate of minor accidents, perhaps due to the influx of visitors. BP was with Charlie and Jack, and she suspected that they, too, were out and about, with no one to impose a curfew.

Eventually, she went upstairs to bed, just before midnight. Despite her weariness, she couldn't get off to sleep. All had been well for the first few years of her marriage; she and Luke were still very much in love, but Luke had lapsed into old habits since the day he took that first drink after a long abstinence.

He can't help it, she reasoned to herself, *it's not his fault. But supposing he lost his job through it? Maybe I could talk to Mark about this, but would that be disloyal to Luke?*

She was out of bed and looking out of the window after hearing discordant voices, when came the hammering on the door and the cry:

'Come down, Missus!'

Clo recognised one of Luke's workmates, one who had recently been taken on at the chandler's; she suspected this was the fellow who led him astray. He and another man, a stranger, had Luke's arms slung around their shoulders, holding his sagging body upright.

'Where d'you want him?' the stranger asked. He wasn't too steady on his own feet.

The smell of strong liquor nearly knocked Clo back. She realised that they hadn't just been drinking beer. She opened the living-room door.

'In here, on the sofa.'

They almost dropped their burden as they heaved Luke towards it.

Clo didn't light the gas. She could imagine the silly grins on their faces. She flashed her torch to show them the door.

'Thank you,' she forced out. 'Goodnight.'

'Goo'night, Missus.' She closed the door smartly behind them. This was a quiet, respectable street; what would the neighbours think?

Luke was groaning. He was horribly sick. Without a word, she fetched a bucket of water from the scullery, laced it with carbolic. She cleaned up the mess on the floor and then filled a bowl with warm water from the kettle on the hob to tend to her husband. It was now that she saw the bruises on his face, the dried blood from a minor gash on his chin.

'You've been in a fight!' she exclaimed, shocked.

His eyes rolled up, and she realised he had passed out. Involuntarily, she recalled Elin confiding soon after the event how she had dealt with Luke in a similar state.

'I can't move you by myself,' she said aloud. She fetched a spare blanket from the cupboard by the stove, and covered him up. She sat in the chair opposite to keep watch.

At some point during the night she fell into an exhausted sleep; she awoke at dawn, feeling cramped and chilled. Luke slumbered on, muttering now and again.

A cup of tea, she thought, unaware that she was crying. *I must have my tea. What a way to celebrate the Jubilee! I'm*

*glad my lad's not here to see this. What can I do, to make
things better – as they were?*

She rested her elbows on the table, waiting for Luke to
stir. The tea warmed her stomach, revived her spirits. She
began to mull over a sudden idea.

'Clover?' He spoke at last, struggled up. 'How'd I get
home?'

'Your pals, if you can call them that, brought you,' she
said evenly.

She rose, struck a match and attended to the oil lamp.
He flinched at the sudden light. 'What's the time?'

'About five. It's Sunday – we might as well get to bed,
I've had hardly any sleep.'

'I'm sorry. You're angry—'

'Disappointed, more like. Come on then. No point in
going on about it now.'

She helped him out of his clothes, turned the bedclothes
back, then covered him up.

'Sorry,' he said again, as she put the light out.

She sensed that he anticipated being rebuffed if he came
too close. Sighing, she put her arms round him, drew him
to her, and cradled him like a sick child.

'I don't deserve you,' he mumbled.

'We'll get over it, I promise you, Luke. Everything will
be all right.'

It was well into the morning before they woke once more.

'Luke, I did a lot of thinking while you were out for the
count,' she told him. 'We've still got most of our nest egg

from your mother, thank goodness. There's that big board-ing house near the front for "sale or rent". It's been a bit run-down, but we could live there while we put that right. We'd have to rent first and hope to take a mortgage out later. We'd need to pull together making the place ready for visitors, not just the summer ones, but all the year round. What d'you think?'

'It would be a full-time occupation for both of us?' He sounded dazed.

''Course it would. But you'd have to be prepared to turn your hand to anything.'

'It sounds like the challenge I need. What about your family, though?'

'Well, I need a new challenge, too. They'll miss me, I know, and I'll miss them. Still, they'll realise that it's about time we struck out on our own.'

'Did I ever tell you how much you mean to me – that I don't deserve you, Clover?'

'Many times, my dear. But don't you ever give up!'

*

After delivering Billie to Ipswich on Sunday afternoon Marian told Jenny, 'We won't stop, if you don't mind – I'll take Elin and Blue home first, then I must find out what those boys have been up to.'

'It might be better if you don't ask, Mum,' Peggy said in her old-fashioned way.

'It's been a lovely weekend, hasn't it? Thank you for taking us,' Elin said, as Mark came down to the gate, close behind Dickie, who was still somewhat wobbly on his feet.

Marian waved. 'We'll see you again soon!' Then she drove off.

Mark hugged Blue, while Elin swung her little son up into her arms.

'Darling, I missed you!' She kissed his fuzz of chestnut hair. He had Mark's colouring. Blue's hair was also darker than her mother's, but just as unruly.

'What about me?' Mark smiled.

'Of course we missed you, didn't we, Bluebell?'

'Put me down, Daddy.' Blue wriggled from his embrace. 'Mummy's turn!'

'Take your brother indoors, then, while I cuddle her! The neighbours will enjoy that!'

'Any one would think we'd been away a week,' Elin said happily, as he kissed her.

'It feels like it to me.'

'We had a wonderful time . . .'

'I'm glad. You can tell me all about it after Blue's had her say, eh?'

'Did Clo come round? She said she would.'

'We saw her yesterday, but not today.'

'Oh . . . I hope nothing's wrong.'

'Don't start worrying the minute you get back! I imagine she and Luke have been celebrating the Jubilee, too. Clo knew I wasn't on call today.'

'Oh, that's it, then,' she said relieved, as they went inside the house.

Clo and Luke walked round the echoing house. Although they'd need to decorate throughout, there was a modern bathroom upstairs and a cloakroom downstairs. Carpets and kitchen equipment were included, which would be a big saving, and some furniture. The owner had recently died; her grandson, who'd inherited the property, lived overseas.

'What d'you think, Luke?' Clover asked, when they'd completed their tour. 'It reminds me of Homeleigh, where the Lamberts used to live, though it's got more bedrooms.'

'Rather musty.' He wrinkled his nose.

'Nothing that can't be cured by opening all the windows – which need a good clean, by the way. A job for you! BP can help.'

'You've made your mind up, haven't you, Clover?'

'Sea views from the bedrooms – what more can you want?'

'We'll be tucked away at the back, I presume!'

'Don't you like it?'

'You know I do, but . . . we'll need to spend a lot to get the business going.'

'Well, let's go back and see the agent, before you think of any more "buts", eh?'

Luke had taken the morning off; later they went together to see his boss to explain.

'You're not the only absentee,' his employer told him. 'I was prepared to give you the benefit of the doubt, Luke; I shall give the other one notice, if he turns up tomorrow.' He looked keenly at the marks on Luke's face, but didn't comment on them. 'So, you wish to leave at the end of next week? I'll be sorry to lose you. Good luck to you both, anyway.'

After Luke promised to be early at work next morning, they decided to walk along to Marian's to impart their news and to see BP when he came in from school.

'There are outbuildings, the old wash-house and privy,' Luke told his stepson, knowing how much it would mean to Clo if BP decided to join them in the new house. 'The agent said they might be converted to a garage, but we don't need a car – we'll be working where we live and shopping locally as now. They'd make an ideal den for you – somewhere for you to have your friends round. The buildings need clearing, but that wouldn't take too long.'

'Could I have the old piano out there? Jack's learning the saxophone now at school and there's a couple of other chaps keen to make music with us . . .'

'I don't see why not. You could entertain the guests on occasion! You want to move in with us, then?'

BP grinned. He was as tall as Luke now, mature for his age and strikingly good-looking. His voice had already broken, and he seemed to have bypassed the spotty, gangling stage which was poor Jack's lot.

'All right. Sounds like there's lots of room. I hope Mrs Lambert won't mind, though.'

Marian ruffled his hair, in passing, having got the gist of what had been said.

'I'll miss you – but don't worry, you'll still see plenty of Charlie and Jack – I shall encourage them to visit you whenever their squabbles give me a headache!'

Clo looked bemused but happy as she let out the table extensions. They'd been invited to supper. BP put the chairs round, counting. Nine of them, with Marian's parents.

Peggy set out the cutlery. She was very quiet this evening. BP gave her arm a friendly pat as she bent over the table.

'I reckon you'll be glad to get rid of me, eh, Peg? One boy less to tease you!'

She abandoned her task, turned and rushed out of the room.

'Whatever made her do that?' he asked his mother, in amazement.

'She's growing up, you all are.'

Luke was not in with them; he was talking to Marian's father in the sitting room. BP had something else to ask Clo.

'Mum – what happened to Luke's face?'

Clo told him the truth. 'He went drinking with his mates last night. Got into a fight.'

'Is that why you decided to move all of a sudden?'

'Yes.'

'You'll be glad to have me around, I guess. Luke's a good sort, in lots of ways, but—'

'He'd never hurt me, I'm sure of that!'

''Course he wouldn't. But you'll have another man about the house, Mum.'

'You're more grown-up now than he'll ever be, BP,' she said, feeling choked.

'We both think the world of you, that's what matters, isn't it?' He gave her a quick hug, while no one else was about. 'I won't let you down.'

'Just remember, even if you did, I'd never give up on you.'

'You said that to him, too, didn't you.'

She nodded. 'Let's go and see what Marian's rustled up for us, shall we?'

The Jubilee was the highlight of 1935, but unemployment was still rife and the coal industry was badly hit by strikes. News from Europe, Germany and Italy in particular, was ominous. Germany was rearming rapidly and had regained the valuable coal-producing territory in the Saar, which had been taken from Germany after the war ended in 1918 and administered by the League of Nations. Italy invaded Abyssinia. The League seemed powerless to prevent them.

There was a general election in November and Stanley Baldwin was once again prime minister of a National government.

In America, Benny Goodman and jazz were synony-
mous. In Southwold, in the old washhouse, BP and his
friends were covertly experimenting with jazz, too; the
classics were abandoned, and the piano was high-strung
for the vibrant, exciting new sounds it produced.

TWENTY-FOUR

The King died peacefully at Sandringham just before midnight on 20 January 1936. The crowd keeping vigil outside Buckingham Palace read the notice posted on the gates shortly afterwards, then dispersed quietly. At home, and abroad, folk gathered round the wireless to listen to the announcement by Sir John Reith. In the morning, in St Paul's Cathedral, Great Tom, the big bell, tolled for two hours. A full-gun salute resounded over the Thames from the Tower of London, and at Hyde Park. There was a new monarch, Edward VIII.

There were more changes within Elin's extended family too: some expected, some not. Early in the new year of 1936, Marian's father returned home after helping Mark with a crowded surgery, collapsed and died. Since then, his wife had become increasingly forgetful and confused. In a way, this was merciful, because she didn't appear to comprehend the loss of her constant companion of the last fifty years. Marian decided to give up her job, to care for her mother.

In March, Richard broke the news that Aunt Ida had passed away in her sleep.

'Will you retire now?' Elin asked him tentatively after the funeral, when they were back at Ida's cottage.

He shook his head. 'I'd rather carry on, like old Doc Clements. Die in harness, like the old pony. She didn't want to give up, either. I've had enough of the heavy work, though – working outside mostly. Luke and Clover have suggested I help out in the guesthouse. They've got a lot of bookings already for the summer. What d'you think?'

'It sounds a good idea, eh, Jenny?' Elin turned to her sister, who was staying with Richard for a few days to support him over this period. It was Jenny who'd prepared the food set out on the table, for those who would shortly call to pay their respects.

'Will they pay you?' she asked somewhat tactlessly.

'You can count on Clo,' Elin put in quickly. *You certainly could*, she thought: Clo was looking after the children this afternoon; Luke had attended the service, but left immediately afterwards to return home. The two permanent guests would require dinner as usual this evening.

Richard sat down abruptly, rubbing his hand over his eyes.

'I reckon I'm the most senior member of the family now, girls. All the old 'uns gone . . . I'll miss dear Ida.'

'That's life, Dad.' Jenny bit her lip, realising the irony of her words.

'I'm not looking forward to living on my own, but the cottage belongs to me, thanks to Ida. It's a special place, as it's where your grandma was born.'

'I can afford to visit you regularly now, and you've got Elin and Mark, of course,' Jenny said.

'I'm grateful to have you so close,' Richard told Elin, 'and Luke and his family, too. Well, there's folk coming up the path – we'd best let them in.'

Over supper one evening, Billie announced her intention of leaving school in July.

'I'll be fifteen then, and it's time to start my career.'

'Oh, and what have you in mind?' Jenny asked quickly, before Ted could open his mouth and express his disapproval. She knew he'd had hopes that Billie would continue her education and make something of herself. She was certainly bright enough.

'I'm going to be a movie star,' Billie said, through a mouthful of sausage and mash. 'Not a second Shirley Temple, Mum, before you say it – I'm far too old. Still, I can act, I get all the best parts in the school plays; I can sing and dance a bit; movie moguls like that.'

'You'll have to learn not to talk with your mouth full, then,' Jenny reproved her.

'Movie star, what's that?' Ted was exasperated.

'*Film* star, to you, Dad.'

'What put that idea into your head? Sitting in that stuffy picture house twice a week, I suppose. What's wrong with the Hippodrome, *real* people on stage there, they don't need a microphone – not that Ma approved of the music hall, either, when I was your age.'

'*You* were already working when you were fourteen. If you don't want that sausage, Mum, I'll have it.' Billie speared it with her fork before Jenny could answer. 'And if you're thinking I don't know how to go about it, well, I do. Miss Tamar—'

'That elocution and drama teacher? I told your mum she'd regret wasting money on those lessons – that you'd get silly ideas – well, now you see what it's led to, Jenny, eh?'

Jenny rose, seized the plates and scraped them noisily.

'Let her find out for herself. You know how obstinate she is, Ted, when she's made up her mind.'

'Let her leave school, you mean?'

'Yes. She'll probably regret it, but—'

'She's too much like you,' Ted said sourly. 'Head full of silly dreams. You have to settle for what life throws at you, Ma always said.'

'I'm not going to argue with you, Ted, and nor are you, Billie.' Jenny blinked furiously as she poured hot water into the enamel bowl in the sink. At least her hands weren't so sore and red now that she used soap flakes instead of soda. She muttered to herself: 'I've tried so hard to be a good wife and mother, but, oh, if only things had turned out for me, the way they have for Elin . . . I'll write to Celia, she's good with Billie, and ask her advice.'

Celia visited the family in Suffolk and broke the return journey at Ipswich to take Billie back to London for an indefinite stay. When Billie went upstairs to fetch her case, Celia took the opportunity to promise Jenny that she'd endeavour to steer her wayward daughter tactfully along a more moderate course.

'I'll be taking her to the places she has in mind, while I'm on holiday for two weeks. If no job has materialised by then, she can earn a bit of pocket money helping out with housework for me, and a friend or two of mine.'

'I'm not sure she's capable of even flicking a duster on the furniture,' Jenny said drily.

'Who can blame her? She's young, impatient and believes she's above such things.'

The house seemed very silent without Billie. Jenny knew she was going to miss her terribly. She'd drawn some money out of the bank and asked Celia to buy Billie some new clothes. Ted still expected his daughter to wear ankle socks, not stockings, and disapproved of make-up. It was fortunate, Jenny thought, that he'd been at work when Billie greeted Celia with startling pillar-box-red lips and an upswept hairdo, which had taken her most of the morning to achieve.

''Bye, Mum! Don't forget to tell Elin to pass on my new address to Alex, will you? Not that I've had a single letter from Bruno, or even from Bertie.'

'I promise, but she hasn't heard from them at all this year. Too much going on in Italy, like there is in Spain – civil war! That's awful, isn't it? You enjoy yourself while you can.'

Jenny tidied up Billie's bedroom. Clothes had been tossed on the unmade bed, cheap scent spilled on the dressing table, and in the grate lay a couple of dead matches – had her daughter been smoking? She poked among the toffee papers and other rubbish, but was relieved not to find any cigarette stubs. Then she sat down on the bed and wept into her upturned pinny.

She's left home, she thought, probably for good. *If my little Ruby had lived, I'd have a child still to care for . . . but now it's just the two of us, and if I was minded to, I could get up and walk out – make a new life for myself. But that would be the end of poor Ted; he still loves me, I know that, but I also know he won't change, it's too late for that.*

'Be happy, my darling,' she said huskily aloud. 'You *will* be a star, I'm sure.'

She was too caught up in her misery to be aware that Ted had returned home unexpectedly, and now stood uncertainly in the doorway, clutching a bunch of pink carnations.

'Jenny, I couldn't concentrate at work – got someone to cover for me, the rest of the day. I should've been here to see Billie off.'

She looked up then. 'Yes, you should.'

'She's my daughter, too, you know ... I think the world of her, like you do. Look, I'm keeping some rock salmon and chips warm in the oven for us and the flowers are for you.'

'Thanks. But ... I just need to collect myself first, Ted.'

'Go and lie down in our room for a few minutes.' He held out his free hand.

She allowed him to lead her next door, to encourage her to rest on the bed. He laid the flowers on the dressing table while he eased off her shoes.

'The fish and chips will keep,' he said.

'Don't you understand, Ted, how I feel?'

'I'm trying to.'

'What I need right now is *comforting*, not food – I want you to hold me tight, and—'

'You've turned your back on me in bed for months now; that made me bitter, angry, even. Didn't you guess how I felt?'

'I'm sorry,' she said simply. 'Come here, let me hug you.'

He looked at the window, embarrassed because it was daylight.

'Pull the curtains, if it helps,' she said softly.

Much later, still wrapped in each other's arms, they exchanged a last, lingering kiss.

It was time for one last confidence from him.

'I came home, Jenny, because I was afraid ... scared that you'd decided to go with Billie, to leave me. When I discovered you weren't downstairs, I looked for a note – there wasn't one, so I panicked, and wondered what I'd find up here ... I couldn't hear any movement, you see.'

She put her hand over his mouth.

'Shush ... I'm ready for my dinner now, aren't you? Even if it's all dried up.' *Like my tears*, she thought. *Yet another new start, but this time we must make sure it works.*

Peggy sat on the old sofa in the den, looking soulful as she listened to the music. BP struck the piano keys with such vigour the notes seemed to bounce off the walls, which Luke had wisely insulated with cardboard. Jack had tired of practising and had sloped off to the beach to meet Charlie.

Peggy wasn't sure that the object of her adoration realised she was still there. This honky-tonk music, she thought, most of it improvised, was exciting – she was tempted to jump to her feet, dance to the throbbing beat, maybe even to sing, but that would break the spell.

Then BP paused, glanced in her direction, and smiled.

'What would you like me to play for you?' he asked kindly.

An idea came out of the blue.

'*Sing As We Go* – you know, that Gracie Fields film, when she and her friends were on holiday in Blackpool.'

'I don't know actually – you sing it and I'll pick it up, eh?'

Because he had his back to her at the piano, she was able to pluck up courage to sing. Gradually, as the music began, she relaxed and allowed her voice to soar to the high notes, just like Gracie, as she led her friends along the golden mile.

'I didn't realise you were a soprano,' BP exclaimed, after the final rousing chorus.

'I suppose you thought I'd sing down in my boots, 'cause I'm dark and dumpy!'

'You've got nice hair, Peg, shiny like liquorice, and you're still growing.'

'I'll be thirteen in September!'

'And I'll be fourteen – old enough to leave school, if I wanted to.'

'Oh, surely you don't? Charlie's going to stay on until he's eighteen, and then he hopes to get a place at university; Mum and Clo were talking about that the other day, and I heard Clo say you were aiming high, too.'

'Well, Billie's in London now, and she's definitely said no to further education. I'd like to join a band, play the kind of music I really enjoy – while my mum thinks I ought to work towards a music scholarship and become a concert pianist.'

'I wouldn't want to disappoint *my* mother,' Peggy said primly.

'Much as we love 'em, they'll have to accept that our generation has its own ideas!'

'Mum is hoping I'll follow in her footsteps and become a nurse.'

'Is that what you want to do?'

'I suppose so. Until I get married, of course.'

'Why of course? You want to enjoy an exciting career before you settle down.'

'Oh, shut up!' she shouted. 'Let me decide for myself, will you?'

'No need to get so ruffled!' He turned back to the piano. 'Cheerio, Peggy. I want to concentrate on a new piece, and get it down on paper.'

She almost collided with Jack outside the den.

'What's up?' he asked, seeing her furious expression.

'I wouldn't go back in there if I were you – Robert Baden Powell Goldsmith is in a composing mood!'

'He usually puts up with *you*, Peg, unlike Charlie and me.'

'Well, he needn't bother any more! He's too big-headed for me.'

Clo, emptying tea leaves into the drain, smiled to herself at this exchange. After all, both she and Marian nursed secret hopes that when their children were grown up, their two families might become even closer.

*

In September, Billie took her first job. Not at the new British film studios at Pinewood, for her letter there had elicited a courteous reply, and the suggestion that she should receive some stage-school training, or acting experience before applying again, but as an usherette in a West End cinema. She wrote to her parents:

It's a start, if a humble one. Don't worry, for the manager is a friend of Celia's and he has arranged for me to be brought home by taxi at nights. I get to see all the latest Hollywood films, in colour, too, and one day it will be ME up there on the big screen, you can count on that. Don't worry, Dad, we wear trousers, not short skirts, a jacket and pillbox hat. (Which makes a mark on your forehead.)

I have a new favourite film star! Carole Lombard. I wish I could dye my hair blonde like hers, but Celia said I would REGRET it, and anyway, I would have to get permission from you, which you are NOT likely to give – are you? C.L. was in My Man Godfrey – *it's a really funny film – William Powell played the butler by that name.*

'Sounds just the same, doesn't she?' Ted said gruffly, after Jenny read the letter to him at breakfast time.

'Not quite,' Jenny said, but she wouldn't be drawn on that.

By the end of the year the new king's brief reign ended in his abdication. Despite all the rumours that had intensified during the latter months, the country reeled from the shock announcement. His successor, the quiet but popular Duke of York, now became King George VI, and his wife, Queen Elizabeth. The family, with their two pretty young daughters, Elizabeth, now heir presumptive, and Margaret Rose, were featured on the front pages of every newspaper. The war clouds were gathering, but there was a celebration ahead, the coronation next May.

TWENTY-FIVE

August, 1939

The guesthouse had been fully booked this summer, but now there were last-minute cancellations. Clo and Luke sat down to breakfast on their own one Saturday morning.

'Luke, listen to me, please,' Clo said, as he tucked into eggs and bacon with evident relish. 'Things are not looking good.'

'Here, you mean?'

'Yes. War will be declared any minute now, everyone knows that. There's talk that the town will soon take some evacuees from London, even though the coast doesn't seem a safe place to be. This place has to pay for itself; we'll have had it if the visitors don't come. I'm glad we haven't got a mortgage on it, as we'd hoped to do by now. I think we should give notice, move out, before we get in debt.'

'I agree,' Luke said, adding: 'I wasn't sure how to tell you this, but you saying that, has made it easier. I've been thinking of going back to sea, doing my bit for Britain.'

'Luke! You'll be called up eventually, but not yet, as you're over thirty.'

'You're not going to try to stop me, are you, Clover? I hoped to go with your blessing.'

'It's a shock, just now, but I expect I'll get over it. But what will I do?'

'We'll get that settled before I leave. At least we don't have to worry about BP.'

'Not just now. Oh, I know I was terribly upset when he left school, just like Jenny's Billie did, and joined that touring jazz band. All them smoky clubs and being up till devil's dancing hours, playing the piano – not that I'm not proud of him, being a success, so young, but he'll be eighteen next month, then he'll get his papers, won't he.'

'He's not the only one; what about the Lambert boys?'

'Charlie's got another year at Cambridge, but Jack's nearly nineteen and him being a motor mechanic, they'll nab him right away.'

'We'd better wait for Richard to arrive, then we'll tell him what we've decided before we go down to the agent's office,' Luke said, pouring them both another cup of tea.

Elin and the children went on the excursion by coach to Ipswich. Jenny met them at the bus station.

'Blue looks more like our Billie every time I see her!' Jenny exclaimed, hugging her niece and nephew in turn. Blue was almost eight now, and Dickie was five and a bit.

'How is Billie?' Elin asked, as they walked in the direction of the market.

'Enjoying herself at Butlin's holiday camp at Skegness this week! She gets a chance to show off on stage when they have the talent contests.'

'Not quite a star yet?'

'No, but she – and I – still have hopes! Guess what, she met Clo's boy at the weekend. His band had a spot in the camp show. She wrote that they had a drink together: "Lemonade, Mum" – but if you believe that, you'll believe pigs can fly!' Mind you, Ted's relieved she got a proper job last year, training as a stewardess with that big shipping line; she was looking forward to those trips abroad, but now . . .'

'I wish *we* could go to Butlin's, Mummy,' Blue said.

'Southwold not good enough for you?' Elin grinned at her daughter.

'Oh, it's the best place to live, but I want to be a star, too!'

'You're soppy,' Dickie said, tugging at his mother's hand. 'Can I have an ice-cream?'

Most of the Italian immigrants who'd arrived early in the century had flourished in Ipswich, and their ice-cream sellers were popular.

'I wonder what will happen to the Italians living over here?' Elin said, as they sat on a bench to eat their cornets. The children were quiet for once.

'What d'you mean?' The Neapolitan ice-cream was made up of three flavours, vanilla, raspberry and chocolate. Jenny licked the chocolate side; it was delicious and cooling.

'When war is declared, Italy will be fighting against us. In the last war, enemy aliens who'd lived over here for years were interned.'

'I imagine that will happen again ... Heard from Erminia, or Alex recently?'

Elin shook her head. 'Nothing for more than a year. I don't suppose we will, now.'

'I've got a bit of news for you – Ted's decided to join up. He was too young last time, and they might say he's too old now, as he's nearly forty, but there's always the Catering Corps, he says. Frying all that fish must count as good experience.'

'What will you do? What about the shop; he's manager there, isn't he?'

'Well, I intend to carry on in his place. That'll be my war effort.'

'Hard work, Jenny; you've been a lady of leisure for some time now!'

'I'm ready for it. How about you: will you stay where you are?'

'We haven't discussed it yet.'

'Well, you should, dearie. The world's about to change – forever, they say.'

'Mummy, can we go shopping now? You promised.'

'Come on then. But don't touch anything – your hands are all sticky!'

It had been a long day, enjoyable, but tiring. The children were at last asleep, and Elin was thinking of going to bed herself, when Mark, who'd been out all evening, came in.

'Did you see my note?'

'Yes, but you didn't say where you were going.'

'Sorry. I had a few things to tie up. Ready to listen?'

She nodded. 'I've got some news for you, too, from Ipswich.'

'Can you tell me later? Elin, I had an unexpected visitor at the surgery today. You may remember me talking about Henry Blake, we were medical students together. He's always been involved with hospital work. He's been co-ordinating a team of doctors, nurses and first-aid workers to help other organisations deal with emergencies in London, which along with the other great cities will be an obvious target for enemy bombing after war becomes a reality. He wants to recruit me, recalling my work with a deprived community in the Depression. I'd like to accept, but I said I must discuss it with you first.'

'What about your work here?' she faltered.

'It's possible that some of the population will be evacuated, that I won't be needed as much here as elsewhere. In any case, I feel it would be advisable for you and the children to move to a safer area until we know just how war will affect us. Marian rang me today. She wants to discuss such a contingency with you, as soon as possible.'

'What about the practice?'

'We might have to close it for the duration; or another doctor may take it on.'

'Mark, I don't want you to leave me – us—'

'I know. And I certainly can't ask you to move to London. We won't even have Celia there. Her firm is moving to Somerset very shortly.'

'Look, I must think about it, what it really means. We ought to get to bed now; talk about it more in the morning.'

'You had some news for me,' he remembered belatedly.

'That'll keep, too.'

She lay awake for a long time, aware that Mark was also sleepless, but neither of them spoke. Then she thought how Jenny had accepted Ted's decision, and she knew that she would follow her sister's example. She told herself she was fortunate that her children were too young to be involved.

She reached out to Mark and he held her very close, still not saying a word.

It was Mark's afternoon off. They decided to drive over to Marian's to impart their news. Elin had woken him with a kiss that morning, then she whispered simply: 'Darling, of course you must go . . .'

'Oh, good, here you are then.' Marian welcomed them. 'Clo and Luke rang to say they are coming later, with Richard. I don't know what that's all about. Peggy dear – can you entertain the children in your room? Now, what were you hinting at on the phone?'

'You tell her, Mark, I'm still in a whirl,' Elin said.

After Mark had explained his plans, he added: 'We still have to make arrangements for Elin and the children – I believe you have some ideas on that?'

'Well, Celia rang me in some excitement to say she was in Somerset, viewing potential digs, and that there was a family house available – she immediately thought of us! Celia, me, Mother and Peggy, Elin and the children; there's four decent bedrooms and we could share, of course. We could squeeze in visiting menfolk!'

'What about schools?' Elin asked.

'Five minutes from the local primary school, ideal for your two! Fortunately, Peggy took her matric this spring, so the move wouldn't be too disastrous for her. She's almost sixteen, so it will be up to her to decide whether she wants to transfer to another school, or stay at home and help me, with a view to getting a job later.'

'We'd have to shut the houses up here,' Mark put in. 'Store the effects. We'd need to achieve all this within a couple of weeks. Are you game for that, Elin?'

''Course I am,' she said immediately.

'It'd be like old times.' Marian sounded excited. 'I thought I might have to convince you! See, I had this card ready to persuade you . . .' She handed it to Elin to read:

Good companion sought by mother, grandmother and daughter, moving shortly to West Country. Children welcomed.

'I might find time to write again. There, does all that remind you of our Holmleigh days?' Marian asked Elin.

'Oh, Marian, it certainly does! I accept on behalf of me, Blue and Dickie.'

Clo and Luke's news was greeted by laughter, and seeing Clo's hurt expression, explanations were in order.

'We've all come to the same conclusion at the same time, it seems,' Mark said.

There was one surprise though.

'Clo's going to keep me company in the cottage,' Richard told them. 'We're inland there, after all. We can manage nicely, I'm sure.'

'I'm going to join the WVS,' Clo said proudly. 'They say my skills in running the boarding house could be very useful, if they have to cater for homeless people.'

'Let's call Peggy and the children and put them in the picture,' Marian suggested. 'Those thumps overhead are rather alarming!'

*

The family had been installed in the Somerset village house for just over a week when war was declared. BP arrived the previous evening to stay overnight. He was on his way to a final musical engagement in Bristol, before going off to his army training camp.

'I saw my mum in her new home – Luke was getting ready to leave, too. They send their love, and so does your dad, Elin.'

On the Sunday morning, after they listened to Mr Chamberlain's broadcast, BP suggested that he and Peggy might go for a walk before lunch. She hesitated for a moment, looking at the children, but he made a little face at her and beckoned her to follow.

They walked along the lane, where the fields stretched out beyond drystone walls, unlike the familiar hedgerows of Suffolk. Peggy pointed out the church, and the school, and the main village street, to the left, with every other house a little shop.

He was much taller than she was now, so they held hands, which made it easier to swing along than if they had linked arms.

'You've grown your hair,' he commented approvingly.

'I've grown up, too,' she said daringly.

He smiled. They stopped by a tree. There was no one about. It looked a perfect September day, but of course it wasn't, for their country was at war. He rested his hands lightly on her shoulders, looked down into her upturned face and noted her earnest expression.

'May I kiss you goodbye? I know you wouldn't like me to do it in front of everyone. I used to think of you as my little sister, but I don't feel like that any more . . .'

She closed her eyes and waited. It wasn't the romantic kiss she'd dreamed of, just a mere brushing of their lips the first time, then he pulled her closer and the second kiss took her breath away.

'I'll write to you, Peg, I promise. Think of me, won't you?'

'I will, oh, I will!'

Elin was out in the front garden when she saw them coming along. She wanted to ask BP to put up the old swing she'd found in the shed, between two sturdy oak trees, for the children to amuse themselves.

She was reminded of herself at around Peggy's age, out walking with Luke the Christmas before she joined Marian and her family.

They look right together, she thought fondly, *but maybe we did too. Life repeats itself, all the time. I didn't know then that I was about to meet the man I would fall in love with, and eventually marry. We've been so happy since it's been just the four of us. Now, after almost sixteen years, I'm more or less back where I started: looking after small children, only this time round they're my own; keeping the home running smoothly for all the family, for I suspect it won't be long before Marian returns to nursing, as her contribution to the war effort. I'll take her frail mother under my wing, if that happens. No one would expect me to remind them, 'How about me?'*

Oh, my darling Mark, may this war not last long, may we be together again soon.

EPILOGUE

1943

Billie was retrained by her employers after the outbreak of war. Her duties were highly confidential. She dedicated herself to a very different role in life from the one she had envisaged. In September 1943 she would be twenty-two years old.

The momentous events of this year proved a turning point in the war. In the occupied countries of Europe there was renewed hope. Euphoria followed the daring raid and breaching of the Möhne and Eder dams; and later, when Stalingrad was freed.

In July there were allied landings in Sicily, and the fall of Mussolini. On 3 September, exactly four years after the war began, the invasion of Italy was launched. Just five days later an armistice was agreed. However, the Germans still occupied Rome at that point, and fought fiercely in retreat. In October, Italy declared war on Germany. The Italian prisoners of war held in Great Britain were now eligible for immediate repatriation.

Towards the end of the year, a great passenger liner, painted battleship grey, which had been used for troop-carrying since the beginning of the conflict, left harbour at dusk, without ceremony or cheering from the ex-prisoners of war on board. There were stewardesses on board, as in the liner's heyday: volunteers chosen for their capability and discretion. Billie was one of these.

In pairs, the women checked the cabins, spoke to the occupants and made sure they were comfortable. The men, who had been trusted to work for local farmers in the vicinity of their camp, spoke good English. Some had been mere youths when they were captured; they were all conscripts, not political activists.

Perhaps, although she was not aware of it, Billie hoped to see a familiar face.

However, she was the one to be recognised first.

Four men sat on their bunks, smiling as their names were called and ticked on the lists, answering politely as they were asked if there was anything they needed.

'I thank you, no,' replied the young man in the naval issue duffel jacket. He'd been regarding Billie intensely from the moment she came in. As she turned to leave, he jumped up impulsively.

'I believe we have met before – ah – Billie Drake, is it you?'

She motioned to her colleague to wait.

'Yes . . . don't tell me you are Bruno! I didn't recognise the name.'

'This is because I changed my name to my stepfather's at his request. And, no, I am not Bruno, I am his brother Alberto, known to your family as Bertie. I have sad news for you. My brother, I have learned since I was in the camp, was killed in North Africa.'

'You look so like him now,' was all Billie could manage.

'Thank you for saying that. I miss him, all my family, very much. Still, I shall see the others very soon now, I hope.'

Nan, Billie's fellow stewardess, nudged her.

'We must get on,' she said in a low voice.

'Goodbye, Bertie,' said Billie. 'I hope we can talk again before we arrive at Naples.'

They met up again on deck as they entered the Bay of Naples. There was the unnerving sight of wrecked vessels, some long abandoned. This was no longer the thriving port so eloquently described in the pre-war cruise brochures. The damage inflicted by the guns of war was all too evident. The greyness of the chilly winter day added to the bleakness.

'I always wanted to come to Italy,' Billie said. Sunshine, olive groves, she thought.

'The last time we met, you were a tiresome little girl – but I still hoped to see you again one day,' said Bertie. The sea breeze tousled his dark hair, and he brushed it out of his eyes.

'I was thirteen . . .'

'And I must have been fourteen; did you ever learn to swim? I hope so.' He gestured at the deep water below.

'Such was my indignation at being rescued by the wrong brother that day – well, I made up my mind to do so, and I did. What happened to the rest of your family – do you know? Elin and Alex were once – well, they were in love one summer, I believe. Before she married Mark, of course.' Other memories, puzzling at the time, were stirred, but were best left unsaid – she realised now that Jenny had also loved, in vain, the man who had become her sister's husband.

'Alex was in the army, too, but he was wounded and invalided out. The last I heard of him, from my mother, was that he had moved with his family, to be with her.'

'Our family seems to be spread far and wide nowadays. Only my grandfather is still near Southwold. My father is stationed in Ireland; at least he gets home on leave now and then to see my mother in Ipswich. Elin and her children moved to Somerset with Mrs Lambert – her boys both went in the army. Mark worked in a London hospital throughout the blitz, and is still there. Did you meet BP, as he was known, our friend Clo's son, I wonder?'

'Yes, I did. Elin wrote of his early success in music. What happened to him?'

'He married my best friend Peggy, Mrs Lambert's daughter, after he came back from Dunkirk. She was only seventeen and he was nineteen. It's so sad. He returned to active service and within a few months she had lost him. Peggy's little son was born after that. Elin looks after him; Peggy wanted to train as a nurse, like her mother.' She didn't add: *I was upset when he chose Peggy, not me . . .*

'This war has touched us all, it seems. So Elin, whom I remember so fondly from my childhood, is still caring for the young.' He looked at Billie, huddled in her greatcoat, her golden hair tucked under her cap. 'I know I am not Bruno, but I hope you will want to get to know me better when this is possible, Billie. My brother would approve of that.'

She slipped her hand in his. *Blow the non-fraternisation warning*, she thought!

'We were meant to meet again,' she said softly.

As they docked, they looked down on a party of nuns, calling out for food for the children they were sheltering. Little boys in ragged outgrown trousers, girls in clumping wooden shoes stared up at the faces looking down at them. Then police arrived to disperse the crowd.

'They're starving, that's obvious!' Billie exclaimed, upset.

'Change does not come overnight,' Bertie said. 'But it will, I promise you.'

ACKNOWLEDGEMENTS

My love and thanks to dear Mimi who told me 'how it was' in the years between the two world wars, when she, like Elin, took the little train home to Southwold.

In appreciation of assistance with my research by the late Miss D. Gamble, stewardess.

Welcome to the world of Sheila Newberry!

Keep reading for more from Sheila Newberry, to discover a recipe that features in this novel and to find out more about Sheila Newberry's inspiration for the book . . .

We'd also like to welcome you to Memory Lane, a place to discuss the very best saga stories from authors you know and love with other readers, plus get recommendations for new books we think you'll enjoy. Read on and join our club!

www.MemoryLane.Club
www.facebook.com/groups/memorylanebookgroup

Meet Sheila Newberry

I've been writing since I was three years old, and even told myself stories in my cot. So it came as a shock when I was whacked round the head by my volatile kindergarten teacher for daydreaming about stories when I was supposed to be chanting the phonetic alphabet. My mother received a letter from my teacher saying, 'Sheila will not speak. Why?' Mum told her that it was because I was scared stiff in class. I was immediately moved up two classes. Here I was given the task of encouraging the slow readers. This was something I was good at but still felt that I didn't fit in. Later, I learned that another teacher had saved all my compositions saying they inspired many children in later years.

I had scarlet fever in the spring of 1939, and when I returned to our home near Croydon, I saw changes which puzzled me – sandbags, shelters in back gardens, camouflaged by moss and daisies, and windows reinforced with criss-crossed tape. Children had iron rations in Oxo tins – we ate the contents during rehearsals for air-raids – and gas masks were given out. I especially recall the stifling rubber. We spent the summer holiday, as usual, in Suffolk and I remember being puzzled when my father left us there, as the Admiralty staff was moving to Bath. 'War' was not mentioned but we were now officially evacuees, living with relatives in a small cottage in a sleepy village.

On and off, we returned to London at the wrong times. We were bombed out in 1940 and dodging doodlebugs in 1943. I thought of Suffolk as my home. I was still writing – on flyleaves of books cut out by friends – and every Friday I told stories about Black-eyed Bill the Pirate to the whole school in the village hut. I wrote my first pantomime at nine years old, and was awarded the part of Puss in Boots. I wore a costume made from blackout curtains. We were back in our patched-up London home to celebrate VE night and dancing in the street. Lights blazed – it was very exciting.

I had a moment of glory when I won an essay competition that 3,000 schoolchildren had entered. The subject was waste paper, which we all collected avidly! At my new school, I was encouraged by my teachers to concentrate on English Literature and Language, History and Art, and I did well in my final exams. I wanted to be a writer, but was told there was a shortage of paper! True. I wrote stories all the time and read many books. I was useless at games like netball as I was so short-sighted – I didn't see the ball until it hit me. I still loved acting, and my favourite Shakespearian parts were Shylock and Lady Macbeth.

When I left school, I worked in London at an academic publisher. I had wanted to be a reporter, but I couldn't ride a bike! Two years after school, I met my husband John. We had nine children and lived on a smallholding in Kent with many pets (and pests). I wrote the whole time. The children did, too, but they were also artistic like John. We were all very happy. I acquired a typewriter and wrote short stories for children, articles on family life and romance for magazines. I received wonderful feedback. I soon graduated to writing novels and joined the Romantic Novelists' Association. I have had many books published over the years and am over the moon to see my books out in the world once again.

Bakewell Tart Recipe:

For the pastry
- 200g plain flour
- 1 tbsp icing sugar, plus extra to decorate
- 125g butter
- 1 egg yolk

For the filling
- 180g butter, softened
- 180g caster sugar
- 3 eggs
- 180g ground almonds
- 1 tsp almond extract
- 200g Tesco Finest raspberry conserve
- 25g flaked almonds

Sieve the flour and icing sugar into a bowl. Rub in the butter. Add the egg yolk and 2 tsp water and mix to a firm dough. Roll out onto a lightly floured board and use to line a deep 23cm loose-based, fluted tart tin. Chill for 15 mins.

Heat the oven to gas 4, 180°C, fan 160°C. Bake the pastry case 'blind' for 15 mins. Remove the paper and baking beans and cook for a further 10 mins until the pastry is dry and a light golden colour. Remove from the oven and leave to cool.

For the filling, beat together the butter and sugar. Beat in the eggs, one at a time, then stir in the ground almonds and almond extract. Spread the jam over the base of the pastry case. Spread the almond filling evenly on top, then sprinkle over the flaked almonds.

Bake for 35–40 mins until the frangipane filling is firm and golden brown on top. Allow to cool slightly and serve while just warm or cool completely in the tin. Carefully remove from the tin and dust with icing sugar just before serving, perhaps with cream or custard, if you like.

· MEMORY LANE ·

If you enjoyed *Far From Home*, you'll love
these other titles by Sheila Newberry . . .

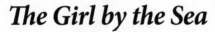

The Girl by the Sea

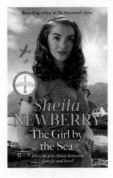

1934

Following the death of her mother, twelve-year-old
Tess Rainbow takes on the responsibility of caring for
her family. When a plane crash-lands near their home on
Romney Marsh, she meets the charming Moray Tann, a
young pilot from Scotland, who turns out to be the son
of one of her father's rivals. Once nursed back to health,
Moray returns to his duties – but not without
leaving a mark on Tess's heart.

With the onset of World War II, the Rainbow family
move to Scotland. Here Tess is reunited with Moray.
Sworn off him, she must choose between her home
and her first true love . . .

The Canal Boat Girl

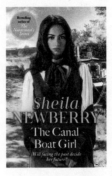

Wales, 1883

Young Ruth Owen, a talented musician with a scholarship to a prestigious music school, has a sparkling career ahead of her. But after a run-in with her mysterious tutor she flees to London, leaving everything and everyone behind.

London, 1897

Fourteen years later, Ruth, now married with two children, finds herself struggling for money and a place to live. Left with no other option, they decide to return to Wales and live on a canal boat. Life on the canals may seem idyllic, but what troubles await her return? And can the past ever truly be forgotten?

The Mother and Baby Home

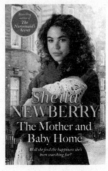

Sunny grew up in the mother and baby home on Grove Lane, London. The daughter of a wartime nurse and a Polish pilot, she was abandoned by her mother shortly after her birth and taken in by Nan, the warm and gentle proprietor of the home.

Never having known her parents, Sunny has always felt like she doesn't quite fit in, but now at sixteen years old, she is ready to find her place in the world. Heading out to start her first job, she finally feels she has some idea of who she wants to be.

As 1950s post-war London is changing at a rapid pace, so is Sunny. And when someone from her past returns, Sunny has some tough decisions to make. Decisions that could affect the rest of her life . . .

The Meadow Girls

Suffolk, 1914

Twelve-year-old Mattie and her little sister Evie lead an idyllic life in the countryside, exploring the meadows and picking watercress in the streams. But little do they know that this perfect childhood won't last. With the onset of World War I, the country is thrown into turmoil . . .

As the years pass, the girls go on to live very different lives. Mattie travels to Canada and America, while Evie remains in England. More than fifty years later, through marriages, deaths, births, war, heartbreak and distance, will these sisters finally be reunited to have their time in the meadows again?

A Winter Hope

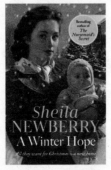

Number five Kitchener Avenue heralds the start of a new life for the Hope family. For pregnant Miriam it is a warm, safe environment to bring up her child. For her sister, fourteen-year-old Barbara, it means independence . . . and boys. And for Fred it provides the security he craves for his young family.

The Hopes settle in, and start to make happy memories in their new home. But World War II is round the corner, and this carefree life can't last.

As the country is thrown into turmoil, can the Hope family come back together and find the happiness they crave?

The Nursemaid's Secret

Tilly, a young maid, is sent away from her home in London to care for a sick child in an old cottage on the Isle of Sheppey, and she little imagines how her life will change . . .

Having settled in with her new family, Tilly dares to believe that the happiness she's longed for could be hers at last, and that she might finally be free from the secrets of her past. But tragedy strikes, and Tilly is forced to return to London, leaving the cottage under the sea wall, and her new life, behind.

As war approaches and new challenges arise, will Tilly be able to overcome her struggles and find her way home?

The Gingerbread Girl

London, 1936

Ill and stuck in hospital at Christmas, seven-year-old Cora Kelly is excited to receive a visit from her mother, who brings her the gift of a gingerbread man. But little does Cora know that this will be the last time she sees her . . .

As Cora continues her recovery on a farm in the beautiful Norfolk countryside, tragedy strikes her family and she moves back to London with her new guardian, Eliza.

Here they live a happy, if simple, life. But, as the Second World War approaches, and the past comes knocking, everything changes.

Will Cora be able to escape the inevitable, or is she destined to repeat her parents' mistakes?

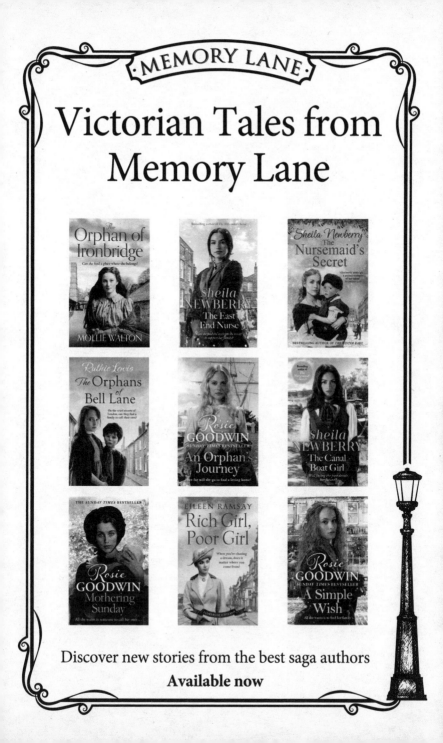